CW01424491

30p   2 8 JUN 1995

ELLA

Also by Dee Phillips

NO NOT I
THE COCONUT KISS
HOLLYBUSH ROW

ELLA

DEE PHILLIPS

HODDER AND STOUGHTON
LONDON SYDNEY AUCKLAND TORONTO

My thanks, again, to E.J.M.
for generous help

British Library Cataloguing in Publication Data
Phillips, Dee
  Ella.
  I. Title
  823'.914[F]   PR6066. H462

  ISBN 0-340-38819-6

To Gwyn, bravest of women. In memoriam.

Chapter One

'Out to dinner,' my mother said into the silence, stirring tea, 'you have to use the outside knife and fork, of course, and work inwards.' She was only addressing Ginny and me. It was a long time since she had said much to our father at meal-times, as if the tediousness of their conversation had begun to embarrass her, with the two of us almost adult, and always listening. 'Naturally, you'd need to watch your step if you decided to miss a course.'

'How d'you mean, "watch your step"?' Ginny asked.

'Well, let's suppose you didn't want the fish. You wouldn't have to use the fish cutlery for meat or anything; you'd feel an awful fool.'

I was trying to keep myself separate for a little longer, wondering about the boy who'd spoken to me on the way home from school. Also there was a painting to be planned and completed for the Painters' Club meeting on Friday, so I was leaving it to Ginny to keep some sort of conversation going, though I knew that wasn't fair.

Grandfather Gordon's death had robbed us of easy things to say during meals. Not that he ever sat with us, but for the two months he stayed, his presence upstairs in the big bed in Ginny's room had kept us alert and talking round the table downstairs. We'd discussed how he'd slept and what he'd eaten, and checked on necessities to bring in after school, like gauze and cotton-wool, or sweets for sucking in the long nights. After the funeral we'd briefly focused our attention on the cat, turning from the table and each other to point out his elegance and laugh at his cute expressions, but when the weather improved and he stayed out till night it was just ourselves again: Mother opposite Ginny, Dad facing me, across the dishes – wondering what next.

It preoccupied us both, and I had started a daydream about a scene remembered from a film, with a tableful of children and adults smiling round at each other, elbows on the cloth, shouting with laughter now and then, and saying things the minute they came into their heads.

'Your father, of course, in his first job, when they had the annual dinner – he was only the office boy at that time, weren't you, Dad – he drank the water in the fingerbowls!'

It was then that, half listening, I looked across at Dad and saw with a sudden flush of the usual excitement that the picture could be about the four of us having tea.

I'd paint it as if from slightly above, to make the table-top central and important. Dad's upper half, front view, could be the top third of the picture, his white hair and pink face and neck bright against the dingy brown wallpaper, which I'd stipple for a bit of texture. The big pink hands, one at his mouth, the other near his plate, would be duller than the face but brighter than the snuff-coloured cardigan, and at the bottom of the picture, the back view of myself with yellow hair and blue sweater would have the wooden rail of the chair-back curling round it.

'A natural enough mistake, I suppose.' Mother was keeping her story going. 'Of course he should've watched the others. Remember that: if ever you're uncertain what to do you can't do better than watch the others.' She got her 'etiquette' snippets from a weekly magazine, and though we laughed at some of them, she had convinced us that life after schooldays would be one long obstacle race with everybody watching, and we worried about things she might have missed or forgotten to mention.

She could lean into the picture from the left, stretching to pass a cup. Thin, with grey hair, she'd need more colour than she generally wore, to lift her from the drabness of everything beyond her in the room, while Ginny, fourteen-and-a-bit, with schoolgirl plaits and restless hands helping her speech along, would face her from the opposite edge. Ginny could become too important for the design if I didn't take care – she was the liveliest thing in the picture.

'I was only Ginny's age!' Dad had perked up in self-defence. 'Got my first job at fourteen – how about that!'

Everyone would slope towards the centre, drawing the eye down to a table full of pattern. On a pink-and-brown checked cloth I could carefully place delicately-coloured dishes, some circular, some oval, so that they covered the hard corners of the checks. There was excitement in making dishes more important than faces, more delicate even, and I had a hunch that this one might not degenerate into just another still-life. So I held it in my head till it grew as real as the reality and I no longer needed to keep looking. One of the subjects on the list they'd given us was 'Seated Group (min. 3 figures)', so it would do.

'Were you still working there by Ella's age?' Ginny kept trying; she could never bear the silences.

'Good Lord, by then I'd had a rise and bought a suit and taken a girl to the pictures.' Dad was addressing me. I always got the answers when Ginny asked the questions. 'You had to be a man at seventeen in those days.'

More than any other age, seventeen had taken me by surprise, with a whole new clamour of other people's expectations. Some-one had always pointed out, as birthdays came, the things that now we should or should not be doing, so that both of us seemed for ever not quite catching up. But we had played at being seventeen, mincing and teetering about, pretending high-heeled shoes, neat legs, beads, handbags. It wasn't just yourself a few years older; it was 'young women', with a great leap forward to be taken, on your own, with too much guesswork to it, and as I watched the others at school, I was convinced that for everyone but me the instructions came automatically with the age. The boy after school was surely some sort of beginning, I would tell Ginny at bed-time.

In the silence I heard the echo of Dad's voice from seconds ago: 'What have they given you tonight?'

'Homework? Only things to finish off.' Work wasn't a worry; they said I was a credit, and kept me at it. 'But I haven't even started my thing for Painters' Club, and there's only two evenings left.'

'Never mind the frills,' he said enthusiastically, 'there'll be time enough for hobbies later on. You ought to think of homework as a privilege.' He waved a hand towards Ginny who had fallen foul of the eleven-plus and attended the Secondary Modern. 'This one's having an easier time of it at the moment, but when it comes to jobs you'll be the one with choices.' In the picture, I decided, no one would be speaking; they would just eat.

Ginny shoved back her plaits. She always took it marvellously, pretending a kind of grown-up nonchalance, and I had grown used to her coping quietly, though there were times when she used words in bizarre ways and needed bailing out as she headed for humiliation.

'Oh, I expect there'll be *some* little menial thing for me to do.' Mother looked nervous, and Dad disregarded her words. 'Anyway,' she went on, 'if the worst comes to the worst there's always the oldest profession, so I'm not unduly worried.' She told me later she thought it meant motherhood.

Dad turned in his chair and stared at her silently, one corner of his mouth twisted into a smile that had no pleasure in it, and the colour rose in her small face and went on deepening. She glanced round at Mother and me in a bewildered way, then turned her eyes to his again, but a few seconds later I had the feeling that she was vainly trying to turn away from his stare. His silence made it awful; he could have eased her torment by saying *anything*, even crossly.

'Don't, Dad!' I whispered softly without really meaning to, and when he looked at me the queer smile had gone, but it was only for a moment, and as he turned to his staring again I found myself planning, as I always did, something to shout, though I had never got as far as shouting it. I even prayed that Ginny herself, with her livelier spirit, might scrape her chair back, run out and slam a door. But anger, at that time, never surfaced in our family.

Mother got up from the table. 'You go and get on then, Ella,' she said quietly as if nothing was happening. 'I sometimes think they give you too *much* work of an evening; it's quite a burden. Ginny will help me with this lot, won't you, dear?' Her voice was always shaky when she was breaking up a moment.

Dad pushed his chair in carefully under the table and strode into the sitting-room humming, picking up the paper with the crossword on the way, while Ginny began collecting dishes, keeping her head down. I went up to my bedroom and the homework which was nearly always more a relief than a burden. The picture could wait till tomorrow; once visualised it seemed already to exist somewhere, and would only need recalling.

At bed-time we would undress back-to-back under our dressing-gowns as we had done ever since Ginny moved in with me to leave her room for Grandfather. She often said she would move back one day, but that if *she* had died she'd hate to see everyone rushing round changing things back to normal, 'mucking up my last foothold on earth', the minute she had gone.

Then in the dark we would invent, as we did every night, a fantasy world of different attitudes, giving ourselves the break we needed without ever realising it.

'How was today, Ginn?' It could only be a whisper across the room; the walls were thin.

Ginny was ready. 'Not one I'll easily forget; a sombre tapestry of sadness, spiked through with bright threads of joy. I've packed in – er – what was his name, last night's one?'

'Ferdinand.'

'That's it. Well, he lacked passion – no, not that – he deceived me. With some slattern from 4C.'

'4C! What a slight!'

'Consummate irony,' she drawled, 'but today I've looked deep into eyes like pools of violet, with laughter lurking at the edges. Eyes which held mine in their untroubled depths, promising the bliss of fulfilment . . .' There were no boys at Ginny's school, but with so much less homework she had time for reading.

'What's this one's name?'

'I'll think of something. There's heaps of time; it'll be ages before I let him have his pleasure of me. For a couple of months I'll just drown in his violet eyes and inflame him with the soft perfumed touch of my raven hair.'

Neither of us had ever known a boy, and I wondered if the one who had spoken to me after school was responsible for the feeling of gathering momentum which had hung over the evening, as in truth there had been nothing else unusual about the day. The idea for the picture was new, and so was Dad's staring at Ginny, but it was not a rarity for tea-time to bring some small ordeal for her, and for me to feel angry about it, though perhaps this time it had taken me a little longer to realise that, as usual, I'd missed my chance to intervene.

Turning over, I said into the darkness, 'I walked home with the rowdy ones today.'

'That's the fourth time. Anything happen?'

'A boy spoke – he said I'm a blonde. Am I?'

'Of course you are, you nit, terrific blonde. That all he said?'

'That's all, it's not important.' It had felt important at the time, the boy turning laughing from a conversation with someone else, saying 'Blondes *never* tell,' and catching sight of me and

11

saying 'Do they? *You* should know.' But I didn't want to remember how I'd blushed deeply and turned away pretending to talk to Lydia, my closest friend, who was used to me reddening and didn't stare.

Why *do* you always blush, I'd wondered angrily for the next half-hour, and it had spoiled the amazement of discovering I was better than just fair-haired. Lydia was beautiful, and never blushed; the two things surely went together, but it was hard even to imagine how anyone with both these blessings must feel.

Ginny said, 'Well, keep trying; something's bound to come of it soon. Goodnight.' I hoped she was right.

Lying on my back I thought of green and blue, a light transparent blue and a dark heavy green, playing my usual game of first visualising them in areas of similar size and shape – which made me feel uncomfortable, almost sick – then behind closed eyelids playing around with them, diminishing the green, breaking it up and softening its shape, while expanding and working at the blue. You discover, gradually, how much of each the other can bear, and go on till you get a marvellous feeling of balance. It was a way I had of getting off to sleep.

Chapter Two

Next day I joined the rowdy ones again, but no one spoke to me. They were a group of girls of my age, nine or ten of them, who bashed their panama hats into non-regulation shapes each day after school, hitching their gingham dresses an inch or so, ready to walk home together past the gates of the Boys' County Grammar. The boys' school was only a few minutes' walk from ours, but higher up the hill, and hardly any girls would have needed to pass it on their way home. When school was over there would be a rush of both girls and boys, downhill towards the shops and buses, and after that the rowdy ones would emerge together to take the long way round. Past the rows of solid red-brick villas, they swung in twos and threes along the pavement, taking up all the space and making too much noise.

I'd joined them a few times since my birthday, impelled by a sense of urgency, not really wanting a boy but wanting to want one as they did. So I pretended along, watching the ones who had money for cosmetics and doing what I could to imitate them, like reddening my lips with my teeth and buffing my too-short nails against my blazer pocket.

As they neared the school the pitch of their laughter would rise, and I shrilled with the rest, never suspecting that their excitement might be no more real than my own. The waiting boys moved off downhill with us, everyone wisecracking at first, and soon a pair would break away to walk ahead or lag behind, while more sophisticated couples turned off along side-streets. Once the boys were with us neither Lydia nor I spoke to anyone but each other. We almost held our breath, and I would leave the remnants of the group at an alley which led through little back streets to home, praying to go unnoticed. It had been the same each time.

That afternoon, as I reached the end of the alley, adjusting my skirt to its proper length, a boy came out of the corner sweetshop. He was looking into a little paper bag and easing out the sweet he wanted from the bottom. I had been taking my time, waiting to feel sensible and easy again before reaching home, but now I hurried on and turned the corner, then heard him shout, 'Hang on a minute, will you . . . please!' with his mouth full. So I stood still and waited, bending to brush an imaginary speck from my dress, as the colour rose from the base of my neck to the roots of my hair spreading infuriatingly to wherever it would show.

He said, 'What's the hurry?' as he caught up with me and held out the bag. 'Take two or three, go on. I know the bloke, and he always gives me a few over the odds.' I'd seen him before, walking with the others in the group – a tall thin boy with the kind of face that looks half-finished, as if waiting for the right expression to grow up with – and as I took the toffees he said, 'Why d'you always hare off like a startled cockroach?' His voice was soft, with a rough accent, but the roughness was genuine, not the carefully coarsened speech most of them had adopted that year, and I fell into step with him, disturbed to think he had watched me before.

'Do I rush off? Must be because I hate hanging about; it's nice to get home and out of these things and forget it all.' It wasn't true – school clothes were the only ones that didn't make me feel clumsy, and homework was something I escaped *into* – but everyone pretended boredom with everything at school.

As we neared my home he seemed to hesitate but I walked quickly past the house, too shy to want to stand chatting at the gate wondering how to say goodbye. He said, 'You girls don't know you're born. No chance of *us* ever forgetting the grind; there's enough work in this bag to keep me shackled for a week.' Then he grinned. 'No, to be honest, I'd read it all even if I didn't have to. I just like History.' So that the first thing I liked him for was that he didn't have to pretend, and I wished I'd been honest enough to admit to spending hours reading set books aloud up in my bedroom and quite enjoying it.

We said nothing for a bit; I was rejecting all the bright things I'd always thought you had to say to boys. It was quite different from the encounters some of the others talked about. Then he said, 'What's your name? Mine's Arthur Knight. It lends itself to limericks, specially if you say "Arfur".' It was surely a name for people's fathers and uncles, not one you'd give a baby.

'Ella Thorne.' Said aloud, it always sounded ridiculous.

'Ella's unusual, isn't it? A tinkling sort of sound, like breaking

14

glass or something. The other day when I wanted to slow you down and didn't know what to shout – apart from "Oi" – I tried sorting out a name to suit you. Came up with Diana . . . tall, I suppose. I've never known an Ella, so I wouldn't know if it fits.'

'I know some Arthurs.'

'And do I fit?'

'Not really; they're mostly bald.'

He opened his eyes very wide, lifted the silly school cap that sat like a button at the back of his head, and dragged his springy hair back from his face, while he covered his teeth with his lips to make a gummy mumble. Then he let go of it all and said, 'Yeah, well – just give me time,' and started whistling very softly through his teeth as he walked.

He made me feel easy, like talking to Ginny up in the bedroom, but I began to wonder what he must think of me walking straight past the house he might have seen me entering before, so again I pretended. 'I'm coming this way to get a few things at the chemist's.'

'And after that? Quick change and forget the day? What will you actually *do*?' It was one of the things I liked to know about people when I wanted to imagine them, and I said, 'I'll work, same as you.'

'Yes, but hating it?'

'Not really. There's a Painters' Club meeting after school tomorrow, so I'll have to do my picture. I've decided what to do, and I generally enjoy it.' We had reached the chemist's shop and both stood still.

'That means you'll be late tomorrow, does it? Want me to hang about till the painting thing's over?'

'Oh no . . . thank you. Some of us have to stay and clear the place up. Anyway, they keep some tea for me at home, so . . .'

'O.K., point taken. Shan't see you then till Monday. Try not to push off quite so fast next time.' He began to walk backwards, then turned, waving the cap with an exaggerated flourish. I went into the shop and queued with the others at the counter for a few moments, then left before it was my turn to be served.

Running back I told myself over and over, 'I've got a boy-friend', wondering if I really had, because it was nothing like my expectations. It wasn't something I could tell the others, at least not in the way they always did. But they would find out,

15

and it would be my badge of membership; now I could stop pretending.

Already it seemed to make a difference to the way I walked. I looked at things and people differently, the way you do immediately after seeing a film or play, and when I reached home and hung my blazer on the hallstand, it came as a surprise that nothing there seemed to have changed. Then I heard Dad's voice call, 'Ella? Come and look at this,' and I went into the kitchen wondering why he was home so early.

'Bit of a cold,' he said. 'Came back at lunch-time; busy with this all afternoon.'

He was holding a new photograph album covered in blue linen, and my stomach turned at the sight of it. Piled beside him on the table were the others I had known for so long, each with the awful Gothic lettering that took him hours to do. None of them had been seen for ages, and I'd held my breath and prayed they were forgotten.

The first of them, chronologically, was white and had 'Ella, born 1941' lettered in gold on the cover. On its front page my mother, on a throne-like photographer's chair, held the bundle in a long christening robe, while he stood behind, smiling. But the two of them did not appear in any of the other pictures, except as disembodied hands and arms stretching in from beyond the edges to prop the lolling baby or show it where to look.

Another of the books, the only one containing pictures of us all, was labelled 'Family', but in the rest there were no pictures of anyone but me: 'Schooldays', bound in dark blue with red lettering; 'At Play', lilac-covered and lettered in green; 'Holidays', striped white and orange; 'Dressing-up', 'Sports and Games', 'Laughter and Tears'. He held up the newest album to point out the cover. He'd printed 'Sweet Seventeen' in white on the blue background, and as he opened it to show the snap he had taken on my birthday, already in its little hinges on the first page, I tried to control a sort of cringing in my shoulders.

'Dad, I wish you wouldn't!' He was beaming like a schoolboy.

'Pretty nice, eh? Developed it at work.' There was little sign of a cold, and I knew he could not begin to understand my distaste, nor even to notice the thin line of my mother's mouth as she bent over her knitting, silent as always in the presence of the albums.

'It's embarrassing, Dad! I mean, I thought you'd finished with

16

it all.' It had seemed normal enough to take the picture on my seventeenth birthday, the sort of thing any family might do, for seventeen.

He laughed, clapping his big hands and rubbing them together enthusiastically. 'Finished! Not yet. You'll see what a beauty I'll make for your wedding. Do the lot myself – bigger album, of course, bells on the cover . . .'

'I'm never *getting* married, honestly!'

He stood up and clamped his arm across my shoulder, grinning and drawing me towards him, simply not noticing how I stiffened. 'We'll leave that to the fellers to decide, eh? A fine strapping girl like you . . .'

'Run up and change your things,' Mother said quietly without looking up, and I was already on my way, longing to shout or slam a door, and terrified I might. 'Ginny's moved back into her own room,' Mother called after me. 'Dad helped me move the bed across. She didn't want Grandad's bed, so we'll get Marshall's to put it in the sale next week.' She had this power to move situations on, clearing them out of sight till the next time round.

Ginny was lying on my bed and jumped up quickly. 'I was just borrowing your bed till you got in; it's lighter in here. We came home early so's the chosen few could rehearse the play. You do look awful! It isn't curse-time yet, is it?' She was talking fast, uneasy, as always, when my calm was threatened.

'I'm bleak, that's all. Dad's got the albums out, and there's a new one.'

'I saw it,' she said softly; then almost cheerfully, 'You shouldn't worry. Honestly, I'd love to be the apple of my father's eye – that's all it is, only it's wasted on you.' She had always claimed she forfeited his affection because of the eleven-plus exam, but I knew better; there had never been an album about Ginny.

'It's getting – well – almost sick! Sometimes I think Dad's awful in some strange way.' For once I couldn't pretend, not even to get Ginny smiling again.

Until a few months earlier, both of us had sometimes brought a friend home, but now we saw to it that no one ever had cause to come, and though the reason was never really discussed I always knew it was to do with Dad. Perhaps it was the different voice he used, pompous with cliché, when visitors were there, especially girls from school; or the way he ostentatiously offered help to Mother in their presence, as if it were second nature to him; or talked indulgently of Ginny – though never *to* her – as if he cared. It might have been the flirty kind of mocking chivalry he pretended to our friends, sweeping doors open for them. Once he kissed Lydia's hand, bending low over it, and she said afterwards, 'Your dad's a proper joker.'

Whatever it really was that made us keep people away, I tried to tell myself that something innocuous, like his false teeth, could be the shameful explanation. They were new and china-looking, and he moulded his lips round them in what Ginny called a pig's-bottom smile; I treasured the snapshot of him smiling his proper smile with his own teeth, and kept it in my schoolbag.

Minding about the teeth, I sometimes thought, was even worse than worrying about the clichés or the acting-up, and as these mean feelings muddled their way in and out of my love, even admiration, for him, I used to long for the simplicity of the old, earlier days when all you ever had to be was good, in the certainty that it would make everyone happy and you would grow automatically into a big girl, then a lady, and ultimately, happy-ever-after, a mother.

'You do still *love* him, don't you?' Ginny sounded embarrassed by the naïveté of her fears.

'Course I do!' And I really did, I told myself, but though I already knew love can coexist with anger, I was beginning to worry if it could survive alongside contempt.

'Promise you won't *do* anything. Don't say anything or start a row or stuff like that.' Ginny dreaded most of all the break-up of our world. She feared the careless, provocative remark, the noisily closed door which someone might think had been slammed, anything which could open floodgates, and had been watching me lately, hanging around ready to placate, as if she saw me as some kind of tinder-box. She kept her nonchalance for coping with Dad, but upstairs when she talked about the things that worried her you could sometimes see in her eyes the look of a little tortured creature, not just an anxious child.

'I won't do anything.'

After a moment she said, 'You don't think, do you, that we might grow up awful – because of Dad, and that?'

'I'm not sure. Anyway, if you really *are* awful, you don't know

18

you are. It's Mother I worry about when he's like that; I reckon she must loathe me.'

Ginny couldn't bear me to be disturbed, and said quickly, 'It's not just you and her; all old people hate younger ones half the time. We had a debate at school, and I suppose it stands to reason, though I'd never thought of it before; when you're old it's like the doctor telling you you're going to die soon. You'd automatically hate the ones who'd go on living, anyone would.'

I felt a need to lift the gloom. 'Depends. Perhaps when you're old you look forward to something like Heaven, with milk and honey flowing through the streets. It wouldn't suit me – I hate honey.'

She shot me a look of admiration and relief; now we could finish it off and get back to normal. 'Oh groan,' she said, 'all that milk; it would ruin your shoes.' And the conversation went the way of all the others that had grown gloomy; we could keep up such silly talk for hours, and already felt better.

'You'll have to go. I've got to do my picture, now and after we've eaten.'

Ginny said, 'You could have another headache, and she'll let you have some food on a tray. I'll bring it up,' and she darted away.

I cleared the old kitchen-cabinet work-top which was my desk, spread newspapers over it, and lifted up the heavy drawing-board as Mother came into the room.

'Ginny says you're painting. Surely you'll do your homework first?'

'I haven't got any, and this will take all evening.'

'Your father wouldn't like your proper work to fall behind, not just for this,' she said, pointing to the board. Whatever she says, I thought, it always seems to be instead of what she wants to say.

'It won't. Anyway, I've got a headache.'

'So Ginny said. Perhaps you should stay home tomorrow.'

'Oh no!' School was the place where colour was, and people with ideas.

'I'll send you something up then. Just keep yourself quiet . . .' She was hovering, uncertain what to say. 'What's it to be this time, I wonder; have you got a list?'

We found it folded behind a postcard on the shelf, and she read it aloud, every word, irritatingly: ' "Stringham Grammar

School for Girls. Painters' Club. Monthly meeting, June 1958. Subject List: 1. Portrait of a Friend; 2. Street Market Scene; 3. The Crisis; 4. Back Gardens; 5. Seated Group (min. 3 figures); 6. Still-life with Bottles."

'Goodness, some of those would be very hard, especially the ones with people in. "Back Gardens" is probably the best for you if your head's bad, so long as you look towards the Carters' and avoid that awful eyesore of a shed.' She went and stood by the window, looking out, and we were silent, secure, I think now, in the knowledge that both of us were thinking hard before we spoke. Then she turned to go, saying, 'You'll probably be as right as rain in the morning.'

When she had gone I sat still, visualising myself perched in a cube-shaped room above the level of most people's heads, and surrounded by a vast area divided up into square houses and rectangular gardens. Then I pinned a big sheet of thick grey paper to the board, set out my brushes and pots of poster paint on the chest-of-drawers, and with a long black stick of charcoal, starting close to the top, drew in Dad's head.

Chapter Three

There was a time – I thought about it as I sketched in broad outline the top halves of the other three figures – when Dad's obsession with snapshots had seemed quite ordinary, a game that fathers played. But even so, the days when I stood still and smiled for him, or endlessly performed some action, or stared where he indicated while he busied himself with equipment, had never had any real connection, for me, with the little black-and-white pictures he showed us afterwards, their corners fastened in the albums. It seemed that nothing was ever recorded of what *I* remembered of the game, and I was puzzled by the unreality of the dull little scene which never told how it was.

'Here's the day we went to see the buttercups,' Dad would say, and I would remember the glory of sun in my eyes and yellow silk petals brushing my face, and Ginny, rolling about in them, kicking her legs and shouting for joy till Mother told her to get up and stop showing her knickers. But when he handed me the picture there was just the blurred image of a girl kneeling to smell black tussocks, and I was disappointed.

Whatever we did, the photos never really told the story. There were so *many* of them, and though in time I recognised that what they revealed was supposed to be what Dad saw when he looked at me, the variety of expressions on the face suggested that a whole host of different little girls had stood there for him. He and the camera, I fancied, had never seen the same thing twice, and I must be for ever changing.

Yet the face that looked out at me from the dressing-table mirror never seemed to change, neither did Dad or Mother, while Ginny, who had made one noticeable lurch from babyhood into girlhood while my back was turned, had only lengthened and fattened since, but always matched the one recognisable face you visualised when she was absent. For a time I was obsessed by the question of how many versions of me appeared in other people's imaginings, and whether they were troubled by the discrepancies.

When the painting was finished I spread it out to dry on top of the wardrobe and got into bed. The room felt strange without Ginny, and sleep would have been difficult even if I hadn't planned to lie and think about the boy. The picture had been done less carefully than usual, and was hard to remember now that it was out of sight, as if the doing had mattered most and I'd hardly noticed the result. I'll only hand it in if it's not unbearably bizarre by daylight, I thought, pushing it out of mind.

By the time all three bedroom doors were closed and the tank in the cupboard behind my head had finished dripping, I saw what a fool I'd been to think you can choose what to worry about. It wasn't the difficulties of having a boyfriend that kept me thinking and fidgeting half the night, but still the scene in the kitchen with the albums. I kept looking back to the time when there had been a reason for the photos, when Dad was a stranger in khaki who only stayed with us for short visits, and needed them for his wallet, to remind him. There had been some of Mother then, and later Ginny, as a baby. It was only after the war, when he was home and started buying albums to store the pictures, that the strange hobby developed round me alone.

In the next bedroom Ginny coughed, and switching on the lamp I saw that it was nearly two. The room looked a tip, with paint-pots everywhere, and thinking about the albums had inexplicably made me want to see the painting, so I got out of bed, sick with fatigue, and pulled it down.

As I did so my hand went involuntarily to my mouth. The thing was like a shout in the night. Several reds seemed to have crept in – though I must have mixed them – when I'd planned nothing warmer than the pink of Dad's face and the checks on the table-cloth. There was black, too, more than I'd ever used before, yet the problem wasn't just the intensity of colour. I had set out to paint something decorative and gentle – a pattern of a family – and though the figures were sitting there, obviously still and caught in their domestic moment, there was no calm in any of their shapes or lines, no order anywhere. It made me feel uneasy and I kept turning away from it.

I could remember working quite carefully and slowly on little bits of it, but the whole thing gave the impression of something painted much too fast and thoughtlessly. For a few moments I stared back at it, wondering what could be done to bring it nearer to what I'd intended, but the thing was beyond adjustment; it was a finished picture, while the one I'd meant had simply not come off. So I pushed it back on top of the wardrobe, telling myself that if I did hand it in I need not even feel responsible, as it wasn't recognisably mine.

'Let's have a look,' Ginny said next morning, finding me rolling it into a rubber-band. 'Oh gasp!' She looked in silence for a moment. 'Won't you get into trouble for rushing it? Couldn't you tidy it up a bit at lunch-time?'

'I'm not touching it; either I tear it up now or hand it in.'

'I'd tear it up. Still, it's up to you.'

We walked together to the bus-stop, the painting under my arm. 'There was something good to tell you after school yesterday,' I said, 'but other things took over. I'll tell you tonight.' Really it seemed stupid to have mentioned it; the flimsy relationship could hardly last till Monday.

In spare moments through the day the oldest of us arranged the exhibits, framing, mounting, or pinning them to boards and making a semicircle of them in the school studio, resting on painting easels or propped against donkeys or table-legs. It was usual to decry your own effort and enthuse or joke at the others'.

'Gawd, look at this! Does which way up matter?'

'Mine's the seated group over there,' I pointed out, forestalling. 'I had a headache.'

There would be an outside critic, we had one every third month, and though we generally saw to it that our own offerings were prominently placed, relying delicately on each other, I hung about when everything was ready and moved mine out of sight behind a larger one. There was no point in getting a bad criticism when I already knew there was a lot still to be done to it, if it was ever to be the gentle thing I'd planned.

For three years I had spent every meeting-day pretending I didn't care, like the others, but secretly wanting and praying and hoping for something I couldn't have put into words. Yet even when there had been praise, I'd always gone home afterwards with a lonely feeling I didn't understand.

This time I didn't give a thought to the painting all day, but hurrying home after the meeting that evening, I recognised the singing in my head and knew there was apprehension in my excitement.

'I won the gold star,' I said, pulling a chair up to the table where they were finishing tea. 'He said I could become a telling painter.'

'Well I never! Isn't that good, Dad! Her picture of our back garden, and she wasn't feeling up to much either.'

'It was the Seated Group; I changed my mind.'

'Us,' Ginny said, 'sitting round having our tea.'

'Fancy that! I hope you thought to give us a decent cloth, and the matching cups and saucers.'

'It was a bit – well – impressionistic,' Ginny reassured her.

The man had said he'd left my painting till the end deliberately, because it treated the subject in a different way from the rest. He said the others had made pictorial records of an actual crisis and how it looked, but mine was about the feeling of crisis itself, and had something to say to us all about the purpose of painting. I grew hot when I realised his mistake, and one of the girls who had seen it in the morning called out, 'I think it's the Seated Group, actually.' He didn't seem to care, and said titles were only literary explanations which we didn't need anyhow, and you could call it 'Teatime', or 'Mr & Mrs Bloggs and Family', or 'The Chequered Table-cloth', or what you liked, but it was a painting of a moment of crisis, almost palpably there like another person in the gloomy little room, stronger than any of the figures, who were all determined to have nothing to do with it but held it between them, 'beautifully balanced'. Then he asked who'd painted it, and I bent down and straightened my stocking and no one gave the game away – they never did.

He said that this girl, who was clearly absent from school, could in time become a telling painter if she could survive the widespread belief that women could only paint portraits and pots of flowers. They all cheered at that, and I cheered with them, though I was longing to get home and up to my bedroom to think about the idea that a painting can carry feelings as strongly as words you have chosen not to speak.

In his hand was the little tin of coloured sticky-backed stars, and he said, 'I'm told I can award one gold, two silvers, and half a dozen other assorted colours. I think this one must have the gold for a brave attempt at working seriously from the inside out, though there's quite a bit of clumsy brushwork.'

The star was exciting, but the 'inside out' gave me the feeling I'd been seen for the first time, which wasn't really something I could mention at home, so I tried to remember the more ordinary things he'd said.

'What took his fancy, d'you think?' Dad was asking. 'Did he say the perspective was good, or the people were life-like . . .' And Mother cut in, 'You could hardly expect the man to judge whether it was a good likeness, him not knowing us. You did tell him it was your family, I suppose?'

'He didn't ask. He said it was . . . balanced, and . . . serious . . .'

'Well, it would be *very* hard to draw people laughing, at your age,' Mother said. I was beginning to see that Ginny might have sensed the painting's danger when she'd suggested destroying it, so I was glad when Dad launched into one of his general condemnations and we could forget about the thing itself.

'Sounds like one of these *abstract* fellers; no idea of what a beginner needs to learn,' he said. 'I was afraid they'd soon be encouraging these passing fads in the schools, and it seems I was right. In my time you'd have got a proper education in the subject – shading and everything.'

As soon as I got away Ginny followed me upstairs. 'What was it?' she asked. 'You know, the thing from the day before yesterday you said you'd tell.'

And suddenly I saw how my world had changed in just a few days. Not so much changed, perhaps, but expanded, making home seem small beside it, just as it looked when we came back from holidays at the sea.

'It's just that I've got a boy, I think.'

'Good grief! How d'you mean though? Aren't you sure?'

'It only started Wednesday and might not come to anything . . .'

'You mean, like – well – doing it, and stuff like that? Aren't you terrified?'

And in a way I was, though not quite as she had meant. It was like having to make a sudden choice between home and something I wasn't sure about, something without even Ginny in it. Not that anything much had actually happened, but I had a feeling that from now on everything would matter, just as it did after you'd thrown your first six in Snakes and Ladders. The way we played it, until you threw that six your counter didn't even reach the board, but once you'd thrown it, all your scores counted.

'When I've done my homework,' I said, 'let's have a game of Monopoly or something; downstairs, with Mother and Dad.'

'But you hate Monopoly; it bores you silly!'

Families, even quite awful ones, are a kind of rest from all the pretending you have to do. For a moment I just wanted everything to stand still and wait for me to catch up.

Chapter Four

Arthur Knight crumbled bread from a paperbag over his shoes and laughed as the pigeons jerked softly round to peck the crumbs from between the laces. We counted patterns on the bobbing heads – brown, grey, white and black in endless different arrangements.

Most days for the past three weeks we had met after school, sprawling on the green-slatted park seat and talking inconsequentially. It was always noisy when we were in the park, partly because it was small – from almost anywhere you sat you could see the red-brick houses at its boundaries. Little children, just out of school, threw bread to squawking ducks, or chased each other, squealing, while barking dogs, freed from houses and kennels and leashes, tore after them. We never had to fear that conversation might falter; there was enough to watch. We made bets about what was coming up in the formal garden beds and argued over the spelling of fuchsia and antirrhinum. Knowing him was a relief, from the worries of home and school and – strangest of all – the business of having to be seventeen and want a boy.

Sometimes I wondered if he really counted as a boyfriend, because there was none of the intensity and innuendo the others talked about. At first we'd told each other a few essential things about ourselves, no different from the way you always started a new 'best friend' even in Infant School days. And after that we seemed to have drawn a line around the two of us, not many yards away, and snatched at anything inside it, whatever offered, for conversation.

It was Arthur's doing. He was preoccupied with the familiar things around and up against us all the time, even quite tiny things. He scraped bits off brick walls with his penknife as we passed, crushing the chips to powder in his hand. 'I hate walls,' he said. 'They're dead, final. Brick-red. But powder's alive.' He let the dust trickle through his fingers; 'Half a dozen colours

27

ready to run and mix again.' He always spoke quickly, for ever pointing things out. 'Look, this fantastic beetle!' 'Quick, don't miss this hat!' – or dog, or door-knocker.

It was nothing like the way Dad was always instructing us where and how to look and what to see. 'Stand over here for the best view,' Dad would say, clamping his hand on my shoulder. 'Notice it's like a patchwork. You can see four counties, let's see how many you can name.' 'If only he wouldn't be so educational!' Ginny would whisper. Mother was always having to jump to her feet and rush over to the window with us to watch some bird in flight. 'That,' Dad would say, 'is the poetry of motion.' Mother never bothered much further than, 'It's very nice, isn't it, girls,' and we would echo, 'Yes, isn't it,' and rarely look. Watching things silently with Arthur was like sharing eyes.

I never told him about my Seated Group with its palpable message which I'd never meant. But standing or lolling around with him and letting images bombard me from outside, instead of endlessly inventing them myself, was what I needed, and I'd already finished my picture for the next meeting – three children bowling hoops on the grass round a circular flower-bed, two running clockwise and one the other way. It was meticulously done, and Ginny said it made her feel light-hearted. Next month, I thought, I'll be braver.

Mother quickly sensed something had changed. 'You're getting later and later home to your tea,' she grumbled. 'What's going on?'

'I walk home with a boy now. I'm old enough.' My heart was thumping.

'That's all very well; meals can't be kept waiting just to suit your convenience.'

'But I'm always in before Dad! No one's *ever* had to wait.' She was liable to turn her back at stressed words, so I continued more quietly, 'It's the only time there is to see him.'

'Your father doesn't like the house being treated like a hotel of an evening. I'm only thinking of your own good. I don't want you getting like – well – Freda from the end.'

Freda from the end was almost the only child in the street we'd ever spoken to, as we were never allowed to play out. She lived in one of the little terrace houses on the corner, well down the street from our semi, a thin, waif-like, laughing little girl a bit older than me. When we were all tiny we'd sometimes smiled and spoken if we passed when she was swinging on her garden gate, but once she was old enough to play in the street she soon became a stranger. Later still, when she walked home from school with boys each day, and stood chatting at the gate for ages, Mother said it lowered the tone, and we learned not to mention her. She had disappeared altogether a few months ago, which was only to be expected, Mother said.

'I shan't get like her!' Chance, I thought, would be a fine thing; I would have loved her ease and gaiety. 'Anyway, she's probably all right now she's grown-up . . .'

'She's not all right. It's always the same, children brought up without a father.'

'Could I go out on a Saturday then? I've been asked.'

'Your father likes us all to do something together at the week-end. He won't thank you for spoiling the family outing just to go gallivanting off somewhere.'

'It isn't gallivanting, and you could all still go. How would I spoil it?'

'Spoil it for Ginny; you've always done everything together.'

Upstairs, Ginny said I was crazy to have told her; I should have invented an alibi using Lydia, the only girl from school who had been more than once to the house. 'Everyone does it, I know that from school. Anything's better than risking a row.' And she tried her usual placating. 'It's not for herself Mother's objecting; she just has to watch it with Dad all the time.' We had never heard their voices raised against each other but assumed from Mother's apprehensive manner that Dad was 'always on' at her in private, the way he tended to behave in public with Ginny.

'Anyway,' she went on, 'it doesn't sound all that exciting yet, you and him. Perhaps it won't come to anything. Will you mind?' She was reeling from an introduction to the works of Mary Webb, and had been waiting almost fearfully for some sign of a developing relationship.

'I quite like it as it is, apart from the difficulty with Dad.' The prospect of 'development', and the lack of it, worried me equally. I think you get used to the endlessly repeated loss and gain, loss and gain, of growing-up, but something was threatening to get out of balance now, and I felt helpless both against Mother's obstinacy and Ginny's anxiety. If I grasped at something outside the family, too many of our happiest times could be in danger.

Then, on a Friday evening, when Dad was at the Gardens and Allotments Association meeting, and Ginny and I were working in our bedrooms, I heard Mother answer the front-door bell then come hurrying upstairs. 'I think it's your young man,' she panted. 'I've put him in the hall, but you could ask him into the front room if you like.' Then she became aware of her own fluster, and added, '*Look* at you! Smooth your skirt down, for goodness sake, and tidy your hair.'

It was disturbing to see Arthur in our hall, like having parents at school concerts, but he grinned and said, 'If we had phones I could ring great thoughts through the minute I had 'em. Look, someone's given Mum a goose; d'you want to come and help eat it tomorrow night? It's her birthday; there'll probably only be us.' Then before I could speak he added, 'I'd love to see you two together.'

'Let me mention it to Mother; there might be something planned.' And though I despaired of it, Mother raised no objection and didn't even mention Dad. When Arthur had gone she said, 'I'm surprised he's such a roughly-spoken boy. I'd have thought you'd want . . .'

'They all speak rough now, even the poshest boys. Should you have asked Dad? Will it be O.K.?'

She made a straight mouth. 'That'll be all right. I suppose you're right about the way they talk. You'd think the young people would want to show themselves in the best light. *We* always did.'

Upstairs, Ginny confessed, 'I had a look at him out of my window; he didn't see me, honest. He's not all that good-looking, is he? Like a schoolboy really, but he looked nice. Hadn't you better wash your hair, to give it time to settle? What'll you wear? D'you reckon she's going to stand up to Dad?'

Her fast talking made me almost tearful. It seemed that nothing could ever happen to you without affecting others and spoiling everybody's calm.

I said, 'It doesn't seem right for her to have to speak up for us all the time . . .'

'Like the Pope, interceding with God.'

We sorted through my few unexciting clothes, but Mother came and vetoed my decision. She said, 'A man likes to think a girl's taken a bit of trouble with her appearance; it's not very complimentary otherwise. After all, you've got the nice navy dress with the little white bolero; it's just right for the occasion – neat, and in good taste.'

And though I protested that skirts and blouses made me feel easier, and navy wasn't a colour, and I didn't want to think about taste, she persisted, saying it wasn't just myself I had to think about – what would people think of her, sending me out looking like a rag-bag. 'It's for your own good,' she said, 'one day you'll thank me,' and when I saw Ginny beseeching me with her eyes not to make a scene, that was the end of it. 'If they *are* people of taste,' Mother added, 'which I doubt, them living in Merton Street, they'll appreciate the dress, and if they're not, at least we won't have lowered our standards.'

At tea-time next day she looked at me approvingly. 'Your hair looks nice; you certainly won't disgrace us with your appearance.'

Dad eased a piece of crust from his denture. 'I hear he's from a broken home. There's a lot too much of that, these days; people push off at the first sign of difficulty without a thought for their children. It's not surprising they turn into these delinquents.' Apparently he hadn't objected to my going.

'He looked happy enough,' Mother said, 'but a bit thin perhaps. A boy does need a father; I daresay those two are eating out of tins.'

Dad agreed. 'We'll have to think about inviting him back some time; arrange some little treat. It doesn't take a lot to amuse a lad of his age, and at least he'd get a decent meal.'

'I daresay she'll have the goose in the oven before you get there,' Mother went on, 'but it wouldn't hurt to offer to help with the vegetables, and of course the washing-up.'

'*He* helps her,' I told them. 'He can cook and everything. They don't eat out of tins. And it's not just the two of them – he's got two little brothers.'

Mother and Dad looked at each other silently, then Dad bit off a piece of celery and crunched it noisily. 'Left her with three of them . . . they ought to deport men like that . . .'

'You should give him the benefit of the doubt,' Mother interrupted. 'I mean, *she* can't have been much, for him to go off like that. She probably drove him to it . . . it takes two. Best not to get too involved with her, dear.'

Perhaps they were doing no harm, but I shuddered to hear them exchanging their words with such certainty, taking my world to bits in terms of their own, as if nothing could be mine, or different, or have any value, if they hadn't given it. I wanted to get away before they made more inroads, and found myself angrily planning a sentence. Then I stood up and said it.

'You needn't worry about him or me or any of them; we've all got our own lives to think about.'

It was a daft thing to say, and sounded terrified rather than angry. Then I went quickly out of the room, closing the door carefully, and ran up and locked myself into my bedroom where I sat listening to my heart thumping. I told myself I'd lost my temper, but it wasn't really that – not when you know beforehand that you're going to do it, and even plan the words.

All over the district, I guessed, girls were scraping back their chairs and running red-faced out of rooms, slamming doors behind them, *properly* angry. That sort of thing must happen suddenly from inside, like sneezing, and probably the nearest I'd ever get to it would be that innocuous sentence carefully planned and politely delivered. It seemed feeble, not altogether genuine, and I grew hot at the thought that my tiny protest was some kind of sham.

Catching sight of my face in the mirror – it *looked* angry enough – I wondered if it would be possible to muster the courage to make a proper stand and change into the skirt and blouse. I got them out and put them on the bed, but the thought of Ginny left behind with two of them to cope with held me back.

She told me later that after I had walked out of the room Dad had leaned over and lifted the slice of cake left on my plate to his own, but no one had said anything.

Chapter Five

The Knights lived in a flat in what Dad, who worked in the Housing Department at the Town Hall, called 'a substantial Victorian property', in a run-down terrace. The house was tall and narrow, and the entire floor had once been two drawing-rooms, one on each side of the landing. One of them was now a living-room and kitchen, and the other had become two bedrooms and a bathroom. All the ceilings were high, and even the one in the kitchen still had grapevine moulding round three of its sides.

Apart from Lydia, whose house was detached, most people we knew lived in semis very like our own – the red-brick, bay-windowed, Edwardian kind, street after street of them, each with a privet hedge, cast-iron front gate, and short path of red tiles leading to the front door with its insets of coloured glass. Others lived in the newer, yellow-brick houses on the small estate, which were lighter and brighter, both inside and out, but Mother said were 'shoddy'. Arthur's home was my first experience of something different.

Ginny and I seldom went anywhere alone, but when we did it felt as if we journeyed on a string tied to the handle of the kitchen door; we were for ever referring back.

'Arthur says you paint,' his mother said as she let me in and led me upstairs to the flat. 'That's a thing I'd love to do. The minute Ralphie's off my hands I'll start in on something like that. D'you reckon it's feasible at my age?'

'Oh, surely, any age . . .' She would have been about as old as Mother but didn't wear a knitted suit and her hair wasn't 'done'. It made a difference which appealed to me.

'I can draw a bit. I used to think I'd keep it up in me spare time after we were married. Only you don't get any, do you? You have your kids then one day you look up and wonder where it's all gone.' She spoke without resentment. 'I daresay you're really good at it; perhaps I could come to you for a few wrinkles.'

33

In the hallway of the flat two little boys of about three and six pushed tiny model cars along the skirting-board, and she pointed to them and said, 'That's Ralphie and this one's Steve. Arthur's gone round the off-licence; he won't be a tick.' She didn't interrupt the game, but hung my coat on a peg and led me into the kitchen, where I gave her the box of three very small white handkerchiefs with edelweiss embroidered in the corners, which someone had brought Mother from Switzerland.

It was difficult to imagine this plump, lively person caring much for such daintiness, and I wished I'd brought the scarf with big pink and yellow roses that Ginny had offered. But as she shook one of the hankies out and draped it over the back of her hand you could see how much it appealed. 'It's not often I get anything *this* pretty. What with the boys and that, everything tends to get a bit clumpy. I'm outnumbered, see.' And, referring back, I wondered about Dad and the three of us.

'Tell you the truth, if I'd known you were going to put a nice dress on I would've smartened up a bit. I love frocks, but you know what it is – Arthur's friends come round and bring their girls, and you'd have to be for ever changing. Besides, I think they like to see you as you generally are, not all dressed up. They take to you easier.' Her skirt and blouse were like the ones I hadn't managed.

'I didn't want to wear this dress; my mother said I ought to.'

'Bit strict, is she? My mum was. I reckon they got it dinned into them when they were girls . . .' She stopped, then said, 'Hark at me going on as if our mums were the same generation! Funny I never got round to feeling my age. Time I started.'

'Why? It's not compulsory.'

She laughed. 'You're good for me, you are.' Then Arthur came in carrying a shopping-bag chinking with bottles.

He greeted us both, dumped the bag in a corner and looked at his watch. 'Right, time's up.' He shouted, 'Ralphie!' And the smallest boy, clutching four or five little cars against his chest, ran in and slid to the floor with his legs spread out straight in front of him. 'Two,' Arthur said, holding up two fingers, 'one red, one blue,' and Ralphie dropped the cars, sorted out what he was to be allowed to take to bed, and held them in his lap. Arthur knelt and took off the little boy's shoes, then said, 'O.K. "Goo'night, Mum, goo'night, Ella,"' and Ralphie lisped the

34

words and turned and followed him across the landing to their bedroom.

'Loves doin' it right, Ralphie does – any mortal thing Arthur tells 'im. Thank God he's like he is, my Arthur; if he was a devil I'd have three devils on me hands.' She started arranging lettuce leaves in a glass bowl. 'Steve gets another ten minutes for being older. Soon as Arthur's seen the little 'un down, it'll be his turn.'

'D'you think I should offer to help him?' It seemed a strange chore for a boy and I could almost hear Mother prompting me.

'I don't suppose he'd like it, not really. We do one each, see, turn and turn about. He gets indignant if I offer to do his one, when he's got a load of homework or anything.'

'I bet there aren't many boys who help like that.'

'They like the cuddle, same as girls. There's not all that much difference. You and your sister help a lot, do you?'

'Ginny – that's short for Virginia – does more than me; they keep me busy at my homework.'

'Got big ideas for you, have they?'

Standing in their kitchen and talking about Mother and Dad made me feel uneasy, as if something new had come up and needed thinking out. I was pretty sure they wouldn't take to Mrs Knight, though I found her a relief from many of the things that worried me.

'You should see my Arthur with the cat,' she went on. 'Real soppy.' She was peeling an apple for salad, turning the fruit slowly in her hand and giving it her full attention as she cut round it carefully with a small sharp knife. 'Steve!' she called, and the six-year-old ran to her and stood looking up at the red mottled peel as it coiled down towards the table. 'It's half-Siamese, and people say they're fierce, but him and Arthur between 'em come as near to a proper conversation as anything I ever heard. Uncanny it is.' She finished the peel and as it flopped gently to the table Steve smiled and picked it up. He carefully wound one end of it round his left wrist, then put the other end into his mouth. 'Five minutes,' she warned him as he ran back to his cars.

Then she shook out a plain red cloth, which Mother would have called 'rough-dried', and smoothed it across the table. Arthur came in and set four glasses round it. 'Ted's coming,' she told me as she brought place-mats. 'I daresay you know him, Ted Forrest at the sweetshop.' Arthur arranged cutlery, she found the cruets; he cleared children's books and papers off the chairs, and told about a motor-cycle accident he'd seen as he carried the bottles home. She said, 'I reckon once they get one of those things their mothers never know a minute's peace.' He said, 'Ted's sweet on Mum.'

They seemed to slot in and out of each other's needs so easily, with no one giving orders. It was as if they were satisfied with each other and where they found themselves, and I couldn't imagine that Arthur was always dreaming of being somewhere else or making up worlds, like Ginny and me. It began to explain the fragments of wall and fantastic beetles.

Ted came half an hour later, bringing a huge bunch of flowers in a cellophane wrapper. He shook my hand, saying, 'I doubt if you'll recognise me in the suit, but I've seen you once or twice.' Then he took two Mars bars out of his pocket and put them on a shelf as if that was what he always did, and went across the landing with Mrs Knight to see the boys. We stood still, listening to their delighted shrieks, and a few minutes later she came back alone.

As she tore away the cellophane to get her nose in among the flowers I thought of Mother, who would carefully smooth and fold away such a nice large piece to come in handy. She would be wondering if I was being a credit, and might not understand my relief that no one was expecting me to do any pretending. Arthur filled a glass jug with water and Mrs Knight arranged the blooms, passing one over now and then for us to smell. Ginny would be happy here, I thought, with no one watching for mistakes.

The goose dinner was the first meal I had ever wanted to go on and on, and I kept turning away from the table to see if I could hold the picture of it in my head. The four figures in it seemed to make a circle, though we were really one at each side of a rectangle the same as at home, but here they leaned into each other's space. And the faces were more important even than the flowers. Things to say came easily, even to me, not only because of the wine – which I'd only been allowed at Christmas-time before – but because you didn't have to edit your thoughts or hoard them till bed-time.

'Kids seem to change quite noticeably when they're six or seven,' Mrs Knight was saying. 'They get the hang of things, I reckon. Look at our Steve.'

'Ginny says that when you're very young you think life's a sort of through-train. You're on it and you've only got to wait to get there. Then you find it's a stopping-train and you have to start worrying about where to change.'

'Too right,' Mrs Knight mused. 'There's no one really tells you, is there?'

She smiled and spooned another potato on to Ted's plate. 'Gawd, it's a bloody stoppin'-train all right.'

All of us joined in all the conversations, and to me it was a new and wonderful way of talking, with every contribution accepted. 'Let's drink,' said Arthur, 'to Mrs Cartwright who gave Mum the goose.'

His mother raised her glass, murmuring, 'Dear old Lily Cartwright,' then spoke to me. 'You keep on looking at those flowers; I bet you're thinkin' you'd like to paint them.'

'Oh no . . . I've never tried to paint anything – well – beautiful.' It was the first time I'd realised it.

'Not a lot of point, you mean?'

'You'd feel clumsy, I should think.'

Ted pushed his glasses up on his forehead. 'What about landscapes and that? Don't you ever want to paint nice places where you've been, to remember them?' He asked as if the answer mattered; all of them asked more often than they stated things. I thought about it.

'I did once try to do a park, all trees and flowers and a lake full of ducks. Only I did it squashed and cramped, pushing up in the middle of a built-up area as if there wasn't room. It's not the same, is it?'

'One o' those strange pictures,' Mrs Knight suggested. 'They'd call it something like "The Struggle", wouldn't they, and you'd stop and wonder why.' She turned to Arthur. 'You can see why people disagree about pictures, can't you? D'you remember Dad when you stuck that Picasso woman on the cork bit on your bedroom wall? All points, she was, and great big tears running down her face. Dad said it was a load of rubbish, and you were ever so indignant. You couldn't have been more than eleven or twelve, and no gift of the gab like you've got now. He said anyone who couldn't paint a proper woman with a nice face you'd want to look at shouldn't paint at all.' To me she added, 'You and him wouldn't have hit it off; still, he'd have had to listen to you.'

They spoke as if you were a complete person already, not just serving your apprenticeship. In any family that kept it up for long, I thought, there would exist a frightening possibility of being, one day, completely understood. Guiltily I remembered a conversation with Dad a few days earlier.

'Here,' he'd said, proudly handing me one of the huge white roses he grew. 'Here's something for you to paint – did you ever see anything this perfect?'

'It's lovely.' Dad rarely left you anything to say.

'That's the sort of thing you should be doing, not the lop-sided stuff they teach you nowadays. A single long-stemmed rose in a tall jar – just a few leaves to give it colour, and you could have a drop of dew on one leaf to convey the idea that it's freshly picked. You wouldn't need a lot of background, just a nice piece of curtain or something. I used to be very good at draped fabrics. Look pretty good, that would, on the sitting-room wall, above the radio. You could look for half a lifetime and not find a more beautiful subject.'

After I'd said again that it was lovely, better really than any picture, Dad had gone away muttering, 'Makes you appreciate Nature's artistry.'

Well, I thought, it's not a crime, talking that way, just a bit . . . bullying; and hated myself for minding so much. But as the easy conversation round the Knights' kitchen table went on, and the comparisons kept presenting themselves, I grew guiltily miserable.

'If you two are off out,' Mrs Knight said as we scraped back our chairs and I started gathering up dishes, 'you'd better push off now and leave this to us – time's getting on.'

'We haven't arranged to go anywhere,' Arthur said, taking the dishes from me and replacing them on the table. 'But don't imagine *you're* doing any more tonight – it's your birthday.'

Ted piled a few plates together then stopped, looking from one to the other. 'Could I suggest something?' he said uneasily. 'Only do say if you don't agree. If you're not going out I'd like to take Doris to the Social Club for an hour or so, for a drink and a dance. I'd give you a hand with this first, while she gets ready . . .'

'Don't be so daft!' Mrs Knight flapped her hands, appalled but smiling. 'If you think I invite a guest to eat then push off and leave her baby-sitting, you've got another think coming. Coffee to make, washing-up to do – no, another time, love.'

'I'm happy to wash up,' I said. 'Don't know how I'll face my mother if I don't, whether you go out or not. It *is* your birthday.'

She folded her arms and said, 'So, it's one day when you don't have to do what your mum tells you.' She spoke light-heartedly, and Arthur put his arm round her shoulder and said, 'It's up to Mum and Ella, but washing-up doesn't come into it. We never do it the same night anyway, so why the sudden worry?'

After some good-natured bickering Mrs Knight agreed to go if Arthur promised to make me coffee, stop me from doing any kind of work, and see me home even if it meant leaving the boys alone for a few minutes. As she went out of the room she beckoned, and I followed her into her bedroom, where she started to pull off her blouse. 'Better get something decent on,' she said, 'with him in his good suit. Look – you sure? I mean, I don't know about you and Arthur, but if you'd prefer it I can stay as easy as go, and no questions. It doesn't *have* to be tonight.'

I wasn't used to having a say in arrangements, and just kept repeating, 'No, really, I don't mind at all.'

'Arthur's O.K.,' she told me. 'Nothing to worry about there – he's a lovely old feller really. Perhaps you'll give me a hand with the zip then.'

She was plump, and I thought her beautiful even in the shabby petticoat. She pulled a green cotton dress over her head and it occurred to me as I watched her floundering in it, hunting for the sleeves, that I had never seen our mother in her petticoat. I pulled the zip up to the neck and smoothed the shoulders at the back, wondering if she generally depended on Arthur, and if Mother looked to Dad.

As the door closed behind the two of them Arthur said, 'Now we'll have some coffee.' He filled the kettle. 'Did you like her? It's a damn silly question; still, I've asked it.'

'A lot – I really did.' She had begun to trouble me, making me feel gaunt and shapeless and only half-begun. It was unlikely, I thought, that anyone would ever bring me flowers. The evening was leaving me with a feeling that I'd wasted my life so far, somehow barking up the wrong tree. I should need to get home and into bed to think it out. I said, 'She's not so . . . well . . . *final* as most people's mothers. And she's more friendly, not always telling you what to do.'

He smiled as he hunted for spoons. 'Having a husband prob- ably finalises people a bit more. Come on, take your coffee and we'll shut the door on this lot and sit by the fire, if that's O.K. by you.'

'A fire! At this time of year?' Then I remembered that though the days were warm, Ginny and I had had goose pimples on our arms for the past few evenings.

Till then, I hadn't seen their living-room, and though there was absolutely nothing splendid in it, it immediately pleased and attracted me, like a picture painted in warm colours. It wasn't tidy, or particularly clean, but everywhere you looked was something *for* you – pattern or colour or shadow-and-light – something to hold your interest. None of the furniture looked as if it would stay for ever in the same position. The chairs all seemed to have just lost an occupant who had left something there and would return to carry on with it at any minute. There were rugs of different colours on the floor, but I didn't even notice walls, or how the place was decorated. There were some shelves of books, some small reproductions of modern paintings mounted on card, and in the corner an old upright piano, perhaps the most valuable thing in the room, open and littered with music-sheets, and with a dirty cup and saucer standing on the top. It was the most lively, friendly room I'd ever seen, and the small summer fire kept the lights and shadows and colours moving and changing.

I know now that you can take a room and clean and decorate away the feelings of all the people who had ever had any in it. You can paper over their enthusiasms and, without meaning to, make a place which the presence of people would only spoil, like litter. In the Knights' room, it seemed to me, no matter what your mood, you could keep your eyes wide open and nothing would jar.

'Sit down,' Arthur said, poking the fire, so I sat on the rug and stood my cup in the hearth, and he drew up a chair and sat with his lanky legs resting against my arm.

'I mustn't be late, they don't like it.' I was trying not to think of them sitting up waiting. Mother would have put a decent dress on, in case anyone brought me home and had to be asked in. They would be in the front room where the one central light threw down a harsh cone-shaped glare, leaving the space beyond it cold and lifeless. They would be listening to something Dad had chosen on the radio, sitting upright side by side on the sofa which was the same green as the two armchairs – a bleak half-green made with too much blue and only ever seen in furniture. There was no other colour – curtains and carpets were beige like the walls, which only existed for privacy and papering. Nothing actually offended, but it was sad, with a poverty I didn't understand. Perhaps the room was about no one but Dad, and though the two of them had worked hard for it and would go on working to keep it nice for ever, it wouldn't come alive. No living-room before the Knights' had ever given me so strongly the certainty that ours was awful.

In my imagined picture of my parents, Mother seemed to be holding her breath, desperate to keep everything unchanged and nice for ever, but only for Ginny and me; as if their own turn at life was over. It made my eyes prickle, and I felt a fool and hoped it was just the wine.

'Well, best to keep on the right side of them, I suppose,' Arthur was saying, 'or they mightn't let you come again. Anyway, *will* you come again? I mean, you don't have to wait for an occasion.'

I couldn't stop my eyes prickling, and turned my head away. A lump was starting in my throat; I was afraid to speak.

Arthur put his hand on the back of my neck. He must have felt the trembling, and said cheerfully, 'You laughing or crying?', certain it wasn't crying. Then, in an amazed voice, as I kept my face averted, wondering what on earth to do against the tears, 'Oh no, don't! Please don't!' He clattered his cup to the floor and held me against his knees with stiff, bony hands. There was such awkwardness in it for us both, and after a moment he said softly, 'I'm sorry. Look, I'm such a fool . . . honestly, I never learn! I just assumed you were happy, same as me . . .'

'I *am*. I loved it all.' How were you supposed to manage the shame of such an outburst? Sniffing and dabbing at my nose I said, 'It's like a kid who doesn't want to go home; everything's lovely here . . .'

He gave a shrill laugh which ended up too high. 'Oh, come *on* – for God's sake – it's a tip!'

'I mean warm, and . . . not bleak. I keep comparing things; it makes you feel so mean.'

'Mean! You? You're crazy!' His voice was unusually loud and shocked me back to sense, as I'd been almost whispering, conscious of the boys asleep across the landing. So I blew my nose and apologised, then told him about my mother not seeming to want anything any more, and about the room at home.

He interrupted. 'What's it matter if you don't like the way they do their place up? What's it matter, if it's what they want?'

And I knew it wouldn't have mattered, if only it had been possible to imagine them sitting in the bleak room and looking happy, but when I tried visualising them with happy faces, the room seemed to fall away from the picture, as if it could never coexist with happiness. I wanted to explain my doubt that anything was really as either of them wanted it, but it occurred to me that he must find it hard to believe in people like us. My face was almost hidden in my skirt as I tried to dab away the signs of misery.

'Look,' he said suddenly, 'why don't you get up – I mean, don't crouch like that. You don't have to hide away just because you're crying.' He got to his feet and helped me up from behind, then leaned his face into the back of my hair. 'You're a daft thing,' he muttered, pushing his thin arms over my shoulders and crossing them in front of me. 'Look.' He was pointing to a small picture we both faced. 'Bet you can't guess who did it.'

He started to walk towards the picture slowly, his long legs gently pushing mine ahead of him as I dabbed with my handkerchief and tried to push the hair out of my eyes. It was a game, and he chuckled, and it reminded me of years ago when Dad would walk us on his feet.

I couldn't see the picture clearly through my tears, though there seemed to be a large expanse of sky with a narrow strip of grass and trees at the bottom. I closed my eyes for a moment as we stood beside it. 'Me!' he announced, without waiting for my guess. 'I did it when I was about twelve, and Dad said, "Clouds don't *go* like that," and I was furious and stuffed it in a drawer. Then after he went Mum tore up all his pin-ups from in the shed and gave away lots of his things, like the model galleon and train-set, and we stuck our own things everywhere, and I put up this picture. Seems daft now, thumbin' your nose to your old man like that. Still, we enjoyed ourselves.'

We stood by the picture and gradually, in the silence, I felt something deep inside me like a great slow pause. It was like being hollow then slowly filling with a sort of tension, palpable as terror, so that for a moment I lost the feeling that I was situated somewhere just behind my eyes, and grew aware that I was inside every part of my awkward body and isolated limbs, filling them out, and knowing their shape and size. It seemed to me that Arthur, too, must be feeling different – I guessed it from his silence, and was glad we were both facing in the same direction. But though it was awkward it was good, and I kept still for fear of losing the sense that we held some kind of certainty balanced carefully between us.

Then he took his lolling arms from my shoulders and rested his hands there instead, and the separate, chaotic bits of me drew together and seemed to come alive at the centre of somewhere absolutely new. And when he said softly, 'Could I take off this loopy jacket thing you're wearing?' it seemed neither strange nor worrying and I stood quite still, letting him push the jacket and then the dress from my shoulders, so that they fell around my knees. For the first time I wanted to be seen, even felt strangely certain that underneath my awful cotton vest I would be beautiful.

We didn't move away from the picture. Arthur still stood behind me, leaning his head against my hair and looking down over my shoulder at my laughable breasts, and when he touched me I felt such richness . . . I was surely big and warm and round and lovely, like Mrs Knight, and vibrant like the room, and it occurred to me that nothing anyone had ever said, and nothing I had ever heard, or read, had told these feelings right.

Arthur said, 'I feel . . . ridiculous. Wondering if my hands are cold or anything. A daft thing like that!' Then he smoothed my hair and shook back his own, and added, 'I feel so bloody *chaste*! D'you mind a lot?'

I was uncertain what had happened, but shook my head and smiled, and felt a bit ridiculous myself. The moment and the feeling were dying, and worries flooding back. Whatever was wrong must surely be my fault. I pushed my arms into the sleeves of my dress and buttoned it up, then folded the bolero, and we sat down on the rug before the fire, leaning against the two armchairs, facing each other now, with our shoes touching.

'My dad,' he said into the silence, 'is full out for the old Greek idea – I think it's Greek – of boys being trained by special women till they're fit to be let loose with a girl.'

'I thought people could make it up as they went along. Surely it doesn't have to be the same for everybody.' I wanted to sound reassuring and with no hint of my confusion.

43

For a time we were silent, and in my head all kinds of different images were getting muddled, images put there by Ginny reading aloud from Mary Webb, other girls' giggled confessions, and Mother's unintelligible warnings.

Then he leaned over and kissed me very quickly – it was the first time he had – and jumped up and ran into the kitchen. I was putting on the bolero as he came back with two of the red-mottled apples, and we sat biting into them, talking in the carefree way we did on ordinary days, only now it seemed another sort of pretending.

He walked with me to the end of the road and I ran the rest of the way home while he hurried back to the boys. Mother was waiting up, neatly dressed.

'It was a lovely evening . . . She liked the hankies. The little boys are sweet. Goose is quite tasty.' I kept talking, fearful of her questions.

'A bit fatty for some people's taste,' Mother said. 'Still, it's nice for you to get out and see things a bit. I can tell you've enjoyed yourself – it suits you.' She brought hot milk for me, speaking with feeling, as if she had missed me.

'What sort of woman is the mother?'

'A lively person, about your age, I suppose. I think the little boys keep her pretty busy.'

'People should think of that before they have them. Specially at that age, if they want their freedom.'

'I was thinking . . . you could go out more now, couldn't you? In the evenings, I mean.'

'Good gracious no, my gadding-about days are over.'

'I don't see why. We're old enough to look after ourselves. Sometimes I think you take too *much* care of us. Mrs Knight goes out quite a bit even now, and when she's got the littlest one off her hands she's going to take up painting. She's interested in a lot of things . . .'

Mother got up and began to tidy cushions. Her neck was flushed. 'So she may be, but you'd better not start coming home dictating the way we should run our lives. Your father wouldn't take kindly to *that*.'

She picked up my mug to take to the kitchen, and added, 'And by the way, we don't want you to make a habit of this sort of outing. You're far too young to think about boys seriously, and you've got quite enough to give your mind to for a long time yet. Anyway, it wouldn't be right for the two of you to go off on your own, and you can't keep imposing on the family, not without asking him back here, and *that* idea didn't seem to please you at tea-time.'

I felt responsible for her confusion and the bitter note in her voice and went up to bed wishing I hadn't tried to get closer to her. Taking off my things I was thinking how unbelievable it was that she and I must once have been as close as any two human beings ever get. I pictured, first, Mother years ago, looking down at me, her tiny new baby, then Arthur an hour ago, standing looking at me from over my shoulder, and I wondered if in some strange way babies too might be aware that they're being looked at and delighted in.

Ginny crept in as I got into bed. 'Tell me,' she whispered.

'The goose was lovely. They're ever so poor, but I wish you could see their living-room. Mrs Knight doesn't go on at Arthur at all . . .'

'Yes, but . . . any developments with him?'

For once I felt much older than Ginny and wanted to keep some of it to myself. 'Well, not really. But don't worry, it isn't like the stuff you read.'

'You don't mean you actually . . .?'

'Oh no! But I think it's all a bit nicer than you'd imagine from the books.'

Ginny looked lost. 'Surely they wouldn't *all* tell it wrong. Anyway, the girls at school say it's marvellous.'

'I think they're right. So don't worry.'

As she turned to go Ginny whispered, 'Dad talked to me quite a bit. He kept asking Geography things though he knows it's my worst subject. I think both of them would have been happier if I'd been the one to go out.'

Lying awake, aware of the shape of myself under the bed-clothes, I knew that although almost nothing had changed I should never again feel quite as ordinary as I had yesterday, and wished I had been able to tell Ginny about the moment in the warm room.

It was easy to see why people couldn't really tell it in words. Surely you couldn't paint it, either – not just the scene. That would only show how it might have *looked*. Yet I *had* painted about a feeling – though inadvertently – in the tea-table group, and I thought how marvellous it would be to stumble on a way of capturing on paper what I had felt that evening. For a long time I lay tense with the worry of just how to trap a sensation, flat, and get a line drawn round it.

Before I went to sleep I came a bit nearer to doing just this, picturing myself with a long empty sheet of grey sugar-paper and a brushful of black, painting the branches of a leafless tree, feathered with small twigs reaching out to the limits of space. I would draw birds in every colour I could imagine; small, patterned birds standing on every branch and every twig, facing in all directions, heads lifted, beaks open, and every one of them singing.

Chapter Six

At tea-time on Monday Dad asked, 'What kind of property do your friends live in? The ones you went to Saturday evening.' He'd hardly spoken to any of us during what had remained of the weekend, and now did so provocatively, in the voice in which he sometimes led Ginny towards humiliation.

'A first-floor flat, one of those tall narrow houses with steps in front and a semi-basement. I don't think it's a property exactly – I mean, they pay rent.'

'Economically, not the most sensible way of living. Years and years of paying out and at the end it's just money down the drain.'

'Hardly down the drain – you do live there for the money . . .'

'Not only uneconomical' – he ignored my remark – 'but when there are children, downright irresponsible.' The other two were holding their breath.

'I don't suppose everybody wants to own things. You don't have to.' It wasn't often I said what had only just occurred to me.

'It shows a sloppy attitude to life. What was the father?'

'How d'you mean?'

'What work did he do – *if* he worked.'

'He ran a taxi-hire thing, had his own taxi.'

Dad's smile suggested that my words just proved what he was saying. 'One of your here-today-gone-tomorrow types; not the most settled race of men.'

'They've lived there fourteen years!'

He leaned forward and took a slice of bread and butter. 'Time enough, I'd have thought, to get their finances settled and a bit of property behind them. What became of that gooseberry jam, Mother? Did we eat the lot?' And I was so unused to being the focus of his hostility that I thought he'd ended the conversation abruptly to help me out. Ginny said later that if he hadn't packed it in when he did, Mother would have done something – 'You get to depend on it.'

As soon as the jam was found Dad smiled round pleasantly. 'I shall be late tomorrow, I'm afraid,' he said. 'Too late for you to wait tea. Got a visit to do.' Now and then he left the office to visit some local housing site, particularly when there were photographs to be taken.

'You're generally home earlier on visit days,' Mother said gently.

'Ah, that's when I just abandon office hours and come straight from the site. This is something different.' He continued with the details as if he were determined none of us should be left in doubt. He would be catching a late-afternoon train to Aldershot – he took a folded railway time-table from his pocket and waved it about, then put it back – to look at some conversions to a large property.

'Aldershot!' Mother said. 'What on earth are they doing out there?'

'It's a *private* conversion. Part of Mr Timpson's personal life, and what you might call "extra-mural" for me – that's why it's important.' He said his boss was having the house converted for his aunt who already lived in Aldershot, and that he felt honoured to have been consulted.

'Will you get paid extra?' Ginny asked, and he shot her a contemptuous look, so that Mother said quickly, 'In that case you'd think they'd allow you time off; not send you there after a hard day's work.'

'That,' he said, 'would hardly be ethical. You can't use the public service for private needs. You should see it as I do, as a compliment. After all' – his voice was growing edgy – 'it's going to involve some contact with the aunt herself, so he could hardly send just anybody.' He said he was amazed that a man couldn't give a little service to another nowadays without the idea of financial reward cropping up 'in some mercenary little mind'. He turned to Ginny as he said it, and Mother at once sent her to the kitchen to fetch an apple tart, which we used as a focus of conversation for a time, while Dad sat silent and annoyed. I think he'd planned his announcement carefully but only envis-aged us listening, not making comments.

'There!' Mother said cheerfully, handing out the tart. 'The pieces are large, but it's never so nice when it's left-overs, and the cat's not a lot of help, not with pastry.'

I said, 'We'd better get a dog, then nothing will go to waste.'

It was one of the things we often said just to help with the talking, certain that no one would take it seriously.

'No thank *you.*' This was Mother's usual reply and we all knew how she felt about dogs, but this time as she said it Dad turned to me.

'What sort of dog? D'you have anything in mind?'

'We couldn't do with a dog!' Mother said quickly.

'I see no reason, if the child wants a pet . . .'

'The cat would never . . .'

'Many people manage to keep both with no difficulty . . .' but I interrupted.

'It was only a joke. I didn't mean it.'

Dad ran his tongue slowly along his front teeth. You could tell he was deciding on an attitude. 'Perhaps it's time we started saying what we mean in this family.' It would be hard for him to drop it now, and he asked Ginny, 'What about you? How d'you feel about dogs?'

She drew in her breath sharply. 'Well, I do love puppies of course,' she began, uncertain where she was being driven. 'I mean, everyone does, don't they? Only I don't . . . think . . . I actually want one.'

'You "love" puppies,' he mimicked her voice, 'but you don't want one.' He shook his head sadly at her, forked around with his apple tart for a moment, then pushed away his plate and leaned across the table towards me, peering at the few crumbs of pastry I had left. 'Was yours soggy at the bottom, or is it only mine?'

'Mine was gorgeous, same as always. I don't suppose either of us will ever get round to making it like this – unless it's something you can inherit.' I wanted to find words to shame him, but placating came easier, when we were face to face.

'You probably swallowed it without noticing,' he smiled, and I got up and started stacking dishes, the only way I had of showing that I wasn't going to sit and play his game. 'If you don't mind,' I called over my shoulder to Mother as I carried plates to the kitchen, 'I'll wash, and leave the wiping to you and Ginny. I've got a picture to finish.' And when she tried to make me go straight up and leave it all I refused. It seemed trifling, but had as much importance, for me, as if I'd fixed Dad with my eye, said 'Watch it!' boldly, and marched from the room.

Ginny was cheerful as the three of us sat down to tea next

day. 'Hen-party, like in the war,' she said. 'Not that I remember any of it,' and chattered on, enjoying her moment of freedom.

I had come home in a torment of doubt and excitement and worry, forgetting Dad's arrangements, and had planned to hurry from the table as soon as possible to talk to her, but as I watched her chattering now, it seemed cruel to cut short her lively mood, for my own reassurance.

'"A little girl with a long tongue,"' Mother said kindly. 'That's what they said about you in the Infants, and I can see their point.'

'*Was* I awful?' You could see how she needed to talk about herself, freed from the fear of humiliation.

'No, neither of you really gave them any trouble. Lots of them did though; they'd got out of hand as toddlers, with the men away.' Even Mother's voice was different, and for once I felt as if we almost made a circle.

'D'you remember VE Day?' I said. 'You stood me on a wall, and held Ginny up in your arms and we looked down a long street packed with people, all singing and cheering.'

'That's right. You had flags on little sticks, and you kept saying "Where's the war?" You thought it was some kind of dragon; they'd gone away and won it, so it was only natural they'd bring it home.'

'In triumph,' Ginny said, 'like the Ashes.'

'There was a street-party in the afternoon.' Mother was narrowing her eyes, remembering. 'I had to lend a lot of plates and things.'

'Everyone was happy at the same time,' I could remember wondering at it. 'It must have been awful for the ones whose people didn't come back, but nobody *looked* sad. D'you think they stayed indoors, hidden away?'

'You didn't see the half of it. There was a terrible lot of sadness everywhere, and more to come. A day like that was wonderful, of course, but then the hard times went on. There was still tight rationing, and lots of the men came back to find their jobs had gone, or things at home had changed out of all recognition.'

Ginny said quickly, 'Yes, but just being home must have made it all seem worthwhile for them.'

'Not for a lot of them it didn't.' Mother so seldom spoke of her memories that I caught Ginny's eye to warn her not to interrupt. 'You must remember none of them was the same as

50

when they went away. They'd lived very different, and done things they'd never . . . You don't just go and fight a war and come back and carry on the same. It was dreadful for lots of the wives and kiddies, with men like strangers coming into their homes.'

I wanted to ask if it had been a bit like that for us, but it would have brought the fragile conversation to an end. Anyway, I could remember some of it. Mother had been anxious about Dad's health, particularly over-solicitous about his bowels, and hounded him with nervous enquiries till he took to forestalling her, stamping out of the lavatory each morning and shouting down the stairs, 'Not a lot of luck', or 'Good clear-out this morning', with occasionally more specific details. She was always horrified, and I used to worry for her when we had visitors. I can't remember that he ever actually shamed her in front of them; just kept an almost palpable tension alive, and I remember Ginny starting, at that time, to pick holes in the elbows of her jumpers.

Now Mother roused herself. 'Well, if you've all had enough we'll clear away.' And when it was all done, and the dishes packed in the cupboards, she said, 'There's no reason why you two shouldn't go up and get on as usual.'

'But it isn't as usual. We thought you'd like a game of cards or something, for a change.'

'Your father wouldn't like you to neglect . . .'

'He isn't *here*,' Ginny insisted, 'so you're in charge. Why do men have to decide everything, even when they're not around?'

'A man likes to feel he's head of the household, even when there aren't children. Look at your Auntie Mary, the way she leaves everything to Uncle Morton.'

'Why look at Auntie Mary? I'd rather copy royalty, and the duke always has to walk just behind the queen.'

'Now you're talking silly,' Mother said, so Ginny took her schoolbag and went upstairs, but I stayed.

'It's only some men that want to be in charge, isn't it?' I asked. 'I mean, what about the ones that don't feel bossy?'

'You know nothing at all about men yet,' she replied unhelp-fully, making a straight mouth so that I knew she didn't want to argue, but before going up I followed her into the living-room and said quietly, 'I never know if you mean that how things are is how you think they ought to stay. Or d'you think people should try and change it all?'

She opened the sideboard drawer and took out her knitting, which she didn't enjoy but kept as 'something to do', then hunted for her place in the pattern. 'The trouble with your generation is that you want to change the lot. It's the way you think you *can* change that's so infuriating.'

I was surprised she thought of me as a member of a generation, when I had to work so hard at being like the rest. 'Doesn't everybody want to, when they're young? I mean, you and Dad's generation even fought a war to get things changed.'

She counted a row carefully. 'People generally fight wars to keep things the same,' she said. 'I don't suppose you realise the shadows they cast, these wars . . . over people's lives, I mean. Most of my lot were born in one war and married in another, think of that. It's all uniforms and heroes to you young people now – that's all they show you in the films.'

It was the first time I had heard her say things which could never have been an echo of Dad's words, and I wanted her to put down the knitting and lean back and go on talking. We could have called Ginny down and made a cup of tea and sat round giving each other a chance, like the Knights . . .

'I daresay we wanted things different, yes; but you soon settle down when you know you can't change them.' She said it with an air of finality, looping up a dropped stitch with a crochet-hook.

I tried again. 'Even when you find you can't, though, don't you still, even now, sometimes *want* to?' But she had started counting again, so I took my things and followed Ginny who had got no further than halfway up the stairs, where she stood with her head bent, listening.

'I just wanted to make sure you weren't quarrelling,' she whispered, then waited till we were in my room with the door shut. 'Everyone in this family is changing,' she said, 'except me.'

'Mother isn't.'

'She was completely different, talking about after the war!'

'Not really, only the same as you – free to say what she likes for once.'

Ginny began to run about, tidying things for me. 'I don't think we ought to say awful things about Dad,' she said gently. 'After all, some men beat their children, or go off and leave them in broken homes . . .'

'Like Arthur, you mean?' I thought of the warm, colourful flat and the living-room fire and the talk. 'Ginn, there's things to tell, but . . .'

'Oh good!' She smoothed the bed-cover and sat cross-legged on it. 'I didn't like to keep asking about him, but I did wonder how you got on yesterday and today after school. Was it any different because of Saturday?'

'I liked it better how it was before. It felt more friendly then, and . . . carefree. But now . . .'

'You mean he wants to make it serious, instead of just a casual relationship. I think that's lovely.'

'Yes, but to be honest, Ginn, I don't really know what you have to do . . . particularly about babies, I mean.'

Startled, she drew in her breath and clapped her hand over her mouth. 'You don't mean . . . Not going the whole *way*!'

All her expressions came from the letters at the back of Mother's magazine, and I wasn't sure what I ought to say, but she went on in a horrified voice, 'You can't! It would be pre-marital sex!' She slid off the bed and began to walk round the room straightening things, her brow furrowed and her eyes almost crossed with imagining.

'He's nearly a year older than me, you see, and going on a training course in the autumn. I'm not really sure how he means, but he does keep mentioning it, since Saturday.'

I didn't want to tell her how worried he seemed, or how his usual easy chatter felt like pretended brightness now, and had made me wonder if he wished I hadn't cried that evening at his flat, changing everything so suddenly.

Reality had certainly changed Ginny. A short time ago she'd been avid for 'developments', and saw it all like one of the romantic books she read, and I believe I'd half expected her to be the same tonight. It was so easy to imagine her crooning, 'So you'll really be lovers? It's absolutely dreamy!'

What I wanted to tell her, but couldn't now, was that one of the prefects at Arthur's school hired out the key of the old unused sports pavilion to boys who wanted to take a girl there after school, and Arthur had asked me to go there on Friday evening. Although it was a Painters' Club evening, I'd somehow agreed, uncertain whether it was awful to go or prudish to refuse, and no idea of how to decide. I wasn't really sure what was expected of me, or who to ask, and was scared by his worried, awkward manner. Now I knew I must keep it to myself.

Ginny took the elastic band off the end of her plait and started to undo her hair, shaking it around her shoulders. 'I know there *are* girls who do it,' she said softly. 'There's this fifth-year girl who went to some clinic to get fixed up, and the girl who was my partner for Domestic Science last term said she had a friend who'd got jujube things from that shop in Plant Street where they've got the enemas in the window. Only – someone in your *family* . . . it seems awful!'

She knew more than I did, and her words alarmed me, but her troubled frown was unbearable. 'Actually,' she added, 'I think boys already know whatever you have to. They're probably born knowing.'

'Well, one of you has got to know, but you can hardly ask them . . .'

Ginny saw her opportunity and began to prance about, calling over her shoulder to some pursuing lover, 'My lord, 'ere upon this four-poster bed you have your will of me, pray answer these half-dozen awkward questions . . .' But her heart wasn't in it, and though we quickly joked the worry out of the conversation, as she plaited up her hair again she added, 'We don't even know the questions; we don't know *anything*, do we? You'd think after all these years and years of people not knowing, someone would write an instruction booklet, if it's as important as they say it is. Have you said anything to Lydia?'

'No, there didn't seem a lot of point.'

'I know what you mean.'

I said, 'Don't worry, Ginn, don't even think about it. It'll blow over. Look, I've got to finish my Street Scene for Friday. You'll have to hop it.'

'At least you won't be seeing *him* Friday,' she said as she left. 'That's a blessing.'

'Nor tomorrow or Thursday,' I lied, resolved now to protect her. 'He's got cricket or something.'

'Good, so we're safe till Monday.'

I kept adding people to my Street Scene that evening, packing them into spaces, completely overwhelming the rather bleak, self-conscious composition I'd mapped out. I didn't feel like painting, but concentrated hard, trying to give myself a rest from worry, kidding myself, as I crowded out the spaces, that I was beginning to be a 'telling' painter.

Down in the bottom right-hand corner I painted the treeful of birds, growing up from the other side of a garden wall. It was quite unlike the rest of the picture but too small to be glaringly out of place, shrunk almost to a kind of signature. All the same, as a pictorial reminder of something that surely *had* been marvellous, I thought it more than matched up to Dad's photo of the day we went to see the buttercups. And by the time the picture was finished I'd decided – although I thought I'd only been thinking about the painting – to ask Lydia to help me with Friday. It wasn't advice I wanted – no one went to Lydia for that – I just needed someone to be in it with me, and there wasn't anybody else to turn to.

Chapter Seven

The Friendly Cow milk-bar, midway between home and school, was never empty. Shoppers went there to rest their feet, while old people, for somewhere to go, balanced uncomfortably on the smoked-glass chairs and stared silently at the murals. At four o'clock the older pupils from the secondary schools flung books and bags down in the space behind the door and raced to the bar stools where for half an hour they shouted at each other above the shriek of the Espresso machine, sharing cups of coffee and gingerly smoking the tensions out of the day. But it was after the evening rush-hour, when the young people back from work took over, that it became 'the place to go', and Ginny and I, who had never actually been inside, looked forward to a time when we would feel sophisticated enough to saunter in, greeted by friends on all sides, and belong, for the whole evening.

It was always dark, because of the grape ivy that trailed and climbed all over the inside of the windows, and the gloom was intentionally deepened by directing a few swivel-arm lights up into the ceiling which was covered with trellis and bunches of artificial grapes.

Lydia and I had arranged to meet there on Friday after Painters' Club. She was to make my excuses at school and bring word of what had happened to my picture, so that there would be something to tell at home. When I'd first asked her, she had agreed at once then said, 'But why don't you just *invent* something to say to them? They'd never know.'

So I had to confess that what I really wanted was to have someone sharing in my little bit of deceit, but didn't want to worry Ginny. 'To tell you the truth, I'm a bit scared. We've only been alone once before . . .'

'Oh I wasn't prying! Of course I'll come. Only, let's meet inside. I'd hate to hang around that doorway.'

Of course I hadn't told her about the sports pavilion. She

was always more discreet and delicate than was necessary, romanticising about my friendship with Arthur with absurd clichés, and I'd given up saying much about us, but it did seem wrong to be too cagey when I was asking for her help, so I told her, 'He's going to France on the School Journey next week, and after that . . .'

'I know, you poor soul, ten lousy days! It's quite true, that bit: "The course of true love never did run smooth."' So I didn't tell her the rest of his arrangements as she would have made a tragedy out of it.

Lydia was just about the dullest person in the class, but flat rather than unintelligent. I'd begun to suspect it in the first days of our friendship when we were eleven and had only just started at the Grammar. She had approached me as I stood alone by the flower-border at recreation-time, pretending to read the labels and wondering how to get into one of the groups or trios or couples that were forming – for the sake of anonymity as much as friendship.

She'd said, 'Can I walk around with you?' and when I nodded quickly and we set off along the border she'd added, 'I'd really love it if you'd be my friend.'

I thought she'd chosen me; it was a compliment. She couldn't possibly feel as I did, desperate for *any* friendship, or she'd never have admitted it by asking. She was the most handsome girl in the class, with a dark, almost adult beauty that marked her out from the ordinarily pretty ones. Her very heavy dark hair fell around her shoulders, her eyes were huge, and because her skin was sallow there was already a suggestion of down on her upper lip. It suggested a sultry, brooding heaviness, though she was actually more slightly built than me, and while the rest of us darted about in runs and jerks, she moved calmly, and I took it as a sign of maturity, fearing she would soon leave me for someone more like herself.

But she didn't, neither did anyone try to take her from me, and we stayed 'friends' as an insurance against isolation. The others came to regard us as a couple, and I found myself collecting and treasuring any chance word that suggested they found us an ill-matched pair. On the edges of groups, before my presence was realised, I heard things which confirmed my own suspicions. 'With a face like that who needs a brain!' Mother and Dad had taken to her at once, and went on inviting her for tea and weekend outings for so long that our relationship was embarrassingly sealed.

On Friday evening, though I arrived late at the Friendly Cow, there was no sign of Lydia, and as I shoved my way through the crowded tables I began to wish we'd chosen somewhere else to meet. Every seat was occupied, and at the bar the customers balanced shoulder-to-shoulder on the high stools, while more of them stood round in groups under the trailing ivy and philodendron plants. I wasn't sure how to get the proprietor's attention as he checked orders at the top of his voice above the noise of the people and the shrieking machine, then how to get the coffee over the others' shoulders and away through the crowd to a safe place. But at last I saw Lydia standing in the shadow of a huge rubber-plant, drinking coffee and trying to attract my attention without drawing any to herself, and I went and rested my cup on the narrow glass shelf where she'd kept a few inches free for me.

'I've been here ages,' she shouted. 'Honestly, I was wondering what to do if you didn't show up. My people are probably on to the police already.' She didn't seem perturbed, just shouting against the noise.

'Sorry, it wasn't easy getting away.' It was horrifying to hear my voice come out between chattering teeth.

'That's O.K. You got a red. She said the lamp-post thing cut the composition in two and you could have done without it; but there were a few lyrical bits. I told her you'd felt sick and gone home.'

'Thanks ever so much.' Having to shout was steadying my voice.

'Was it all O.K.? Don't worry, I'm not actually asking, only you don't look all that – well – radiant. Not like I'd expected.'

'I'm fine, really.' I wanted to sit down, at least to be quiet, and had to force a smile.

She said, 'That's better. Look, I'll have to go,' but she didn't, and we stood looking round at the excited crowd. She said, 'None of these people are from school, all out at work, I suppose, though I reckon some of them could be younger than us. It makes you think.'

Looking round I wondered how on earth I'd get to be like any of them in just a year or two. 'Perhaps going out to work changes you a lot,' I said, but Lydia thought it had more to do with how you choose your parents. 'Next life,' she said, 'I'm picking more carefully.'

Her parents were wealthy and she disliked them openly, but without the rebellious indignation, or any of the distress, that other girls with parent trouble often showed. It was as if she'd consciously decided to dislike them, rather than felt actual dislike. She also accepted, easily, as if she'd decided on it, the mediocrity of her work and ideas, and her poor performance at creative subjects and all games, and seemed to see herself as a permanently half-baked, once-and-for-all fact.

'Don't forget,' she said now as she turned to go, 'red star, awkward composition, lyrical bits. That enough?'

'Thanks, Lyd. I'm coming too. Look, could I pay for your coffee or something?'

'Don't be daft. Just do the same for me one day.'

Outside, the street was full of strollers enjoying the first cool of the day, and despite the traffic there was relief from noise. As we walked Lydia said, 'Don't answer if it's a cheek to ask, but did it happen?' I nodded, and we continued to the corner where we took different directions. As I walked on alone I was trying hard to justify to myself the day's deceit. Surely it's not the same when it's for other people's sakes, I told myself, and with Ginny in her prudish phase I'd had no option. I tried hard not to think too much about Ginny now, and remembered with shame that I hadn't even asked Lydia what had been said about her own picture.

'Never mind,' Mother said, bringing tea and sandwiches. 'No one can always be the best, and you've had some good stars this year. Anyway, it might have been even better if you'd had a proper visiting critic.' Dad said a bit of failure never harmed anyone; it had made Ginny pull her socks up, hadn't it? Ginny opened her mouth then shut it and smiled, settling for the scrap of implied praise. I hoped she would leave me alone this evening, but she was watching closely and went up when I did and followed me into my room.

'Listen,' she said at once, 'I've done something awful. Can I tell you? Only I don't want you to do anything about it . . . is that O.K.?' You could see her agitation in the way she waved her hands about. 'We had our Maths test today and there was one thing I couldn't get – I worked it out but it was a silly answer and I was terrified of not finishing in time and couldn't bear to start again, so I cheated.' She was blinking a lot and biting her lip. 'I moved myself around in my seat till I could see Maria Clarke's answer and simply copied it. I'll never own up though.'

Dad was after her about her Maths and I knew what it meant to her. 'Shouldn't worry,' I told her. 'It's quite a little thing.'

'You probably don't think it's much, but I've never done it before. They say you should confess things like that in your prayers, but I think that's dead easy. It's a lot harder to tell an actual person, and makes you feel better . . . I think.'

Any other day it might have disturbed me. What would she do, I wondered, with my burden of deceit! A magazine was lying open on the dressing-table and she picked it up. 'I left this for you earlier – oh God, you'll think I'm an awful drip, or preachy or something, what with that *and* this. It's a letter about what we were saying, from someone called Marlene who's got this boy who keeps on at her. It's a good answer. I believe in it.'

We'd read them before, dozens like it, letters and answers, generally aloud to each other and making fun, using stupid voices for the questions and a ramrod schoolmistress voice for the answers – a voice, Ginny said, with a bun at the back, sitting bolt upright with pursed lips, and peering as if through pince-nez.

We'd never really understood the problems and must have made fun to distance ourselves from them. But reading the sickening stuff now I felt unbearably irritated and flung the book down. 'You're crazy to even read such rubbish!' None of us ever shouted. It came out like a pressurised hiss, so that Ginny looked around anxiously, fearing it could rise out of control. 'All this about "this deep and very beautiful experience that I know you will wish to share some day with someone very special . . ." Who said it is! And all that about self-respect and owing it to yourself, and mothers waiting for you to bring your questions and confidences . . . You know damn well Mother would sooner *die* than listen to ours. It's rubbish! First you make up all that stuff about eyes like violet pools, then you go all prudish when anybody's *really* wondering what on earth to do . . .'

'No, honest . . .' Ginny was clasping her hands together. 'I expect you're upset about the red star. It must have been awful, with all the others there . . .'

'It wasn't, and I don't give a damn!' It was getting hard to stop now, and I knew I'd tell her, against my better judgment, about my own deceit, already wondering if I would have told if she hadn't mentioned hers. 'I didn't even go. Lydia went, and she told me about the rotten star.'

Ginny's eyes were screwed up in bewilderment and I sat down on the bed, longing to cry, but with anger trapped somewhere in my head and chest still pulling me about. 'All right, two guesses where I've been, and what I've done, and you can feel ashamed of me if you like but *I'm* not ashamed – I just feel awful.' And I lay face down on the covers, trying to hold back the tears and shut out the sight of Ginny with her hand clapped against her mouth.

A few moments later, in an even voice at last, I told her about the arrangement with Lydia and going to the sports pavilion. It seemed right to tell now, about the arrangements at least, and because she so clearly minded I felt at last that somebody was really in it with me.

For a time she was silent, then said softly, 'They say you feel all besmirched, the first time. *Do* you?'

'You shouldn't listen to what "they" say. None of it's right.'

'But . . . the other day you said you knew for sure that it would be marvellous. Wasn't it?'

I didn't want to talk about it, and shook my head.

'But . . . it's supposed to be like – well – rapture! You're supposed to blend . . . into one person!'

I couldn't keep the tears back any longer, and pressed my face against the pillow, scrabbling for my handkerchief.

'Oh Ginn, it's an *awful* thing to do to anybody!'

Ginny sat down, and I felt her hand on my arm. 'Gosh, you're shivering like anything.' She was still for a moment then burst out, 'Why do they all go on about it all the time, if it's so awful! It can't be . . . not something *everybody* does. You're the first person I've ever heard . . .' As I cried into the pillow I felt her jump suddenly to her feet.

'Ella's a bit upset. I was trying to help.'

Mother was in the doorway, frowning, with a pile of newly ironed pillow-cases on her arm. She put them on the chest-of-drawers then took one from the top of the pile and shook it out. 'If you're going to upset yourself every time you're disappointed you'd better forget about the Painters' Club altogether, and join something else,' she said as I sat up and handed her the pillow to change. 'There's no sense in spoiling your proper work for it.

Look at you! The skirt of that dress will need ironing now, and you know I don't like you lying on the bedspreads, not with your shoes on.'

When Mother had gone Ginny whispered, 'It's O.K. She didn't hear anything.' She had moved away from the bed and sounded as if she was ready to go.

'I'm sorry I told Lydia and not you. I just didn't want you feeling ashamed of me.'

'I don't, honestly.' And I believed her. But when she added, 'I bet even Dad and Mother wouldn't be all that wild, either, not if they knew you didn't like it,' it sounded unpleasantly cynical, for Ginny.

At the door she turned and asked, 'Does he know you didn't like it? Did you tell him, afterwards?'

'I couldn't – Lydia was waiting. Don't let's talk about it any more.'

When she had gone I lay trying to exorcise the memory of the evening by imagining that it had continued as it had begun, in a warm, unbelievable tenderness. But in the end I found myself remembering, over and over, only the growing anguish in his face, and the sudden clumsy hostility of his body. Ginny had said you blend into one person, but clear through the panic and pain and resentment I'd felt a shock of utter loneliness. It was something I'd never read about, nor heard about from anyone else, and it was probably, finally, the only feeling that he and I shared.

'The water's hot, if you'd like a bath,' Mother called up the stairs. But I hated the thought of taking off my clothes, and at bed-time kept my vest on under my pyjamas.

Chapter Eight

Arthur's group left by coach for France on Monday morning – for nearly all of them it was their last week as schoolboys. And once they had gone we 'rowdy ones' grew unusually calm and sensible, each of us recognising in the others the girls we had known terms ago, before the pretending began.

Summers were always sunny and hot and good, and the last week of the summer term had become my favourite part, even more of a high-spot than our annual fortnight at the sea, which was beginning to be marred for Ginny and me by agonies of embarrassment in the dining-room of the Coppice Guest House where Dad, as a visitor of long standing, tended to throw his weight about.

That year formal lessons were suspended for us older girls, and we worked alone in the library or laboratories or studio, finishing things off, and made time in the afternoons to sprawl in the long grass round the tennis courts, endlessly talking. I could always see, as I lay listening to the others' confident chatter, that behind the shared ideals were many different points of view, and found to my shame that I could agree with almost anybody who could put their own into words.

No one, surely, was ever so easily pulled about as me, and I envied them their attitudes, and passions, and sometimes courage: a few had walked to Aldermaston with the nuclear disarmers in May that year; there had been three or four dramatic religious and political conversions; the head girl had joined the Roman Catholic Church against her parents' wishes; the captain of hockey had signed a pacifist pledge; even Lydia had become a vegetarian.

Beside them all I felt an ignorant sham. I'd never even found the voice to challenge Dad's most bigoted pronouncements, and retreated into daydream at the first stirrings of annoyance with him. I'd probably believed him when he told Ginny, 'Neither of you are old enough to know your own minds,' though she was less gullible and had waited till we were upstairs then whispered what she had 'felt like saying'.

I think my only certainties were visual. What I found ugly I avoided with exaggerated loathing, but knew just where to turn my eyes, even in imagination, to find enjoyment intense enough to keep me ticking over and not thinking much.

This, I thought, was to be the summer when I would put myself together, using the break to think and read and dream myself into knowing where I stood. Arthur would not be part of it; he had won a long training course with British Railways, to start in the autumn, and had planned every moment of what he saw as his last free summer. After the School Journey there would be Cadet Camp, then a short interval at home – while we would be at Hythe – followed by a long visit to his grandmother in Nottingham, where he'd found a vacation job in a factory. The little boys were going with him to Nottingham, and a new term would have begun for me before he returned to prepare for his course.

As usual, Ginny's term would start several days before mine, and this year I was looking forward to the time Mother and I would have alone. Though I'd never enjoyed these days together much before, I needed them now, and had invented a fantasy about her wanting to confide in me.

But by the time those few important days came round, my summer was already wrecked, and my resolution forgotten. On our first afternoon together Mother and I sat in the kitchen. Shivering on a chair by the window I watched her shelling peas. 'It's not often we get a bit of time to ourselves,' she said. She was tossing the peas into the white enamel colander and dropping the pods into a carrier-bag on the floor at her side. Dad was at Aldershot and would be late – it was getting to be a regular occurrence.

I let the image of Mother fill my eyes, with nothing else in focus around her, and concentrated hard, waiting for courage for the words I had to say. I'll never forget any detail of her appearance: grey hair with regular, artificial waves; brown and grey flecked cotton skirt, pink blouse, small neat white summer shoes and the thick beige stockings that hid the lumps beginning in her legs. She seemed more relaxed than she'd been for ages, and it made it harder.

'You'd have died laughing . . .' She was telling about the gas man, come to mend the Ascot. 'He's always been a bit of a sobersides, that one. Never says a word, makes you feel uncomfortable, as if it's your fault the thing's gone wrong. Anyway, he'd got little screws and bits all over the draining-board and didn't seem to be getting anywhere, so I said, "I'll make some tea – would you care for a cup?" I thought surely that'd raise a smile or something but he never moved a muscle, just went on staring into the Ascot and said, "No thank you, Madam – spoil me dinner."'

The time was getting on and I said quickly, 'Mother, I think I'm going to have a baby.'

She was quiet for a moment, head on one side, smiling. 'Properly put me in my place he did. I felt quite sinful having a cup myself.'

'Mother, I think I'm . . .' She looked at me with narrowing, uncomprehending eyes, and said kindly, 'You shouldn't joke, dear, not about something serious like that.' Then she shelled a few more peas and I had the feeling she was trying to hold the moment back where it had been, not to allow the dreadful idea even to begin.

'I've missed my monthly; twice I've missed . . .' My teeth were chattering. The memory of the past weeks, worrying by myself, were more than I could bear, and I covered my eyes with my hand and heard her say, without conviction, 'You can't have missed, you had your towels as usual.' She always gave us our towels herself, a day at a time, and I'd kept up the pretence and hidden them away.

Now when I looked at her it seemed we had begun a different life already, as if the world we had been sitting in seconds ago, with the gas man for news, had gone the way of all our easy, childhood years. I said, 'I hid them in my drawer.'

She had stopped shelling peas, but now began again. 'I daresay it's just a mistake. People miss for all kinds of reasons, like nerves. You've been quite jumpy lately. You've got no other symptoms.' She wasn't asking.

'My chest feels tender' – I couldn't say 'breast' to Mother – 'and the past couple of days I've got ravenous in the after-noons.'

'You're always hungrier in the holidays, with less to fill your mind.' I began shaking my head, desperate for her to believe, and after a moment or two she said quietly, 'You mean . . . that boy?' I nodded, and as she turned away I saw her chin was trembling.

'Please, please don't mind!' I begged, and bent my head. It was a relief to cry, and I thought we were crying together.

'Don't *mind*! My God, that's rich! What the *hell* d'you expect . . . And it's not a bit of good you piping your eye like that.' I looked up and saw she had controlled her chin and set her mouth in its straight, disapproving line. 'You should've given a bit of thought before, but no, not one scrap of consideration for anybody else . . . nothing but your own pleasure!'

'I didn't even enjoy it!' I sobbed, and Mother snapped, 'That's enough of that sort of talk. A bit of a girl of your age! I don't know what on earth you could've been thinking about. It's not as if you've been allowed to run the streets! I've told you time and time again . . .'

'You never told me anything . . .'

'So it's my fault, is it? There you are, you see, you girls just will not be told. You might have known you knew nothing at all about such things, and neither should you, at your age. Good God, you're no more than a child at school!' The things she was saying were confused and confusing, things no one could answer, and I ran upstairs and shut myself in the bathroom. Perhaps she would use the moment to recover, I thought, as I sat trembling on the lavatory. Perhaps she would cry.

When I returned she was calm, staring down at her hands holding the edge of the table. I said, 'I'm sorry, terribly sorry,' and waited for her to say I should have thought of that before, but she began to talk softly, as if to herself. 'I don't know what on earth we can do, I really don't. We'll have to get advice. Your father, he'll have to get some advice.'

'I don't want . . .' I began, and she interrupted sharply, 'The time for thinking what you *want* is over now, you silly little bitch. Can't you see what you've thrown away! You could've kept out of this lot for another eight or nine years! My God, what I'd have given for what you've . . .' It was almost as if she had said it all aloud without meaning to – her eyes seemed half-crossed as she stared into space – but for a moment it warmed me. I suppose it must have sounded more real than before, Mother putting herself into words with real anger, but then she seemed to come to with a jerk, and carried on in the carping voice again.

'What thought have you ever given to what *we* want, though

it's little enough. We've given you every possible chance, made sacrifices for you, and all you do is bring this disgrace on us then turn round and say you don't want . . .'

'I was going to say I don't want Ginny to know.'

'I should just think not. She'd never stand the shame; none of us will. It's like young Freda from the end – they'll never hold their heads up again. Goodness only knows how we'll manage.'

And though I'd begged her not to mind, I needed her to, and in a way the muddle behind the bleak hostility of her words was reassuring. Then we heard Ginny's key in the door. 'You're not to mention this to your father either. I'll speak to him.'

Ginny was glowing and appeared not to notice the tense atmosphere or my red eyes. At netball practice she had shot six goals in a row, and the games mistress, who was getting together the new First Team, had called her aside and told her to stay behind on Friday for the trials.

'I always knew there was something I could be marvellous at,' she said. 'I'm going to make it the most important activity of my life, and do breathing exercises and go running before school.'

Mother said, 'I'm not at all surprised. After all, you've got a nice athletic little figure.' Ginny smiled blissfully, and though, later that evening, Dad was to tell her that if she did stick to her resolution it would be the first one she'd ever managed, she was not discouraged.

'I've never been nearly fifteen before,' she said. 'It makes a difference.'

He sucked his teeth. 'Ah, yes, it'll soon be your birthday. One thing occurs to me – having a dog to take for a run would certainly help to keep you up to your word.' Then he disappeared behind his newspaper, leaving her silent and apprehensive.

The very sight of Ginny, that evening, with her small, lithe body, had suddenly made me feel grotesque, and when I went up to bed early with a headache, it was a shock to catch sight of myself in the long mirror on the landing, and remind myself that nothing at all had visibly changed.

At ten, Mother brought me milk and biscuits. She closed the door, put the glass on the bedside table, folded my undies from the seat of the chair carefully over the back, then sat down and said, 'You'd better tell me, I suppose, what happened.' She sounded resigned and it felt kinder, and I told her about the sports pavilion but not the evening at Arthur's home, because she would have blamed his mother. I couldn't have found words to tell her about what happened when we were *in* the pavilion but it was almost a relief to tell how I'd deceived her about the Painters' Club meeting.

This time she didn't interrupt or speak bitterly, but when I'd finished she said, 'I despair of you. A boy comes along and says this is what everybody's doing and you lap it all up . . .'

'Lots of boys get hold of the key . . .'

'How do you know? D'you know these boys, or the girls they take there?'

'No, but the girls wouldn't talk about it, would they . . .?'

'Oh wouldn't they! And when they did you'd soon see they weren't girls like you at all. They'd be the sort who are left to themselves while their mothers are gallivanting off enjoying themselves – the sort of thing you've been trying to get *me* to do.'

It was getting angry again, with no hope for anything I might say. She was so marvellous, as a rule, at moving awful moments on – Dad's awful moments, when she saw them coming. Suddenly she stopped herself in full flow, and said in a sensible voice, 'Now, this boy . . . what does *he* say about this . . . business?'

'He doesn't know. He's been away . . .'

'Then see to it he *doesn't* know, and keep away from him.'

A little knot of anger began to form in my chest, but all I said was, 'Have you told Dad?'

'Don't be silly, not with Ginny about. Besides, your father's in no mood to be told tonight.' I'd noticed it for the past two or three Wednesdays.

'He's always strange after Aldershot. Why is it?'

She turned away, then got up stiffly. 'You just give a little more thought to your own life,' she said. 'Attend to your own concerns.'

Ginny put her head through the door and called 'Goodnight', and Mother bundled her out with her as she left. I was glad of it. Being completely dependent on Mother I couldn't afford anger, and needed to be alone.

She had made me think and talk of Arthur, and now I realised that since my first awful moments of suspicion of pregnancy I'd hardly thought of him at all. My strange, unhappy situation seemed to have been visited upon me like an act of God, and

68

the foreign thing inside me, which was so hard to believe in, simply felt like something that should not be there, certainly no part of me or anybody else.

I didn't want to think about any of it, or have to make decisions. All I wanted was to be back to a few weeks ago, though without concern for things like freedom or a life of my own. I wanted school, with double periods of History, exams and Painters' Club, and nonsense talk with Ginny, and nothing more important. I wanted Dad and Mother to set the pattern, and Ginny and me to go on grumbling about it and dreaming of something different. I didn't want to be a woman.

In the dark I lay shivering and praying, unable to use the awful name of what it was I wanted, but begging that Dad and Mother could do something to get us back to normal. I began to plan another picture, trying to keep my mind occupied till it would all be over and too late for thinking.

Chapter Nine

Next evening after Dad returned from work Mother came and talked to me again. 'Your father's been advised you should have a urine test. He's heard of a doctor who could probably help us, but there's no sense in getting involved in such expense if it might all turn out to be a false alarm. I'll get you to give me a specimen in the morning and he can take it in when he leaves for work.'

'I could run it round to the surgery myself . . .'

'It isn't *going* to the surgery,' she snapped, but though I waited, she didn't explain.

'Will he know, when he comes home from work?'

She shook her head. 'It takes a day or two.'

'What then – do we have to ring?'

'Look, just leave it to your father. He'll do what has to be done, from the office.'

For the next couple of days I watched their faces for clues, but nothing showed and nothing was said about it, not even at the weekend when we were all at home. Dad hadn't so far given the slightest sign of even having been told about me, and I remembered how Mother had insisted I should say nothing to him myself, and wondered what she was up to.

Then on Monday, the first morning of the autumn term, she handed me a note to take to school. Ginny was on her morning run and Dad had left for the office. 'It's asking them to excuse you for tomorrow morning,' she said. 'We can be back by dinner-time.'

I wasn't really surprised, but scared, by the new certainty, and my own helplessness. I wondered if she would tell me anything at all if I didn't ask, but perhaps she was trying, like me, to avoid thinking or discussion.

'Where are we going?'

'Harley Street, ten-thirty. Have a good bath tonight and put on clean undies in the morning. You'd better wear your weekend clothes, but wait till Ginny's on her run.'

'But Harley Street! That's terribly expensive!'

'Far too expensive for people like us, but it's got to be managed. Your father's going to have to borrow.'

'Who from?'

'Mr Timpson, of course. Who else does he know! And I hope you're not so thick-skinned you can't see what all this is going to do to your father's pride.'

'Couldn't we go somewhere cheaper though? Couldn't we ask our own doctor to recommend . . .'

'We certainly could not, and if we're to be able to hold up our heads he's to know nothing at all about this. It's all very well for you to talk, but your father and I are not prepared to get involved in anything dubious. We'll go for the best, and if the expense upsets you, you've only yourself to blame . . .'

'What will the doctor do?'

'Now you're asking me something I can't possibly know, can I! It's our first experience of this kind of thing and I hope to God it's the last.' She still seemed more angry than worried, and ready to demonstrate it afresh with every question she answered, but she must have sensed the unpleasant harshness of her voice and went on more gently, 'Check up, I suppose, and advise us what next.'

Although Mother wasn't spelling out her hopes in detail my instincts told me, though I avoided thinking of it, that she and I must surely want the same outcome, with everything back to what it was before. I couldn't be so sure of Dad, but needed her to get her way. So I kept silent, and the next morning we walked to the Underground with barely a word between us. I was keeping my mind empty of everything except the childish prayer to which I'd reduced my fears and hopes – 'Please God, don't let me *have* to have a baby' – and filled the time with it, repeating it silently over and over against the rhythmic clatter of the train.

But as we stepped out into the sunlight at Regent's Park station some sound or smell, or a feeling in the air, reminded me of days when a ride on the Tube was delight, with something lovely at the end. 'When we came this way it was always to the zoo,' I said.

Mother hesitated for a moment, walking beside me. 'I've never cared a lot for the zoo,' she said softly, 'but I'd give all I've got

71

if we could be going there now, with all these other people.'

It didn't sound carping this time, and I walked on in silence with a lump in my throat, staring at the pavement and hunting for words, jostled by the summer visitors with their cameras and picnic lunches. The place was too public for the words Mother needed from me, and anything I might say could risk a retort beginning, 'That's all very well, young lady . . .' Somehow or other I let the moment pass as if she hadn't spoken, then she turned right suddenly, and I looked up and saw that it was Harley Street.

I couldn't remember seeing it before and stood still, looking along the terrace with its great running, repeating design of steps and doors and basement areas, windows and iron railings, over and over, in gracious, easy proportions.

Mother looked back. 'Come on. There isn't time to hang about.'

'Isn't it lovely? The whole street's a pattern.'

'I don't know about that.' She was hurrying on. 'Old places like this are hard to clean and cost the earth to heat. They're mostly let to doctors for consulting-rooms; there's not a lot of people living here. Come *on*!' She sounded more than usually irritated and I hurried alongside.

'I just didn't know it was so – elegant.'

'It's elegant all right – so will the bill be. It's hard to get you to understand the seriousness of anything.' I couldn't tell her, and tried not to notice myself, how much I needed irrelevancies to crowd our awful problem from my mind; how much I wanted to be rushed, thinking of other things, to a point beyond decisions.

There was a handsome black front door and an old man in a baize apron still cleaning the five brass plates. Then a large waiting-room with a huge polished table in the centre and five or six people sitting round the walls. I made for a chair by the window and sat looking out, praying, letting the lovely regularity of the street accompany the prayer. When I glanced round I saw that the people were all old, surely too old to need a gynaecologist. None of them were reading, nor really looking at anything, but imagining or staring inwards, and I guessed that like me they were repeating something endlessly, wanting one thing, perhaps one answer, hoping to ensure it through the repetition of their words. Perhaps they're praying not to have to die, I thought. It made my own despair seem silly and unworthy and I jumped up and took a *Country Life* from one of the neat piles at the end of the table.

The doctor was small, middle-aged and raffish-looking, completely at home in his elegant room, so different from the partitioned-off surgeries we'd always known. He wore a pepper-and-salt-coloured suit and a monogrammed tie, and on a hook behind the door hung a brown curved-brim bowler and a checked raincoat, which made me think he'd fitted us in on his way to the races.

He had a way of inclining his head in Mother's direction, smiling acknowledgment but disregarding her words whenever she tried to answer the questions he put to me, and when he came to what he called 'questions of a more personal nature' he said it was his duty to ask if I preferred to be interviewed alone. He said it was normal procedure, but I guessed that no girl, surely, had ever sent her own parent back to the waiting-room.

His questions appalled me and I felt Mother fidgeting in her seat, but he helped out blandly with words to make sense of my excruciating answers, and told us, smiling gently from one to the other, that more and more young people were taking advice on contraception, while Mother kept opening her mouth and shutting it again. The clock said ten fifty-five; at school they would be starting Modern History. Ginny didn't even know we were here.

As I undressed behind a screen I prayed that Mother wouldn't emphasise to him the tragic aspect of our visit. He was trying to discuss the weather as they waited, but she said she'd hardly noticed what it was doing, not for days. 'When something like this hits you, you're walking round in a daze, aren't you, wondering where to turn.' She told him that neither of her daughters had ever been involved in any of this rock-and-roll nonsense the young people were getting up to, and were devoted to their studies. 'We certainly don't want them growing into these . . . adolescents you hear about,' she said.

It was the first time I'd been examined internally, but he put a blanket over me and was gentle, and used no instruments. It seemed unbelievably clever to be able to tell what was going on simply by touch, without looking, while he talked to me about school and future plans. Once he cut in, 'You're fond of children then?' and I replied, 'I suppose everybody is.'

73

He smiled. 'That's a dangerous supposition. Let's say most people think they are, particularly if for some reason they can't have them. Having them, or having to teach them, often alters things. But perhaps, like my daughters, you find that cynical.'

Suddenly I felt the need to justify my presence to this man and said quietly, 'I suppose there's quite a danger in having a baby too early, isn't there? I mean, before you're old enough to know how to look after them. Just as dangerous as having them – the first at least – when you're getting on?'

He laughed quickly. 'Tell you what. I daresay you've heard, there's a worse danger. Every fourth child, they say, is born Chinese. Good, everything seems to be fine. Just dress and come and sit down, please.'

He told us that in his opinion I had begun a perfectly normal, healthy pregnancy. For a few moments he sat in silence, looking down at his hands, then said to me, 'And you have quite made up your mind about a termination?'

I thought it a better word than 'abortion', which made me think of drains, and as I hunted for a reply which would do for both him and Mother she said quickly, 'Anything else would be quite impossible.'

He took no notice of her words and waited till I nodded my head, then took up his pen and a very small sheet of paper. 'As a gynaecologist I'm of course almost entirely concerned with childbirth and obtaining healthy pregnancies for those who have difficulties. I can only give you the name and telephone number of someone who may help you; a first-rate obstetrician. Ring him for an appointment, and when you go, say you were advised that a D and C would be required.' He wrote on the paper, then said he would be obliged if we would avoid actually mentioning him by name; the man would understand – they'd worked together for a long time.

He handed the paper to Mother, saying, 'Give your daughter two or three weeks afterwards, then make a further appointment with me. I like to check that all's well, and perhaps we can help then with some contraception.' Mother's neck grew quite pink but she quickly asked what she must pay and hid her face in her handbag. As we followed him to the door she said urgently, 'We want to do the best for her, you see. It's a difficult decision . . .'

He inclined his head. 'I'm sure you and your husband and

daughter have considered very carefully. Good morning to you. Good morning, Miss – er – Thorne.'

In the street Mother looked flustered. 'I'm not sure I understood about the Chinese babies,' she said.

'I think it was a joke.'

'Hardly his place, I should've thought, to make jokes at a time like this. I didn't like his manner – made me feel quite uncomfortable. He does very well out of it all, I daresay.' She took the slip of paper from her bag. 'A foreigner, this one, by the look of it, German I should think. Earl's Court he said – your father'll have to take you there, I don't think I could stand an ordeal like this again.' I was walking backwards, looking away down the street, which seemed even more beautiful now that something was nearly settled.

At school that afternoon, unusually inattentive, I imagined the doctor at home, talking about his day to the woman I'd seen in the photograph on his desk. 'Another seventeen-year-old. Came with her mother – bitter sort of woman, bulldozing her into a D and C. I made the right noises about the options, but the kid doesn't stand a chance.'

I'm a hypocrite, I thought. I didn't *want* a chance, nor even to know about options, and must have thought up the bulldozing idea to shuffle off responsibility. I'd have liked the doctor to see Mother getting us through some of Dad's awful moments though, to balance things a bit. When it's over, I promised myself, I'll do something about hypocrisy and not knowing what to say to Mother, and allowing myself to be pushed around. I'd also choose a friend for myself, not just put up with Lydia. Looking across the classroom I thought of several girls I would have liked to know more closely, and wondered why I'd never done a thing about it. It was a feeling I'd often had in the past, but not recently, not since meeting Arthur in fact. Then I wasted more time being mildly surprised at how difficult it was to feel that he was linked in any way with my new predicament.

With Ginny not allowed to know either, I was unbearably lonely with my secret, and felt a sort of relief next evening when Mother told me Dad had made us an appointment at Earl's Court for Friday, the day after tomorrow, at five thirty.

Chapter Ten

'Post!' Ginny shrilled, jumping up from the breakfast table as the letters flapped through the front door. She brought in a little sheaf of them. 'Buff one for Dad, card from Uncle Arthur – Mother better have that one – "L. Thorne, Esquire" from Kentish Town, and a thing from the milkman.' She dropped the letters by their plates. 'I'll get the paper-knife, Dad, it's in the kitchen.' Her lively voice had broken into the silence of that awful Friday morning like a benediction, and I took my first real breath of the day, thankful for the new energetic Ginny, picked for the team, with her morning runs and early nights.

Mother looked up from the card and said quietly, 'It's not from Uncle Arthur, it's for you.' She pushed it towards me and I reddened at once and without picking it up read the words, 'Flaked out. Not my scene at all. Longing for home and everything that goes with it. Same as ever, Arthur.' Then I turned it over to the picture side as Ginny came in with the knife. 'Can I see it next, please?' she said to Mother, and leaned across the table to pick up the card.

Mother said softly, 'It's Ella's,' but at the same moment Dad flapped his buff envelope across her hand. 'Put it down!' he snapped, so loudly that she jumped with fright and snatched her hand away.

I said under my breath, 'It's not from Uncle Arthur. It's Arthur Knight, he's away.' It took her a moment to realise what was happening, and I could see from her colour that she was struggling with embarrassment and anger.

'I didn't *know*!' She was addressing Dad, and her voice was excited and aggrieved. 'Everybody makes mistakes – not only me!' She swallowed hard, looking from one to another of us in the silence, then burst out, 'What's the matter with everyone!' and turned and ran out of the room, leaving the door open behind her.

'The child wasn't to know,' Mother began quietly, 'She was out of the room . . .'

'All right, all right!' Dad dumped his letters in front of her. 'Allotment rent's going up, and Beckers can't get the fence-posts for another three weeks.' Then he stood up and brushed the crumbs from his lap on to the floor, bent to peck Mother on the forehead as he passed, and stopped at the door. 'You'd better meet me outside Earl's Court tube at about ten past five,' he said to me. 'The place may take a bit of finding. And don't turn up in that rig-out,' waving a hand at my school uniform. 'No need to rub it in.'

Mother saw him off as usual, and when she came back said, 'Go up and have a word with Ginny. I don't want her late for school or anything,' and began collecting dishes together.

'Will she be told about this evening?'

'Not if I can help it she won't.'

Upstairs, Ginny was coming out of my room with something in her hand. She looked flustered. 'I was just getting something I left in there. I didn't know he was away.'

'Nottingham, I told you last week.' I beckoned her into the room and closed the door.

'I know you told me, only I thought you were – well – pulling my leg again. What's up with Dad? He practically hit me!'

'Only with an envelope.'

'That was just luck. He could have had *anything* in his hand. I didn't know what on earth to do. Did it look dreadful running out like that?'

'I don't suppose they liked it, but I was glad.'

She beamed. 'It's a lot easier when you're already standing up.' And as she brushed the fringe out of her eyes she dropped the little box she was holding and bent in confusion to pick it up. 'It's just – it's those jujube things,' she said. 'I left them for you, but as he really *is* away I thought I'd better get them back.'

The thought of what she must have gone through to get hold of the things appalled me and I could have wept. Suddenly it seemed wrong to be keeping a secret from her as if she were a child, and without stopping to consider I told her my news, adding, 'I'm going to a gynaecologist with Dad tonight. Heaven knows what they'll tell you, but please don't let on that you know.'

She had turned towards the window, biting her lip, but after a moment began to cry silently, and dab at her eyes. Her handkerchief was a blue-patterned one with 'Tuesday' written on it and a cat's face in the corner, one of a box sent at Christmas by an aunt who never saw us and couldn't keep up with the years. At last she said, 'I can't bear it. Being too late, I mean. Aren't you frightened to death?'

'They're going to . . . help me. I've already been to Harley Street.'

'You don't mean . . . not an abortion!' She was the first one, so far, to have used the word, and must surely now, I thought, begin to feel the shame she'd expected and I'd dreaded, but after a moment's silence she said, 'We had a debate at school. There were only seven of us on the side of life, but anyhow it was about a mother, not a schoolgirl.'

I couldn't bring myself to tell her I was trying not to think about it in terms of choice and didn't want anyone to make me make decisions, and when she added, 'How d'you actually feel about it?' I said at once, 'Just that it isn't fair and – well – hurry up.' Then we stood silent for a moment, looking down at the little box in her hand.

'D'you want to look at them?' She drew the lid off the box. Each one was wrapped separately in silver paper.

'Not really. Have you seen them?'

She shook her head. 'I couldn't bear having them in my room. Better not unwrap one – the paper would get all creased and then they'd never take them back.'

We walked together to the bus-stop and for the first time ever I would have liked to be getting on *her* bus, instead of the one taking me to forty minutes of Garibaldi in the opposite direction.

Strangely, telling Ginny my news, and having her reaction, had made me believe in it myself, while Mother's response had made it seem unthinkable enough to be unbelievable. If I'd been in the debate, I wondered, and had come down on one side or the other, would it have determined my feelings now that the problem was real?

It reminded me that I'd intended using the holidays to take up attitudes to things. Now I decided that there must be some people who think out their attitudes to everything before they ever need to, and stick to the decisions in times of crisis. While others, like me, depend on the crises to find their attitudes and make decisions, and once they're made, must keep their heads filled with other matters and prayers, and their eyes with patterns, to save themselves from thinking. I'd depended on Garibaldi to get me through till break-time, but it didn't work, and I began to despair.

As we hurried out, eating Milky Ways, to find a place in the sun, I told Lydia, 'There was a rumpus at home this morning. We've got these friends at – er – Aldershot, with a daughter just a bit older than us, and she's pregnant. The indignation, when my parents read the letter! Her parents are bulldozing one way, and mine think she ought to go the other way . . .'

'Well, there's only two things she *can* do. Who's side is she on?'

'Nobody mentioned that.'

'I'd want to decide for myself.'

'Me too – but I don't know what I'd decide.'

'That's because you're not in it. You'd know all right, if it was you.'

'She's probably wondering what's the right thing.'

Lydia laughed. 'I bet she's not. I don't think anyone thinks much when they're up against it. You know in your guts what you want, I reckon, then you work out reasons why that's the right thing. You choose the thing you're least afraid of, don't you?'

It sounded less corny than her usual opinions, and though I guessed it was full of holes, I didn't want to look for them. Perhaps I recognised it, like an old friend, as one of the uncomplicated certainties from childhood. And when we got back to lessons it wasn't so difficult to pay attention.

I couldn't remember ever having seen Dad embarrassed before that evening at Earl's Court. The house was less elegant than Harley Street but much more comfortable – a home where people lived, and we waited in their richly furnished dining-room. The minute they were rid of us, I thought, the housekeeper who had let us in would snatch the pile of magazines from the end of the great oval dining-table, bring out the lovely plates and silver that could be seen in the glazed cupboards all round the walls, and a family would sit down to a lavish dinner.

'Take a bit of upkeep, this lot,' Dad said, looking down at his shoes half buried in thick carpet. And minutes later, upstairs in the doctor's study, he appeared to be sinking lower and lower in his chair as he struggled with the problem of saying we'd been sent, without revealing who'd sent us.

'Come now' – the doctor was short, square and heavily built, with kind eyes behind thick spectacles, and a middle-European accent – 'Come now, how would you *expect* me to react? You bring your daughter, a minor, and ask me to perform an illegal operation which could bring – let's make no bones about it – bad trouble to yourself as well as me, and all suggested, you say, by a friendly, first-class medical man whose name is not to be revealed! Who convinces me that you are not, for example, police?' He held his plump hands wide and smiled.

'Oh, nothing like that!' Dad was crushing his trilby hat between restless hands. 'It's just that the wife made this promise.'

'Then there was perhaps some mistake! My work is in conjunction with several consultants but never one of them has asked a patient . . . Now look, perhaps his name begins with an A.' He was looking at me. 'B? C? Wait a bit, it isn't . . .?' When he mentioned the right name I must have looked relieved, and he laughed loudly. 'The old devil, what does he think he's playing at! One of my oldest friends – for years I work with him!' He began to fill out a card, like the other doctor, but smiling and joking to Dad. 'I will have a few words with him – you can be sure of that,' though Dad appeared not to be listening but sat absolutely still, staring down at the floor as if permanently humiliated. Then he was sent back to the waiting-room while I went with the doctor down three steps into the most modern, best-equipped surgery I had ever seen.

The clean, efficient-looking stainless steel reassured me at first, but when I caught sight of the examination-table with its leg-rests, wide apart, raised high up at one end, I was appalled, and wanted to snatch my clothes and run. Surely they can't *make* you lie like that, I thought angrily, and heard my own voice, unsteady with anxiety: 'The other doctor checked. Is it necessary again, please?'

He looked amazed, and lifted his hands, wide apart, as he did almost every time he spoke. 'Why are you so afraid?'

The gentleness of his voice brought tears prickling to my eyes, and feeling like an idiot I could only climb on to the thing and let him adjust the rests to my legs. Ginny was the only one I'd tell about the visit, but not this part. He snatched a length of soft paper from a roll and handed it to me.

'Dry your eyes and try not to cry. I shall help you, but there are many girls who get no help at all,' he said. 'It happens all the time.'

'You mean poor people? It would be nice if it was free for everybody.'

'It would be nicer if it were unnecessary for anybody.' His amused face helped to diminish the discomfort.

'It's a bit frightening, the first time anything like this . . .'

'The first time will also be the last. We shall help you, and if again, in the future, you should consult me it will be different – and *good*! You are a very healthy young woman.'

When he had examined me he came and stood at my side. 'You have thought? Huh? Thought of all the possibilities?'

'Oh yes.'

'You are healthy; all is well . . . What of your friend, the man?'

'He doesn't know. He's not a man exactly, just a bit older than me . . .'

'Nevertheless a man, and the father of a child. Is this wise that he does not know? I am not moralising, you understand, but a man – or boy – might wish to know. Perhaps for him too it might be important.'

'He's going away to work. I don't think we'll be friends any more.' I could hear the anxiety in my voice and knew that what Lydia had said – about knowing in your guts what you want, and thinking up some reasons later – was right. Yet some part of me was in danger of listening to this man – almost in danger of telling him about keeping myself from thinking till it was too late.

'Get dressed, please,' he said, 'and come back to the other room.'

I found him writing on a piece of yellow paper. Dad had come in and sat looking away from me.

'So.' The doctor gave me the paper. 'This is the address of the clinic I should like you to come to – it's a turning to the right some two hundred yards further down this road – next Thursday, at three in the afternoon. An overnight stay will be necessary because of anaesthetics, so you will require night-clothes and a sponge-bag. I will come there in the evening for this very simple operation and there is nothing whatever for you to worry about. You must make some arrangements to be absent from school for Thursday afternoon and Friday.'

81

Then he spoke to Dad. 'There is a waiting-room where you or your wife may be present, should you wish, but you must be there by a quarter to seven. After that time the door will not be answered. The young lady should bring one hundred and twenty pounds in an envelope in her handbag – in cash, please. It could be done more cheaply with only local anaesthetic but I would not advise this with a young girl.'

I found it reassuring that he reeled off all these details parrot-fashion, as if he'd been doing it for years and years.

'Now I must stress to both of you what you already know, that no mention of this should be made to anyone – for the sake of us all, you understand?' When he had pressed the bell for the housekeeper he added, 'My fee includes, of course, a check-up afterwards. I like to give my own clean bill of health.'

Outside, Dad stood up straighter, and though I would have liked to say I was sorry about the humiliation, I didn't want to risk an outburst of bravado, and we walked in silence till we were passing a big brown corner pub. He stopped, and said, 'Would you come in and have a drink with me?'

'I can't – I'm under-age!' I'd never been inside a pub, and was amazed he'd asked.

'A few months off, that's all. You could have a tomato juice or something.'

'Isn't it illegal though?' At once I saw what a stupid excuse I'd given, considering our errand, so, afraid of humiliating him by refusing, I followed him in through the half-empty saloon lounge to a small round wooden table standing almost in shadow at the other end.

While Dad was at the bar I looked round cautiously, and found the place quite beautiful compared with the modern but cold angularity of the milk-bar. There was warm colour, dark wood, red upholstery, shining brass, and I appreciated the anonymity. At the bar itself two men stood side by side in silence; a few yards away a middle-aged couple worried over something private; and at a table near the door a young man sat with one arm round the shoulders of a girl who had been crying. It seemed there was no special way to behave; you could come here with whatever feeling was possessing you, and not pretend. It was a warm bolt-hole.

Dad put the juice in front of me and I asked what was in his glass. 'Bitter,' he said, taking two packets of crisps from his pocket. 'Pint of best bitter.'

'We mustn't be long. Mother will be . . .'

'Just take your time.' He lifted his glass. 'There's no prize for getting back early.' He was drumming his fingers on the table.

'I'm sorry about the money, Dad. Is it too much? Will Mr Timpson . . .?'

'Mr Timpson?'

'Mother said you'd have to borrow from him.'

He smiled. 'Ah well, perhaps he does owe me a favour. Your mother will have to come with you next Thursday. I can't make three o'clock.'

'Or I could go alone.'

'Shouldn't do that.' He stood up and took my glass. 'Same again?' It was all so different from our usual 'Please may I have . . .' and for a moment I felt I now belonged more with Dad and Mother than with Ginny. It was ages since I'd felt any kind of ease with Dad. With the juice he brought another pint of bitter, though the first was unfinished. 'She won't need to go in,' he went on. 'Just take you to the door.' Then he finished the first pint in one long swallow, took a swig at the next, and sat looking down at his fingers, no longer drumming.

'Make you feel like . . . nothing, don't they,' he said, unusually softly.

I'd often wondered why people drink together when they can't possibly be thirsty. Now I curled my finger round the stem of the glass and sipped, and put it down, then lifted it and sipped again, feeling that we moved on through awful moments without it seeming awkward not to speak – just like the two men at the bar. In a few moments Dad began again, but in his usual voice: 'Real oily customer that one, and as for the other bloke – the one your Mother saw – up to 'is neck in it behind the big brass plate. Won't soil *his* hands though, oh no. The foreigners can do the dirty work.'

'I never thought of that.'

'Sticks out a mile.' His words troubled me; they sounded as if he hadn't worked them out before he said them – freed for a moment from having to be, above all, a father. Soon he had drunk three pints in quick succession and went up for a fourth, and I noticed that before he brought it to the table he drank something from a small glass, downing it in one gulp as he stood at the bar. Looking round, I saw that nothing in the pub had changed; no one had come or gone. It seemed a good place.

When Dad stood the glass down he had some difficulty getting it on to the beermat. He sat with his arms folded, looking into space, and nodded his head now and then. Once he laughed bitterly to himself as if he thought he was talking to me. Then he said, 'You were a love-child, of course,' making it sound like the middle of some other conversation.

'What's that?'

He took a long drink. 'I won't say you were actually born out of – er – wedlock, because you weren't. But we had to go to church a bit sooner than we'd planned. I don't suppose your mother's mentioned it.'

I felt my face redden, wondering if it meant I was illegitimate. But though Dad's words had shocked me, it was the shock of surprise. I'd never understood why people in plays and books, discovering their illegitimacy, reacted with such shame.

'Is that the same as being illegitimate?'

'Good Lord no. Your mother and me were already engaged, and couples everywhere were making up their minds in a hurry; long engagements are no good in war-time.' He was screwing up his eyes, trying to read a poster on the wall above us. 'Ginny, though, that was solely for your mother.'

'How d'you mean?'

'Wasn't my idea. I'd seen too much of the war by then. Didn't make me keen to build up a family. Still, your mother was determined. Funny the way wars change the women. Lovely young woman your mother was, though never what you might call particularly . . . welcoming. I suppose I thought perhaps . . . However, once she'd got it, that was it.'

He surely couldn't have meant to tell me any of it, but it made them both sound more like other people. I sat absolutely still, terrified he would suddenly notice me, realise what he'd been saying, and react unreasonably. He closed his eyes for a moment, and though I'd have been scared if he had really dropped off I half hoped he would doze for a moment, then wake up feeling better and with no idea of what he'd said.

Knowing that I was a love-child didn't feel particularly like a problem, perhaps because I already had enough to worry about, but the unbelievable part of Dad's revelation was that Mother had been in a predicament like my own. I wanted to ask how much she'd minded, and what Granny and Grandfather Gordon had said, and sat wondering whether Mother would have behaved differently towards me if I had been engaged.

One of the men at the bar said 'Goodnight then,' and walked out, letting the door swing to and fro behind him, and Dad came to. 'You don't say a lot, do you,' he smiled.

He held my arm on the way to the Underground and neither of us spoke, but as we were coming up the station steps at the home end he said, 'There'll be no need to mention to your mother that we stopped off on the way. She's got strong feelings about such places.'

'Oh no, I won't say anything.'

'Or to Ginny,' he added, and suddenly I felt an urgent need to cash in on his unusual mood before it evaporated, for Ginny's sake. It might be years before he would seem so available – or I feel so courageous – again.

'Dad . . . *about* Ginny – erm – I think she's terribly fond of you.'

'So?'

'Well, she wants to please you, and, well, you seem to make it hard for her.'

'Meaning what?' There was a hint of sarcasm in his voice, and I knew he'd go on pressing me now, exacting all the embarrassment possible. I wished I hadn't started it.

'Well, you are sometimes a bit awful to her.'

He rattled the change in his pocket for a moment, then said, 'You know, you're hardly in a position to dictate to me – or any of the family – how we should behave to each other. What good d'you reckon this little lot will do Ginny? Eh? Thought about that, have you?'

It was the same as Mother, and I knew they'd rubbed out the past, both theirs and mine, and reinvented me as wicked. It was a completely new way for Dad to talk to me, and I was glad of the dark.

For the rest of the evening everyone behaved as if I hadn't been anywhere, and at bed-time Ginny said she had asked where I was, to avoid suspicion, and Mother had told her it was time for me to lead a more private life, now that I was seventeen, and she wasn't to worry me about my comings and goings.

'Was it terribly sordid?' she asked. 'I've been imagining him, like some vulture . . .'

'No, he was kind – a different sort of man from any we know.'

'We don't know any – only Dad and the uncles. You can't count film stars or men in books.'

We'd always been to all-girls' schools with female teachers, had no boy cousins, hardly ever visited the doctor or spoke to the vicar, and with the neighbours 'kept ourselves to ourselves'. It only left men in shops, and bus-conductors.

'Everyone says they're all the same,' Ginny went on, 'but I don't believe it.'

Neither did I. I was remembering Dad and the gynaecologist sitting side by side, with Dad slowly sinking through his chair.

'Dad didn't tell you off, did he? I think he'd let you get away with anything.'

'He made it clear that he thinks I'm wicked.'

'Do you *feel* wicked, Elle? I mean, they used to turn girls out-of-doors, and things like that . . .'

'Well, I feel awful about the terrible expense, and upsetting Mother and Dad – and you. Not wicked though. It's God . . . or something, that I feel guilty towards, for sort of mucking-up the balance.'

Ginny shrilled with laughter. 'What balance! You haven't half got some funny ideas,' and I heard Mother come to the foot of the stairs. 'Ginny, get to your bed,' she called.

But I meant it, even if I'd only put it into words because of Ginny's question. What was *I* doing with a baby inside me? I'd jumped a queue, upset the order, and forced God's hand – 'Make one like *me* now!' The idea of me being a mother was crazy, when I still had to pretend about being like the others, or wanting a boyfriend.

Starting next Friday, I'd take the things that worried me, one by one, and learn to cope with them, gradually get to know the ropes, and by the time I'd come to see things in an adult way, such difficulties as decisions would be much easier. Everyone knew it took time. After all, people who are really old even know how to manage death – that wasn't something you could do at seventeen.

For the first time ever, Mother knocked at my door before coming in. 'So it's settled,' she said, as if she had come success-fully through a fight. 'Better take a nightie, not pyjamas, and you can borrow my thin dressing-gown, it doesn't show the creases. Stay home Thursday morning – we'll say it's a bilious attack and just hope none of your friends come wondering where you are. How d'you feel?'

I think I wanted her to mean how did I feel *about* it, and said quickly, 'After next Friday I'm going to think more about getting things right. I'll pay you back the money, once I'm earning. It'll be a lot easier when I'm through this . . . phase; you've always said seventeen's an awkward age, haven't you, but by the time I'm a proper adult I'll manage things better. I suppose once you're through *that* obstacle . . .'

Mother sighed deeply, looking past me and out of the window, then she stood up and straightened the bed-covers. She said, 'So you think seventeen's hard. What makes you think thirty's any easier . . . or forty, or fifty?' Fifty was what she was just coming up to. She bent over and kissed me. 'Goodnight. You've got a lot to learn, young lady.'

Chapter Eleven

'Now don't take a lot of rubbish,' Mother said, looking into my case where I'd packed my Palgrave's *Golden Treasury* and a little wooden mouse with a leather tail that Ginny had given me for luck. 'They'll be too busy to want to bother with it.' The bitterness had gone from her voice. She folded the uncrushable dressing-gown neatly. 'I daresay the class of person you're likely to meet there will have bed-jackets, but it's hardly worth the expense of getting you one.'

It was awful not knowing what to expect, and I needed a picture in my head. 'Clinic' meant a place with rows of chairs where you waited till your name was called then went into a curtained cubicle for treatment. 'Overnight stay' suggested a hospital ward. 'D and C', whatever it meant, was less criminal, more medical, than 'abortion' but a shamefully naïve mental picture of it broke through now and then. There were not even leg-rests in it, just some minute, unattached thing, a woolly-dressed dolly, half a thumbnail long, being taken from my body – I was not sure how. It was dry and clean and plastic; nothing to do with me. How would they keep your identity secret?

We went in silence, separately worrying, till Mother said, 'Should one go in, I wonder? Dad thinks they wouldn't want me to, but they can't expect people to know the correct procedure.' I suggested it probably depended on how much room they had, and she must have remembered this when we found that the place was just a private house. A small woman in a white medical coat opened the door and Mother said at once, 'I've brought Ella Thorne; my husband will be in touch this evening,' then kissed me on the forehead and ran back down the front steps almost as if she feared infection.

'The mothers – they worry. It is only to be expected,' the woman said in a Czech or Polish accent as she closed the door behind me, then led me up to a small first-floor bedroom which had a bathroom opening out of it, and overlooked a garden.

'Please have a bath now, and get into bed. I will come later, but if you need me you should press this bell.' She looked friendly, and smiled with her eyes all the time she was speaking.

I undressed quickly with a vague sense of trespass, folding my clothes away into the case, uncertain whether I was expected to use the cupboards and drawers as I felt sure it was somebody's bedroom. There was an orange rose in a vase by the window, and I pictured the owner clearing her things out and forgetting to take it with her. But gradually I began to feel that for a time the room was really mine, and the rose cut and put there ready for me. The money I had brought would pay for everything, like in a hotel.

It was the nicest bedroom I'd ever occupied, carefully furnished and carpeted, very warm and light, with none of the do-it-yourself look of my room at home and no big old-fashioned junkshop furniture like the bedrooms in the boarding-house at Hythe. There was a good deal of white and light grey, but little real colour, apart from the blue bed-cover and the rose.

Here, I was hidden-away and safe, and more private than people in families are used to feeling. The others would be coming home from school, a new generation of 'rowdy ones' tarting themselves up in the cloakroom. Sitting up in bed, warm from the bath, with the *Golden Treasury* open on the covers, I filled out the time till it would be too late to change my mind, with daydream.

Mother had vetoed my zipped shoulder-bag as unsafe, and lent me 'a proper handbag', navy-blue and impregnable, with handles and clasps, studs, flaps and private pockets. It was awkward to carry and obtrusive, a bag that accompanied but was never part of you. Now it lay on the floor by the bed, holding the buff envelope with the money, and Arthur's card, in which he, like me, longed for the world we had known before the holidays. Dozing, I realised that I was in a place where no one who knew me had ever been. They could not even visualise me here. The threads which always seemed to attach me to other people were muddled, in the new surroundings, so that I felt completely disconnected.

I could get up and dress, take the envelope and card out of the bag and put them in the case, walk downstairs to the front door, and out and away without hurry, to the Underground, then Paddington or Waterloo. I could choose somewhere to go from the Arrivals and Departures board, eat something in the station buffet while waiting for the train . . . The girl in the daydream showed no sign of worry. Someone at school had done it, it was not illegal and I was old enough. It was the first time I had ever allowed myself even the dream.

Some time after four the woman came and stood by the bed talking pleasantly, but without referring to my situation till I found the courage to mention it myself.

'Is there only me here? I thought there would be other girls.'

'You do not want others, not just now.'

'No, but do many come? Do they seem to mind, a lot . . .?'

'You are worrying, I can hear it. So many girls do not get help, remember . . .'

'That's what the doctor said. It makes you feel awful.'

Slowly she said, 'You are here, and they are not.' It seemed the easiest way to look at it, temporarily. 'Soon it will be over.'

'Will it hurt?'

'Afterwards? Yes, the same like a heavy period. We will give you something for it. Please relax now. It is the best thing to do.'

'Please could you tell me your name?'

'Mostly I am called Mrs B. It does well enough.'

After that she looked in once or twice but didn't stay, and at six thirty came and took me downstairs, in Mother's dressing-gown, to a bed in a ground-floor surgery. 'You must please bring your handbag,' she said.

The surgery was like the one along the road, and I lay looking round at the modern equipment and the couch with high leg-rests, but this time found it a little less appalling. The doctor brought a younger man, an anaesthetist, who busied himself making adjustments to the table. 'I will just listen to your chest,' the doctor said. 'I'm told you have been coughing, so we must check.' As he folded away his stethoscope he said, 'Good', then pointed to the handbag. 'You have brought the money?'

When at last they were ready for me, and Mrs B. came to help me out of bed, I found the few steps that I must walk from bed to couch, cringing with embarrassment in my blue nightie, the hardest part of all.

'May I please go to the toilet again? I'm sorry.'

They looked at each other in silence, then the doctor nodded and Mrs B. took me to the door, but when she opened it I saw only a blank white wall instead of the hall through which we had come in, and felt irrational terror. Then she pressed something and the wall slid back and the hall was there. I'd never heard of double-doors and my alarm was momentary, but it made my teeth chatter. 'Have either of my parents come?' I asked, and she shook her head.

It was night when I woke, still in the surgery bed, and I lay surprised at the pain and the feel of blood. The doctor was sitting in the lamplight beside me with the buff envelope in his hand. He said, 'You've taken longer coming round than we expected; I have been home and back again twice. Under the circumstances, thinking I might not see you till morning, I took the liberty of getting the envelope out of your bag; it is all correct. Now we shall give you something for the pain and my nurse will get you back upstairs. I shall come again tomorrow morning.'

It was terrifying climbing upstairs, leaning heavily on Mrs B. and trying not to drift back into sleep, but longing for the ease of it. She gave me two pills and tucked me in. 'Did anybody come?' I asked.

'The doorbell rang just after they started, but of course I couldn't answer it. It's hard for anyone to be punctual, with those tube-trains. There was a man across the street a little later, just standing looking up, for quite a time. It could have been your daddy.'

The pain was easier by morning, but I had to stay in bed till the doctor came. He sounded brisk and business-like. 'Now, everything is away – the after-birth, everything – and you will have nothing at all to worry about. Keep your breasts tightly supported, we don't want any trouble there.'

'Trouble?'

'Your body has started to get ready for a baby; now we are asking it to stop. It takes a little time for it to accept the disappointment.'

It was one of the saddest things I'd heard, and I sat by the window waiting for Mother in a terrible welter of imagining. An after-birth, whatever it was, would have been soft, with blood on it.

'I'll take the case,' Mother said, smiling and thanking Mrs B.

We walked to the station in silence, and she went slowly for my sake. By Monday, I thought, the pain should be quite gone and I'll be feeling free and wonderful. In a few weeks we'll both have forgotten it and be back to where we were. It'll be October, with Ginny's birthday and half-term. And as you can't really talk against the noise of the Underground I sat thinking how hard I'd work now, so that some day I could pay them back for the second chance they'd given me.

At the other end we walked home through the back streets, and Mother stopped at Ted Forrest's corner sweetshop. 'Just wait a minute – I'll get a few Liquorice Allsorts for the weekend.' She went in and I stood well beyond the end of the window, thinking I was out of sight, but after a minute or two, when I was watching for her to come out, I heard heavy rapping on the glass and turned to see Arthur's mother beckoning me from inside.

Reluctantly I went in. She was counting change into Mother's hand and shouted, 'Hello! I'm helping Ted out for a couple of hours. You heard from Arthur?' You could tell she didn't know we were together, so I nodded quickly then introduced them to each other; it seemed unavoidable.

'Oh, I *am* pleased to meet you!' she said cheerfully, putting the last coin into Mother's hand, but Mother snapped shut the fastening of her purse, said, 'Thank you, good morning,' and walked out of the shop.

For a moment Mrs Knight and I were silent, then she said, 'Don't worry, that's O.K.' and smiled. 'Oh look, she's left her Allsorts, you better take 'em.' As she handed me the sweets she added, 'Don't know when I've known a summer go so slow, him being away, I suppose. Starts his course end of October, I expect he told you. Still, he'll be back for a day or two before then, so perhaps we'll be seeing something of you.' I didn't know how to answer, so I smiled and nodded and hurried after Mother, whose hostility, I felt sure, would not last long, and I should soon hear her saying ordinary things in her ordinary voice.

She opened the front door and I followed her in and put the Allsorts on the hall table. She took a hanger from a hook and as she was putting her coat on it said, 'I've washed your skirt and blouse. You'd better get them ironed ready for school on Monday.' Then she went into the kitchen, where I found her setting out two cups and saucers. 'Well,' she said as she poured water into the teapot, 'I hope you realise that no decent man's going to want to have anything much to do with you now; not after this they're not.'

No one mentioned Earl's Court that evening, as if it hadn't happened, but at night when all the lights were out Ginny tiptoed into my room and crept into bed with me without a word. There was too little room and we clung to the edges of the bed and giggled helplessly, but I was glad of her warmth.

Chapter Twelve

For a few days after Earl's Court nothing was very different from usual. An abortion's a hard thing to believe in afterwards, with nothing like a scar to show for it, and sometimes I wished I knew another girl who'd had one. But it soon became clear that the old familiar world I'd expected to lean back into wasn't really there.

At home the others had only changed in small ways, like people moving gently forward on an escalator, but I began to feel I'd jumped clean off the end of something high-up, without checking for a place to land. Mother went on helping us through bad moments, but couldn't keep the little barbs of bitterness out of her voice when she spoke to me, and Dad seemed to be always on the verge of a snub like the one on the night we walked back from the Underground. It never came, but I stayed tense for it at meal-times, longing to sag into daydream.

At school I found it hard to stay alert, and began doodling round the edges of my books, wondering where to find the old enthusiasms. Instead of concentrating I kept worrying about how to smuggle little bits of milk chocolate to my mouth behind handkerchiefs or books. It seemed the richest thing on offer.

'You're tired, that's all,' Ginny tried to reassure. She still talked nonsense round the things that worried us, but never resumed her romantic saga of imaginary boyfriends. She quickly recognised that I was starting to have trouble getting up in the mornings, and began cutting short her morning runs to hurry back and get me out of bed at the last moment. I woke too early, and lay with my arms crossed tightly round me, longing to postpone the day and visualising all the things that might go wrong with it.

'I see you've started another picture,' Mother said, handing me the marmalade. 'You'd only half finished the last one – what happened to that?'

'It wasn't right.' I couldn't finish anything.

'The latest one looks even harder. What's it called?'

'At the Theatre!' It was the front view of a girl with a box of chocolates on her lap. Her arm curved down the centre of the picture, the fingers taking out of the box a huge round chocolate in a brown frilled paper-cup, and the image had begun to obsess me. I'd worked at it till the arm and hand threatened to topple the whole design with their importance.

'The girl's supposed to be watching a play, is she? Wouldn't it have been simpler to do her from the side? Legs coming towards you aren't all that easy.'

'Foreshortening,' Dad said triumphantly. 'That'll be your trouble – just a few easy principles involved – but I don't suppose they teach a thing like that nowadays.'

'The legs are O.K. There's a box of chocolates in her lap and . . .'

'You're not supposed to take those boxes home, of course,' Mother said. 'Did you two know that? Even if you haven't quite finished the chocolates you have to drop the box on the floor when you leave, don't you, Dad? I always thought it was a dreadful waste, though I suppose the cleaners stand to benefit.'

Dad clattered his cup down on the saucer. 'Don't talk bloody silly! That sort of caper was before the war, and even then it was more fool you if you hadn't got the guts to . . .'

Mother had turned her face away after the first few words. 'I think you'd better moderate your language,' she said coldly.

It was happening quite often, the coarse, hostile manner bursting through into Dad's conversation when he was address-ing Mother. He was at least speaking to her more often, but though it was not exactly anger yet, Ginny and I could feel a row in it and would sit rigid and ready.

The third Thursday after Earl's Court, Mother called after me as I left for school, 'Now hurry back tonight and get working a bit earlier. You'll have to take tomorrow evening off, for Ginny's birthday, and you're already slacking quite a bit. You do know, do you, that there's been a letter from the school?'

'They said they'd probably write – about me seeing a doctor . . .'

'Yes, well, we'll have to see. Your father's promised not to mention it till the weekend, because of the birthday.'

The reminder to hurry was just one of her barbs, as I was never late home. Every day now I hurried back from school alone, thinking of nothing but half an hour in Dad's deep armchair – the only comfortable one we had – before he came in.

It was raining at home-time so I put my head down and ran. Round the corner from the sweetshop a small grey moped was parked at the kerbside, and a few yards further on Arthur stepped out from an office doorway where he'd been sheltering. He said, 'Sorry about the shock!' – though I wasn't really shocked – and we dived back together into the doorway which was so narrow we could only stand face-to-face, with the rain dripping from his oilskin jacket on to our shoes.

'I only got back half an hour ago and I'm off again on Saturday,' he said. 'Thought I'd better come straight round to see if we could fix something up for this evening.'

'I've promised to be home early and do two evenings' work.'

'Tomorrow evening then?'

'I can't – it's Ginny's birthday.'

He clicked his tongue. 'What could we do then? Damn nuisance you've got school all day.' He'd lost his outgrown look, and the filled-out face and springy hair belonged with his jauntier manner and different clothes; he seemed more what Ginny used to call a one-piece person.

In my mind he'd never had anything to do with Earl's Court, and talking to him was easy again, a relief after the failure of my day – *every* day, but I surprised even myself when I heard my voice saying, 'Why don't I just stay off school?' It sounded like somebody else.

'*Would* you? You amaze me! It would be terrific, we could go into the country or something.' He pointed at the moped. 'These things don't carry pillion passengers, but there's always the Green Line bus – we could pick it up at Filey's Corner.'

We didn't talk about anything or ask for each other's news, and as I ran the last bit of the way home, with still a little time left for Dad's chair, I wondered at my lack of surprise at being with Arthur again. Perhaps it had always seemed inevitable, and that was why I'd spent so little time considering it.

Next morning I went off at the usual time, carrying my schoolbag, and headed for Filey's Corner, which took its name from S. R. Filey and Sons, Builders' Merchants, whose offices had stood at the junction of two roads for over seventy years.

Next to the bus-stop was an underground public lavatory, and I went down there to take off my school skirt and tie and the beret with its badge, and stuffed them into my bag. Then I put on a cotton skirt I'd hidden in the bag – the change was easier than it would have been in summer with the dress and panama – and went up to stand by Filey's entrance, watching the typists and clerks arriving in twos and threes. Several of the girls seemed younger than me, but you'd never have mistaken them for schoolgirls, and I wondered how long it had taken them to pick up the things to say and do, the way to walk . . .

Neither Ginny nor I had ever truanted, though we'd often envied girls who did – not so much for the truanting itself, but because it showed they didn't care. I was already finding the anxiety a burden, and fell back into dreaming of what the day might offer. Though my expectations were vague I knew it wouldn't be like the evening at the sports pavilion – he'd hated that too much. There were two pictures in my head. In the first, the clearest, we walked about in green fields and lanes, with Arthur looking and sounding and behaving exactly as he was before the evening at his flat. It would feel like a holiday, with easy talk and no pretence, and the change would do me so much good that next week at school I'd find concentrating easier, and manage again. The countryside in the second, vaguer picture was much more lush than you can really expect so close to London. No one else was about, and we wandered hand in hand through dreamy landscapes, and Arthur was the new one I'd seen yesterday, unconnected with earlier times. Though I tried not actually to picture it, recognising even then how much it owed to Ginny's romantic saga, with its feeling of happy-ever-after, I did think we might make love somewhere, perhaps at the end of the walk, and it would be good – good enough for me to be able to reassure Ginny – and we would realise that last time had been some sort of misunderstanding or mistake, and something would have been solved.

Arthur wore the waterproof jacket, but with the pockets full of chocolate bars and sweets and crisps. We started eating them as soon as we got on the bus, and it prompted me to tell him about eating chocolate at school and not being able to concentrate. I told it lightly, as if I believed everything would revert to normal once I tired of chocolate, and he considered this as we sped past suburban villas.

'I reckon nearly everybody gets to the stage where they've *had* school,' he said. 'I only recognised it after we got to France and I thought, God, you're well out of it, and wondered why I'd never kicked against it before. Then, when I started the job at the factory I'd have given anything to get back to the County. If you've got a mingy job, like I had, on some rotten machine, you get to feel guilty if you even think your own thoughts for a minute – you wonder if anything's gone wrong, or something's gone through while you were elsewhere. There seems to be no time, ever – time when you're not just doing what somebody tells you to, I mean.' He stretched his arms above his head then clasped his hands behind his neck. 'Felt quite a heel when I left – it was only to finance the holidays, you see – and all the others had to stay behind. I used to think privilege was about having things that other people can't, but now I know it's not having to do things that other people must.'

He stared straight ahead and I knew he was no longer really talking to me because he didn't expect me, inhabiting another world, to understand. He'd got it wrong about my troubles at school – I'd have given all I owned to be able to fit back in, and things to be as they were before – but that was my fault for telling it so lightly.

We walked from mid-morning till some time after two, eating continuously. We drank beer in a pub which was full of collections of things – horse brasses, teddy-bears, chamberpots – but didn't have the warm red feel of the one I went to with Dad. We walked backwards, hand in hand, up a green gentle slope towards a field full of grazing sheep, and looked down over clumps of fiery autumn trees, and he said, 'Since you came to us, Mother's always looking at things and saying, "That's nice – what d'you reckon young Ella would make of a thing like that?" What are you painting now?'

'I keep starting different things. The last one I finished was a street scene. I only got a red for it.'

'You were on that the last time I enquired! Ages ago – when did I last see you?'

'The day before you went to France.'

'That's it.' He said nothing for a moment, then began to laugh, and pulled me by the hand, closer to him, his arm round my shoulder, to share the joke as we walked. 'That bloody awful sports-hut day, wasn't it, when with gritted teeth you endured my callow schoolboy fumblings. Christ, I reckon I'd forgotten that because I was so ashamed!' We walked in silence for a bit, then he said, 'I'm so *sorry* about that day – I really am,' and turned and kissed my forehead quickly, and I hoped he'd say no more about it. 'You were sweet about it, of course,' he went on, 'and I was bloody lucky – there's not many girls who wouldn't have given me a thick ear, as I've since found to my cost.'

I would have liked to be able to act up, like Ginny, but couldn't start. 'More and more,' he said, 'I begin to agree with my dad, that a boy's first time ought to be with someone in the know. I mean, when it's first time for both there's too damn much at stake, isn't there? You could wreck it for ever for a girl.' He turned and kissed my forehead again. 'But I didn't, did I, or you wouldn't be here. I must say, if it hadn't been for you I wouldn't have stood a chance at the factory. I was . . . grateful, if that doesn't sound too patronising.'

I think it was precisely at the moment he finished speaking that I saw to the left of us, perhaps two hundred yards away, a big Alsatian dog race up towards the top field, leap the hedge easily, and bound in the direction of the terrified sheep who, sensing the threat, had already drawn close together and now ran, huddling and bumping together, towards the trees that grew close to the farthest hedge.

There was no sound from any of the animals, and no one in sight. Watching the creatures' terror I felt a great rage let loose inside me and in seconds I was over the stile and racing, shrieking, up the slope. Arthur ran close behind me, whistling at the dog who'd managed to separate an old ewe from the rest and bring her to the ground. She lay now in a shapeless woolly huddle, without a flicker of fight or even resistance, while the dog shoved his sharp nose into the wool of her back.

I can't describe that rage I felt as we raced over the field – it wasn't fear, not even for the ewe. As the dog heard us he lifted his head, then stood back for a moment, as if he felt ashamed, while the old sheep just lay there without moving, and the rest of the little flock stood apart, watching, panting and huddling together. 'He's *killed* her!' I called, almost breathless.

The dog bounded away a few steps as we approached, and the ewe, perhaps frightened by us, got to her feet and bumbled off towards the hedge. And now the dog, excited by her movement, took up the chase again, and would easily have overtaken her, but Arthur took up a stone and lobbed it towards him. The stone hit the ground just in front of the dog, who jumped around, stood for a moment watching us come closer, then lowered his head and ran off.

The ewe had reached the shelter of the hedge but galloped out as we came near, then circled round to join the flock and they ran off together, all baa-ing now, as if in welcome. Lower down the field the dog was cowering at the feet of a man. We heard it yelp, and then he had it on a lead.

'I'll go and have a word with him,' Arthur said, running off, and I stood still, wondering at the intensity of the rage inside me. When he came back he said, 'He'll have to watch it; says there's been trouble before. Nice bloke. They'd have to shoot it, y'know, if it was persistent.'

'I didn't know a dog would *attack* a sheep. I thought they only worried them . . .'

'To death, if you're not careful. That was a young dog; they do it for the sport. The danger's that the sheep could die of fright, and you wouldn't take kindly to that if you were a farmer with capital invested in a few of them, then ended up with a carcass. She's no chicken, that old girl, but I reckon there's quite a bit of lambing mileage in her yet. That's her, right over on the left, the one with twenty-four printed on her back – see how he's pulled quite a bit of wool out of her backside. Daft things, sheep. She'll be O.K.' The things he was saying were filling me with a sort of exaggerated resentment, which seemed crazy when no harm had been done, and I began walking back down the slope, waiting for it to ease.

'You're quiet,' he said. 'Out of breath?'

'No, not now. A bit miserable about the ewe; nothing to defend herself with, and legs not even any good for running away.'

'Oh come on, stop worrying. You *eat* them, don't you?'

'Yes, but they kill them painlessly, not frighten them silly.'

'You kidding? Lambs are so scared they panic, sometimes, and their systems burst. That's another dead loss, the meat's not edible then.'

We caught a bus to get me home no later than usual. The sweets were finished and we sat with his arm round my shoulder. He asked if I'd enjoyed myself a bit, and when I nodded, kissed my forehead and said 'Bless you' again. At Filey's Corner I put my school things back on, wondering whether I'd be home in time for Dad's armchair, and we walked together to the corner of my road.

Because we seemed so separate I guessed we were doing what girls at school called 'packing it in', though for no clear reason. Quite a few things he'd said had irritated me, but he'd also seemed to be acting a bit, trying to show me that he had moved on into a world where I wouldn't stand a chance. It was strange that he'd come looking for me.

At the corner I wished him luck with the course and new job, and he gave me a message from his mother, inviting me to look in at any time. I walked the last bit alone, and kept telling myself that there had been no ease with this new Arthur, and there was nothing I could do but let my stupid imagination latch on to the idea that the old one, lanky in his outgrown school uniform and unconnected with the new one and with Earl's Court, was still in Nottingham, hating it.

'Things go any better today?' Mother asked, and I nodded and smiled. 'I've put your present, and mine, by Ginny's place,' she went on, 'and Dad's bringing his in, same as last year. You run up and put something nice on, and by that time he should be back.' But I hurried, and there were still a few minutes left for the chair.

When Dad came in he carried a fawn mongrel puppy, and I saw Ginny's eyes glaze over with fright when he set it down in front of her. As she bent to pick it up I wanted it more passionately than I'd ever wanted anything before. If only it had been *my* birthday, I thought, as warning bells rang in my ears, he might have given it for the right reasons. Mother had gone into the kitchen the minute she saw it, and I guessed he hadn't cleared it with her first.

Ginny, red-faced, began to act up, thanking Dad fulsomely and kissing him on the cheek, and he handed her a plaited leather dog-lead, saying, 'This is for training it. It'll be your responsibility, remember; your mother's got enough to do.'

'Training? What, walking on a lead– that sort of thing?'

'Dogs have to learn obedience and cleanliness. That means beating it into them, there's no other way.' He watched the dismay on her face for a moment and I tried to push out of my mind the pictures of the distress his loathsome little plan could bring to us. Then he turned to me. 'You're in my chair again,' he said cheerfully. 'It's getting to be a regular thing.'

Ginny put the puppy down and I jumped out of the chair and snatched him up. 'Keep it away from your face,' Dad snapped, and Mother, carrying in the birthday cake she had iced in yellow, said, 'I'll say it now so you can all hear me. I'm certainly not having it in the bedrooms. I shan't say it again – I don't want to spoil the birthday – but if it does get up there it'll simply have to go.' Dad was already doing the crossword.

While we had tea the puppy, who was fat and seemed reluctant to move, settled on an old cardigan in a corner. Dad said he was already called Bonzo, but Ginny said at once that she wanted something more dignified, 'like Liberty only not that exactly', and that she didn't see why animals should always have names that sounded like a leg-pull. This one, I thought, *looked* like a leg-pull – silly and lovable and helpless, and so right for Ginny that Dad couldn't have chosen anything better to hold just out of reach from her. You could tell she feared his motives but could only play along. 'You did say he was my responsibility,' she simpered bravely, taking advantage of the restraint expected even of him at a birthday tea, 'so I ought to choose his name.'

I watched her blow the candles out. 'Now that you're fifteen,' Mother said, helping her cut the first slice, 'we must give *you* a chance to decorate a cake, mustn't we, Dad? My birthday's next – you must show us what you can do.'

Big deal! I thought angrily as she put on the grateful delight they expected. It was the sort of cynical thought I'd never have had a month ago. Mother had patronised her since the eleven-plus, perhaps to counter Dad's disapproval, but had only managed to make her feel no one expected much of her, though she was in fact the brighter of the two of us.

When we got up to clear the plates Ginny said anxiously, 'I'd better take him for a run in the garden, poor little thing's probably bursting.'

'Oh no you don't.' Dad sounded as if he'd been waiting for her to say it. 'I don't want it cocking its leg on the lawn. Take it down the road – there's plenty of verges.'

'But how will he know it's not O.K. on the grass at home, if it's all right out there?'

'That's what the lead's for. It'll know right enough.'

She picked up the little dog and with the lead in her hand

started towards the door. 'Put it on the lead before you go,' Dad said. 'That way you're in control.' She fastened the hook in the lead to the ring in his collar, then with half an eye on Dad set him down and moved towards the door again, but the fat little thing sat trembling where she had put him, and didn't budge.

'What shall I do?' Her face was red and anxious.

'Get behind it and give it a tug . . .' Dad was pretending exasperation.

'Oh not from behind, it'll hurt his neck!'

'That's what we want, to make it move. It'll learn, same as you would if somebody tugged at a strap round your throat.'

Without a word she went back to the dog and gently pushed the toe of her sandal against his rump on the floor, but Dad jumped up and snatching the lead from her gave it a jerk which sent the puppy sliding along the floor with a squeal of pain. Then he thrust the lead towards her but she pretended not to see and didn't take it. She bent quickly and, gathering the dog up in her arms, ran out and through the back kitchen door with the lead trailing behind.

'Not on her *birthday*!' I shouted at Dad as I jumped up to follow her. 'It's her birthday! How can you be so *awful* . . .!' I ran to catch her up; it was the first real spark of life I'd shown for ages, and I'd felt it coming on all day.

'I'll never hurt him like that,' she murmured, when we were well past the house, dabbing her eyes. 'He could choke!'

Round the first corner she sat down on a low wall, still holding the dog upright in her arms. We sat in silence and he rolled himself into a ball in the crook of her elbow. I said, 'It's staring us in the face, isn't it – Dad's an outrage at times.' I felt like a traitor – not only to Dad but to Ginny herself, as she worked so hard at pretending we were no different from any other family.

And still she would only placate. 'He's disappointed, that's all, same as you'd be if you gave a nice present to a cack-handed thing like me who didn't even know how to cope with it.'

'But you do know how to.' The little dog was peaceful, snuffling towards sleep. 'And Dad isn't disappointed. He's doing all right – he's paid out all three of us for the various things we've done to him.' I didn't want to spell out the cruel hold over her that the dog would give him, and she was too wise to ask. She was crying freely now.

'Don't say anything though, Elle. Promise you won't. It

frightens me, the different look you've had just lately, as if you're ready to come out with awful provoking things and start a row . . .'

'It's another bone of contention, you see, and if you don't do something quickly, even if it *does* mean a row, we'll all be miserable for ages.'

'How d'you mean, "do something"?'

'Like refusing to have the dog.'

'You *can't!*' A month ago I would have said the same.

A man in a dark suit and bowler-hat was coming towards us and seemed to have noticed her tear-stained face. He stopped and raised his hat. 'Is anything wrong? I mean, can I be of help?'

'Oh no, thank you, we were just resting. The dog's not used to walking yet.' As she spoke, Ginny kept shoving back her fringe with her free hand.

'He looks a nice little fellow. What d'you call him?'

'I haven't decided – he's a new present, from my father.' The man was busy conjuring up the idyllic picture she intended. 'Perhaps I'll call him Bone, short for bone of contention,' she shrilled. You could see she'd get to be an awful little flirt.

When he had gone she was serious again at once, and said, 'We couldn't have told him what was the matter. No stranger would believe it – I hardly can.' I wished he hadn't come along, dispelling the beginnings of our anger.

We wandered back, the dog trotting happily for a few seconds at a time and getting used to it, and as we went I mentioned some of my fears, to alert Ginny. 'He'll threaten to send him away if he makes a mess, and have you on pins day and night, trying to protect him. He'll try to make you beat him, and if you won't, he will, so you'll have to for the dog's sake. He'll say he's too fat and put him on some diet or other, and you'll be creeping round smuggling bits to the poor starving little thing . . .' But Ginny was shaking her head; she didn't want to think about it.

When we got back the cat was in the kitchen, and Ginny stayed there for a time to reassure both the animals, while I went through to the front room where Mother had set up the Monopoly board. Dad was holding a letter.

'Your mother says she's mentioned this to you already – it's from the school.'

Mother turned a red, angry face to him. 'We agreed not to discuss it till after the birthday!' But he ignored her.

'What do they mean? They say you're finding the work difficult, surely not . . .'

'Not difficult – I just can't concentrate, that's all. They said I should see the doctor and check it's not anaemia.'

'It isn't.' Mother's mouth was straight. 'And we can keep the doctor out of it. It's nothing that can't be put right by pulling yourself together. You could start by getting up a bit earlier of a morning.'

Dad looked upset and I could see his concern was real, though I was sure he'd first brought it up in a fit of pique because I'd shouted at him. 'You should've mentioned it, to me or your mother,' he said gently. 'What's put you into this state?'

'I just didn't settle in after – Earl's Court. Only I can't say so, to them.'

'We've all agreed to put that right behind us,' Mother said firmly, and Dad came over and put his hands on my shoulders.

'You mustn't let a thing like that upset you. You know the hopes I've got for you, and you mustn't let anything, *anything*, get between you and your ambitions.'

'I don't seem to have any, not any more. Look . . . may I please leave school?' Then, before they had time to react, I heard Ginny come into the room behind me, and knew that the three of us would behave, now, as if I'd never asked.

Ginny went over to the table where Mother sat, and started to open the box of chocolates I'd given her – I gave her one every year and we always ate them the same evening, playing some game or other. 'Come on, you two,' she shrilled, doggedly trying to keep us all happy. 'I suppose you're going to have your usual fight over the hazelnut cluster . . .' Dad turned an angry face towards her, annoyed by her interruption, but I took his arm and said, 'Toss you for it,' smiling and leading him to the table, and he stuffed the letter into his pocket and came like a lamb.

In bed there was time to face the idea of not having a boyfriend. It settled like a grey, sad veil all round my head, but the sadness wasn't wholly unwelcome, because perhaps it showed I *really* wanted one at last; since Earl's Court I wasn't just trying to be like the others.

Dad and Mother behaved as if I'd never asked to leave school, and I was grateful, and pushed it right out of my mind, because surely I couldn't have meant it.

Chapter Thirteen

Yet on Monday morning, walking to school because I was early for once, I hesitated at the junction of the High Street and St Michael's Road, thinking of nothing in particular, then turned off to the right instead of going straight on; and my schooldays came to a sudden end.

I felt strangely dreamy as I walked, for I'd neither decided this action nor considered it, but halfway along the road, close to the church, I felt the first moment of fear and began to make decisions again, walking as if I were going somewhere, taking off my tie and beret as I went, till I came to the public library at the end.

Up the broad steps, through the swing-doors, across the patterned tile foyer to the Reference Section and Reading Room, where I sat down at the far end of the high, echoing room and spread out *Religio Medici*, a notepad, biro, pencil and rubber, on half the table, and without looking round, started to read a long passage I'd been staring at for ages, unable to move on.

But it was no easier here than at school, and as I felt the familiar lethargy creeping on I looked up and stared all round the room, searching for something to latch on to.

By the wall, two old men read newspapers secured to broad ledges, and one of them jotted down information. A third sprawled at a table, turning the pages of an outsize book very fast. At the librarian's desk a young man who used to serve at the bacon counter at the Co-op accepted a book from the assistant, and I thought how they were all gathering information, which must be a good thing, while I got nowhere because of an unintelligible paragraph, which must be bad. An ant distracted me, tickling my wrist, and I flicked it off. 'If this isn't satisfactory,' the assistant was saying to the Co-op man, in a carefully lowered voice, 'let me know and we'll send someone downstairs for the Crabbe and Wolfsson – they'd almost certainly cover it.'

I got up and went over to the desk, doing something I was

always dreaming of – that is, doing something the minute it occurs to you instead of just dreaming of doing it in the future – and when the assistant smiled up at me I asked, 'Could you please find me something on . . . ants?'

I followed her to the shelves where she flicked over the pages of a huge red book and handed it to me. 'There's an excellent potted biological study in this, pages forty-three to . . . fifty-two, but I expect you'd want something more comprehensive – organisation of colonies, social set-up, that sort of thing.' All the time she was talking she was stretching up and down to take books out and turn the pages very fast. The telephone rang at her desk, and she handed me the thinnest of the volumes. 'Garner and Petersen,' she said. 'Let me know if it isn't what you want and we'll try again. Excuse me.' I carried both books to my table, opened the smaller one at the beginning, turned to a clean page in the notebook, and lost myself for two hours.

At twelve o'clock I packed my schoolbag, exhilarated by the morning's work, returned the books to the assistant and went out to the Friendly Cow milk-bar where I spent one-fifth of my dinner money, the day's allowance, on coffee and a sandwich.

I allowed myself one hour exactly, then walked back to the library, growing more fearful, as the day stretched on, at what I'd done, and trying not to think about it. But I didn't feel guilty and was encouraged by the certainty that at least I'd stopped the rot. That afternoon I studied the Poor Law till two-thirty, then, slowing down a bit, various editions of *Whitaker's Almanac*, and walked home at about my usual time, but through the small back streets to avoid the others coming out of school.

I'm sure I intended to say nothing to anyone, and to get myself back to school as soon as possible, with the new certainty that I could still concentrate, but Dad had rung the headmistress that afternoon, at Mother's insistence, to make an appointment for the three of them to talk about my work, and heard that I hadn't been at school since last Thursday.

'It was the nearest we've ever been to a proper row,' Ginny said upstairs at bed-time. She looked as if she felt betrayed. She had spent her weekend almost entirely with the dog, taking him out or just being with him in the kitchen, as if determined to keep the little creature out of sight of Dad, who rarely went in there.

'I couldn't *believe* how calm you were,' she went on, 'not riddled with guilt or doubled-up with terror, as I'd have been.' I couldn't understand it either, but had hung on to the feeling that I'd reversed the downward trend.

'The worst thing was,' Ginny went on, 'they were on at each other more than you.' It was what she'd always feared. 'Will you really never go back, or were you just saying it?'

I wasn't sure. The things they'd threatened me with, like having to get a job, had scarcely entered my head. I simply knew I couldn't bear school at present, but hadn't really considered alternatives. So I'd just hung on, telling them over and over, angrily, that I didn't want to go back, surprising even myself. I think sometimes you only find what you really mean when something forces you to put it into angry words.

'I just want something new,' I said to Ginny, but she said she couldn't even bear to contemplate anything as new as going out to work. She was staying on at school a bit and didn't plan to leave till the Christmas after next, but you could tell she hoped something would keep cropping up to stretch it out almost indefinitely.

That night I lay awake worrying over the different attitudes of Dad and Mother. Mother's was based on blame and punishment. 'Then if you won't go back to school you'd better start looking for a job; nobody's going to keep you moping in idleness at your age. You've had your chance – it's up to you.' Dad was trying, perhaps, to salvage some of his hopes. 'All right, all right, it'll get no one anywhere, carping the way you do,' he shouted at her, then turned to smile at me.

They would go to school tomorrow, he promised, and ask if I could be given till half-term to pull myself together. And if not, *he* would get me a job, something with prospects to match my potential. 'There'll be no drifting into any old dead-end thing,' he said to me, then to Mother, 'She's still our girl, and we'll go on doing our best for her, no matter what you say.'

It seemed to me to mark the end not so much of my schooldays as of the genteel pretence they'd kept up for years. Mother had got up quickly and gone into the kitchen where she found Ginny weeping, her face against the dog's head. 'Keep that animal away from your eyes – I've told you time and time again,' I heard her say. And later Ginny told me, 'Even when Dad goes on at her I still seem to want to stand up for *him*; it doesn't seem normal.'

My own behaviour in the days that followed seems to have been pretty short of normal too, but at the time I couldn't see a choice. Each morning I left home at the usual time and walked to the library where I kept my head down, studying whatever appealed, from the 1944 Education Act to the principles of Phrenology, excited by the variety of what was on offer. I enjoyed the freedom from having to pretend, and felt no guilt so long as I kept to my time discipline, certain that something important was being salvaged. In the evenings at homework-time I went upstairs and painted – a pub interior with people slouching at the bar; a huddle of sheep by a hedge. For the sheep picture I had to make dozens of sketches from book illustrations at the library, but always after a quarter to four when I'd done my academic stint, so that it wouldn't seem a theft of time.

Mother and Dad didn't seem to want to tell me about the interviews with the headmistress, and never showed me any of the letters that passed between them and the County Council, and after half-term Dad said he'd arranged an interview for me at Filey's, the Builders' Merchants. I'd been trying to ignore my fears about the future, and it was a shock.

'Have I been . . . expelled?'

'No, you've "terminated your studies".'

'Did you tell them about . . . Earl's Court?'

'We did not,' Mother said quickly.

'Some of the girls once told me a sixth-former was allowed back after – after leaving, like me; three years ago. Just for the exams . . .'

'Some families,' Mother said, 'have no shame.'

'What's the job, though? I mean, I can't think of anything I can *do*.'

She began, 'It's a bit late to start thinking . . .' but Dad interrupted. 'Everyone starts with General Office Duties, and they train you.' He was smiling, eager to convince me. 'There'll be prospects, with a big firm like that; no knowing what you might rise to, a girl of your intelligence, if you play your cards right.'

'Is it through Mr Timpson?'

'Er – that's it,' Dad said, and Mother, looking up from her

knitting, added, 'You'd better wear your little navy suit. They do a nice midday dinner in the staff canteen, I'm told.'

In bed that night I cried, but I'm not sure whether it was for the future I used to look forward to, or school, or the end of the few marvellous days I'd spent in a kind of airtight bubble on my own, with plenty to do, no rules, and nothing to pretend.

Chapter Fourteen

There were no curves and no warm colours in Filey's order office, just khaki metal filing-cabinets, and four desks facing into the centre. Cheryl and Lynne, who were about my age, had sellotaped pictures of Russ Conway and Frankie Laine to the wall behind their heads, and Jennifer, twenty and engaged, had pinned to the front of her desk a newspaper cartoon of workmen sitting on scaffolding high above the town, drinking beer out of cans. It said, 'Danger, men at work', and she had inked out the 'm' and substituted a 'J'. She had little fringed mats for standing things on, and a box of Kleenex tissues which she folded between her cup and saucer to avoid drips. She seemed to use dozens of tissues, dabbing her lips and wiping the tips of her fingers all day, and made me feel grubby and oafish.

All three of them typed a great deal. Cheryl and Lynne, copy-typists, had metal baskets full of work waiting on their desks each morning, while Jennifer, who was called a secretary, went off now and then with her dictation-pad to one or other of the men who were not yet eligible for a secretary of their own. My work, described as 'general office duties', which sounds quite varied, turned out to be mainly the checking of lists of figures.

In a separate space beyond a smoked-glass partition sat Mrs Heather Boyd who was in charge of us. She was heavily pregnant and had interviewed me with the younger Mr Filey – 'Mr John'. When I told Dad he said, 'She'll be the one to watch. People are always leaving and needing to be replaced and everyone goes up a step. You could do worse than take note of the way she goes about things, give yourself something to aim for.'

She was pretty in the same plump way as Mrs Knight, and worked 'extended mornings', which meant doing without a lunch-hour and leaving at two each day.

'She used to work ordinary hours,' Cheryl told me, the first afternoon. 'She's only just started this new arrangement, for personal reasons, hasn't she, Jen?' She and Lynne referred back to Jennifer for everything and seemed to admire her – not that she was pretty, but I think she felt and made others feel that she was glamorous, with her olive skin and heavily-painted eyes. Her prim mouth was straight, but after speaking she would quickly draw back her lips in a sort of smile which showed very white teeth just for a second. She talked in a rush, using her smile like a full-stop.

Now she was filing her nails. 'I wonder if we ought to put Ella in the picture a bit,' she said to the other two, who nodded eagerly. She surveyed her nails from different angles, then said, 'We're a friendly bunch, and we thought you'd settle in a lot easier if we spelt out the lie of the land, as it were.' She did her smile, and the other two were nodding; no one was doing any work.

'We expect you've guessed that Mrs Boyd's likely to be leaving in the very near future.' I nodded. 'We're all ever so fond of her – loyal, aren't we, you two? She's been here ages – used to be Mr John's secretary, left when she married, then after she was widowed she came back, only in a different job, of course.'

'Has she already got children from her first marriage?'

They looked at each other and Jen began to use the nail-file very fast. 'Funny you should ask that. No, she didn't manage it.' She checked the glass partition to right and left behind her, and leaned forward. 'The thing is – she didn't marry again, she's on her own.' They were all looking at me and I nodded absently.

'Ah, we guessed you'd be mature enough not to be shocked, didn't we, you two? We're not shocked either, of course, we just wanted you to know so's you wouldn't say anything out of place, and so on. I'm sure she knows how we all support her, and it must help – she's on her own, you see, and getting on a bit, nearly thirty-eight.'

She put down the file and unscrewed the cap of the nail-varnish bottle. 'We think it's ever so good of Filey's really, keeping her on and not making a fuss like some firms would.'

I wasn't sure whether they wanted me to say anything, no one was looking my way any more. Jen waved her left hand about to dry the glazed nails, and studied them carefully, first holding them up at arm's length, then letting them hang down in front of her face. 'To me,' she said suddenly, 'the saddest thing is that she's probably missing out on all the lovely before-hand part – getting all the pretty bits and pieces together, both of you, and everyone knitting and talking about it . . .'

All at once I began to feel dreadfully irritated. 'O.K.,' she was going on, 'so the best place for children *is* inside a happy marriage, we'd all agree, wouldn't we, you two, but no one should be denied such a wonderful experience just because they're still waiting for Mr Right to come along. After all, it's the most creative thing any of us will ever do, isn't it?'

She gave her smile, the other two were looking dreamy, and I heard my voice say, 'I don't know about creative, but I do agree there's . . .'

'Not creative? Childbirth not creative!' She stared at me, ap-palled. 'What more marvellous thing *is* there to make, than another human being?'

'Oh yes, I think it's marvellous too, but you don't really make it, do you; you only have it. I mean, you don't have a lot of say about it all, do you?' I wished I hadn't started, they were all aghast. 'I mean, the only real say you *can* have is whether or not to have one, and not everybody gets even that much choice.' I'd never really thought of it that way before.

Jen screwed the cap back on the bottle. 'Well, you're a very strange person if you don't mind me saying so, the way you manage to make such a beautiful experience sound quite sordid.' She began to type very fast, then stopped. 'D'you mind if I ask you something – personal?' I shook my head, furious at my own stupidity. 'Have you got a boyfriend?'

My face was getting red and I turned aside before I lied. 'Yes, I have.'

She made her smile, then said slowly, 'Well, I think we all have to go through a few relationships which aren't all that meaningful, before – well – the real thing, and you're still young, aren't you? But I do hope you get to feel less cynical about it – I really do wish that for you.' She smiled again, and as if at a cue from her the three of them bent over their work.

I went on checking figures against a list, the only thing anyone had asked me to do so far, and wondered, as I had once or twice in the morning, what I was doing there. I would have liked to retrace the events which had brought me, certainly not kicking and screaming, to somewhere I so little wanted to be. No one else had wanted it either – I was the only villain. It seemed ironic that the only thing I had to do here was concentrate, and Filey's export lists were less fascinating than the subjects, like ants, that I'd chosen at the library.

At half past three Lynne said, 'I better go and start the tea, it's – you-know-who's week, isn't it?' Cheryl ran to the back window and looked down into the car-park. 'Yes, he's here,' she said, 'I'll come and give you a hand.' Before she followed Lynne out she carried an upright wooden chair with arms, which stood in one corner, into the very centre of the office. I kept trying to think of something to say to Jen while they were gone, to recover the friendlier atmosphere of the morning, but before I managed it she said, without looking up, folding papers together, 'Mr Filey looks in for an afternoon every two or three weeks – that's Mr *Henry* Filey, Mr John's father, son of the one who founded the firm. Doesn't do anything, of course, he's long past it, but I suppose it helps to convince him he's still alive. I think old age is terribly sad – it's really just a case of jollying them along, isn't it, and we all pull our weight with Mr Filey.' She didn't smile or seem to expect anything of me any more and as she started typing again the door opened and Mr John came in with a very old man, tall but stooping. Jennifer jumped up and moved things out of their way, the younger girls came back into the office, and the old man sat down on the wooden chair with his hands folded in his lap.

He was all soft blue and grey, like Grandfather Gordon, without a hint of warm colour, even in his face. His limbs and hands were long, and below the high forehead his eyes were opaquely blue, and I had the silly fancy I'd had with Grandfather that he'd somehow reached down into the extremities of his body, gathering the remaining vitality, and centred it all behind his eyes where he could still be in control of it. 'Like moving your possessions,' Ginny had said, 'from a great rambling house into a small neat bungalow.'

Beside the old man his well-built son had an ugly, explosive look. 'One new recruit, Father,' he said, rubbing his hands, then beckoned me. 'Miss Ella Thorne, who started today, taking Miss Pearson's place.'

The old man stretched out and held on to my hand for a few moments. He smelt of milk, like a baby's pram, and recited his welcome in a thin but warm voice. 'We are glad to have you with us and hope you will be both happy and successful here.'

114

Then he turned to his son. 'Is this . . . the girl Heather suggested?'

'That's right. Look, Father, I'll leave you for a few minutes – one of the young ladies will come with you in the lift when you're ready.'

As soon as he had left, the other three came from behind their desks to sit on the front of them, crossing their legs. They talked slowly to the old man, with raised voices, sometimes praising him as if he were a child who has managed his own buttons, and now and then speaking aside to each other about him, or giggling behind their hands.

'Will you be coming to the staff party this year, Mr Filey?'

'Good! That's good, isn't it, Cheryl! There's no stopping you, is there, Mr Filey?'

'Looking forward to it, are you, Mr Filey? That's right. Something to look forward to, eh?'

Jennifer said to me, 'Mr Filey always has a dance at the party, it's marvellous really. He dances with Miss Gilchrist – she's the longest-serving member of staff, then the newest recruit, if there's time.' She raised her voice. 'You always have your dance, don't you, Mr Filey?'

He gave short, shy answers to their questions, smiling round kindly at us all. 'You'll be able to dance with Miss Thorne this time. That'll be nice, won't it?' Cheryl giggled.

I hated the things they were saying, but didn't like to go back to my desk, and when after a few minutes he began to rise slowly, saying, 'Well, ladies, I must leave you now,' everyone was suddenly at his side – 'Steady now', 'Easy does it', 'All right, Mr Filey?' He thanked them gently and turned to me. 'Perhaps you, Miss Thorne, will come with me to my son's office?' And simply because of the way they had spoken to him I was surprised he could remember my name.

We walked to the door together, slowly, and he said, 'Thank you. Good afternoon to you all.'

'Good afternoon, Mr Filey.'

'All the best, Mr Filey. We'll bring you your tea in a jiffy.' Cheryl held the door open, and as it swung to behind us I heard a burst of muffled giggles.

Neither of us spoke as we went along the corridor and up in the lift, and I had the feeling he might be unable to walk and talk at the same time. A secretary was typing in the small open office in front of Mr John's, and when she came to greet him and helped him to a chair I turned to go, but he reached for my hand and held on to it till his breath returned.

'I wanted to ask . . . what you are interested in? What do you like to do?'

'Painting.'

'Ah . . . now that *is* something. Something to talk about.' Suddenly he laughed. 'Except, of course, that my breath begins to fail me, and you are new, and shy, and haven't found your voice yet. We shall manage. I hope you will be at the staff party.'

'Mr Filey generally manages to dance with the newest employee . . .' the secretary began, but he interrupted. 'Her colleagues have just told her, many times. We mustn't frighten her away, Mrs Coates.'

Back in our office Jennifer was alone, and went on typing for a moment after I went in, then stopped and said quietly, 'Look, don't you think it would have been kinder to mention that you had some connection with Mrs Boyd, instead of just letting me go on – well, making a fool of myself?'

'I don't know what you mean.'

'Well, we all heard that old – goat, saying she'd recommended you, didn't we?'

'Oh no – that was a mistake. It was a Mr Timpson at the Borough Council. I expect she was just the one he got in touch with, to mention it to Mr Filey. I'd never even heard of her.'

'Oh, I'm sorry then.' She didn't sound convinced, and there was no more talking in the office that afternoon.

'Well,' Dad said at tea-time, 'sounds as if you've done yourself no harm by your few words with the old gentleman.'

'Quite an honour, it'll be, dancing with the very head of such a prestigious firm,' Mother added.

'It's automatic,' I protested, '*every* new recruit . . .' but Dad persisted.

'You've always under-estimated yourself. Just look ahead and see where it could lead, if you play your cards right.' I didn't tell them about the tension in the office, though I described the girls, and Dad said, 'Little people, ten-a-penny people, no need to concern yourself with them. Raise your sights a little.'

Upstairs, I told Ginny more about them, but she grew depressed. 'God, how I hate reality! I've got a mental picture of

116

them now, and it's a lot different from the one I'd made up before. Mine was full of gorgeous accountants and rugged-looking executives, not just one sweet old watery-eyed man and a few bitchy girls.' I asked if the dream was for me, or for herself next year, and she said, 'For Dad really. He's happy about you again and it makes him a lot easier to live with. No trouble with Bone, or anything, once he'd set up this thing for you.'

She was only keeping trouble at bay because she worked herself silly making sure the dog never put a paw wrong. He took up all the time she had meant to dedicate to fitness, but it hadn't spoilt her success in the team. She still lived in terror of upheaval, and in the days that followed I strictly edited the things I said at home about Filey's. I didn't mention to any of them Maurice, the clerk from Accounts who got Cheryl to call him over to our table in the canteen, and later asked if I'd go to the National Gallery with him one Saturday.

Gradually I found it was as important at work as it had been at school to have a boyfriend to talk about, though the risk and secrecy and half the excitement had gone out of it. The three girls included their boys in the domestic news they brought in on Monday mornings. Lynne's Reg had helped her father decorate the kitchen, Cheryl's Dave had turned up with marvellous table-cloths and sherry glasses he'd bought in the market, and Jen's Martin had driven her and her parents to High Wycombe for dinner, to celebrate her mother's birthday.

I think they were proud that they hadn't had to look to Filey's to provide their boys, and flirted in a patronising way with the ones who came in and out of our office. But though I despised it I would have loved to be able to do it myself, and kept my head down, pretending I wasn't interested in the wisecracking, fearing my give-away blush.

'You don't sound as if you even want to *go*,' Ginny said as we shopped together for fabric to make my dress for the staff party.

'I don't. It's all this fuss about dancing with the old man. They keep giggling about it; it sounds as if they want me to make a fool of myself.'

'Then don't go. Surely once you're at work you can do as you please.'

I couldn't tell her how seldom I ever did anything I pleased at Filey's. It was nothing but a tyranny of figures; you had to give

117

yourself up to them entirely, for whole mornings or afternoons at a time, without a moment to think your own thoughts, so that the idea of school, even with the lethargy and bits of chocolate, seemed exciting by comparison. Also I hadn't reckoned with the need to behave in quite new ways, almost like reinventing yourself, every time you join a new group – it's a lot freer to stay among people who've known you for years and take it for granted that you're there. Sometimes I lay awake in a sort of excited horror at what I'd done, and how easily, it now seemed, Mother and Dad had allowed it.

We made the dress together. I drew it and Ginny translated it into a paper pattern. She could adapt, cut out, and do all the processes of needlework just as well as me and often better, and threw herself into it enthusiastically, though she seemed to be always listening, ready to spring up at the first sign of trouble about the dog.

Once or twice on Saturdays I saw Lydia, who told me how they envied me at school now that exam pressures were building up. 'At first they thought you'd done a Mavis Lacey' – Mavis had started an affair with a married man and been asked to leave – 'but mostly they thought it was babies, or Approved School for pinching – something like that. I told them what you said in your letter.'

She admired my break from school, but felt that in her own case freedom from family was more important. She had made a new schoolfriend, a girl whose parents were active in some left-wing political movement, who had helped her to see what 'a politically ignorant lot' her own parents were. She had no time for painting now, but sometimes went to meetings and demonstrations with her friend.

I didn't tell her about my dissatisfaction with Filey's, and had never mentioned anything about Earl's Court. In my letter I'd used Arthur's words about coming to a time when you know you've *had* school.

He would certainly have understood about not being able, because of the figures, to think your own thoughts now and then at work. So would his mother, surely, and one cold November Saturday I felt depressed enough to take him at his word about the invitation to visit her.

That afternoon I walked about by myself in the little market in the cul-de-sac beyond the end of Merton Street; I often went there for the colour and clatter and brilliance. If you stand in an ordinary street, gazing around you, people wonder what you're up to; but no one wonders at loiterers in a market. That afternoon I really went there for the opportunity to walk twice past the Knights' house, in the hope of being seen and invited in. We were never sent shopping there – Mother didn't like the way stall-holders shouted out what you'd ordered, making your business public, and Dad said you didn't have the same rights about taking back imperfect goods as you did in a shop.

For a long time I stood near the roasted-chestnut man with his glowing brazier, and it reminded me of how the Knights had had a coal-fire even in summer. Then I walked out of the market towards Merton Street again, thinking, I'll ring the bell if no one sees me this time; I've been invited.

Not far into the street the market noise always seemed to die suddenly, and a little further on I heard a shout and Mrs Knight was hurrying behind me, a heavy shopping-bag in each hand, trying to catch up.

'I saw you by the chestnuts,' she said when I joined her, 'but a shout's wasted in there.'

I took one bag and we walked slowly. 'What do you do with the boys when you go shopping?'

'My neighbour and me take it in turns. I had her three the other day. What about coming in for a bit of tea – they don't need collecting for half an hour or so.'

Nothing was entirely as I remembered it. There was no fire in the bright living-room, which looked quite a tip, and as she turned on a gas-fire and moved heaps of clothes around to make room for us I told her I was at Filey's.

'Ah . . . He said you'd had enough of school. Sit down and get yourself warm, you look perished. I'll get a cup of tea.'

I think she used the tea-making time to think out what she wanted to say, and started to talk as she brought it in. 'I've been hoping to see you ever since the day you went off on the Green Line with him' – she always mentioned Arthur as if we were already talking about him – 'I almost plucked up courage to come round your place, then I thought, well, better not. I was just worried how you'd taken it, and whether I'd done *right* making him tell you. He didn't want to, you know, but I told him I was completely against that. I've been hoping you wouldn't hold it against me . . .'

'Oh no.' I was completely at sea, and didn't know what else to say.

'You wouldn't be here if you did, would you, but I did wonder. I thought to myself, there's some you can play fast and loose with and they don't give a damn, but I said to him, "You tell her now, it's only fair with a sensitive one like that." He'd have told you in any case, of course, but perhaps not till afterwards.' I could only keep nodding.

'I won't say I wasn't terribly upset at first – I mean, what mother wouldn't be – then after a bit I thought, O.K., so he's made a mistake, but I didn't really see the necessity for going *that* far and I told him so. I said he ought to wait a bit – it was such early days she couldn't have been all that certain, and there's many a slip . . . but he'd made up his mind.'

She looked down at her plate and silently flicked a few crumbs around. 'He kept saying I ought to be able to understand that there was no question in his mind – he'd marry her, and certainly wasn't going to hang around, offering a marriage that was conditional upon a baby turning up. He's lovely, y'know, really, he still is.' She reached into her sleeve and dabbed at her eyes. 'It's just that I always think it's such an awful thing for a man to do to himself, to make that sort of marriage.'

I said, because it was time to say something, 'I expect it's the best of the possible solutions, for him.'

'That's right. Thank God they never contemplated abortion . . .'

'Ever so many girls do . . .'

'*He* couldn't muck around with life . . . not like that. No, I know they've done right. I only wanted him to give it time. Anyway,' she forced a smile and pushed the hair out of her eyes, 'it means a lot to me that you don't hold it all against us. I daresay you look on it pretty much as I do – right or wrong, you *have* to like Arthur.'

There was silence for a moment then she said, 'I knew you wouldn't want to talk about it, but it was myself I wanted to justify a bit, not him so much.' She tilted the teapot over my cup and winced. 'What say I make a fresh pot – this is pretty lousy.'

Over the fresh tea I told her about Filey's and my misgivings.

'I know what you mean. Boring's one thing, but when you've got to concentrate all the time and give it all you've got it makes you wonder . . . unless it's leading to something good.'

'There's nothing I really want at Filey's.'

'I wonder you don't get yourself a little factory job to tide yourself over till something comes up. It's *real* boring, but at least you can think while you're shovin' on the flippin' lids or whatever.'

'Arthur said you can't. He said you worry about what's happened while you were thinking.'

'Ah, that was machine-tool stuff, semi-skilled. That was a nerve, setting a lad to that! No, I mean one-handed stuff – I caught up with myself that way, doing a couple of months at Savill's, on the containers, years ago.'

I didn't ask for any details about Arthur – when or who or where, and anyway the pictures that had formed in my head as she talked were so hard-edged and clear they would take a lot of shifting. There didn't seem to be any point, either, in wondering why he'd behaved as he did on the day I played truant. It all gave me an awful left-behind feeling, like standing at the edge of a group while the others decide what to do and go off to do it. On the way home through the dark streets I thought how reassuring it was to hear someone of Mother's generation talk about catching up with yourself, as if there was an important part of herself that she'd managed to keep intact right through her life, like a sort of core. It was more hopeful than Mother's obstacle-race attitude, with other people's rules the most important. So I decided to try and be more of a doer, instead of just letting things happen to me; but it wasn't the first time I'd made that decision.

Mother kept finding fault with the way the dress was proceeding. She didn't like the colour, and said we should have chosen white – 'It's what a young girl would be expected to wear' – but she couldn't spoil Ginny's pride in it.

'It's a super fit,' Ginny said, pinning up the soft yellow fabric, as we tried it on for the first time.

'Super it may be,' Mother nagged, 'but they certainly won't expect her to turn up in anything as tight as *that*. Let those seams out a bit, Ginny, there's hardly room to move.'

When she had gone Ginny put all the pins back to where they'd been before. 'The minute *I* get a bit of shape I'm going to reveal it,' she said.

Chapter Fifteen

Filey's Christmas decorations went up well before others in the district. Dusty old paper-chains came out from store and each office planned its own, with little Miss Gilchrist, the longest-serving member, supervising the corridors and canteen.

Everyone talked about the annual party, which was sometimes called 'the dance', but when Lynne referred to it as a ball Jen said it only showed her ignorance – 'A ball is always a long-frocks affair, with formal dress for men. The Filey family are the only ones who dress, but I'm sure they do that every evening.' It was to be held at the Claremont Room in the Town Hall, where I'd seen people going in on a Saturday night past a Borough Council notice on a stand by the door – 'Jiving is not permitted in the Claremont Room.'

'Ah well, there's always the corridors,' Maurice, the boy from Accounts, said. He had already been to one Filey's party and asked me if I would go as his partner. 'It's O.K. so long as you've got someone to go in with,' he said. 'Everyone looks so different you think you've walked into the wrong lot. Little bits of girls done up like duchesses . . . It's a lot different to your average office booze-up, round the desks.'

And because I had already wondered about going in, and what on earth to do if no one spoke, I agreed. 'That is, unless I'm expected to go with the others in my office.'

'You won't be – not your lot. Jen would see to that. She's something altogether different, done up for a party. Ordinary days she makes you feel you've got filthy dirty fingers; it's the white blouses. Mind you, she wasn't that prim before she got engaged – oh no. Sellers, from my lot, he cut his teeth on her, as you might say. Livened up many a dull old lunch-hour for me, he has – he's got the knack of telling a good story. Tell you another one that's really stunning dressed up – Heather, your supervisor.'

'She isn't coming.'

'Ah well, there's not a lot you can do, is there, with a bun that big in the oven.' I didn't like him.

Mother said I ought to give a little thought, at the party, to the way I held myself. 'There's nothing people notice in a woman so much as poor posture.'

'I dispute *that* . . .' Dad began.

'And smile. Smile when they ask you to dance . . .' I was already worrying that no one would.

'Ask?' Dad was scornful. 'You're going back a bit, Mother. From what I hear it's all snatch-and-grab these days.'

'Not at the Claremont Room – there's none of that sort of hanky-panky. The Town Hall don't hire those rooms out to just anybody.'

One afternoon when everyone had been talking about it and Jen and I were left alone in the office, I asked her, '*When* exactly do I have to dance with Mr Filey?'

'Oh, no fixed time or anything – it's not all that important, if you know what I mean. Miss Gilchrist though, she has her dance at the beginning, after Mr John's said his welcome.'

'Perhaps they'll forget about me then.'

She opened her thick-black-edged eyes wide. 'Look, if you're worrying – just don't. As my mother used to say when I was shy, "Stop fretting. No one's going to look your way – there'll be too much else going on." Know what I mean?' She smiled.

On the Wednesday before the party old Mr Filey made one of his afternoon visits. Lynne saw him from the window being helped from his car. 'He doesn't look up to much,' she told us. 'You'd think he'd stay home in the warm – after all, he'll be seeing us all in a couple of days.'

A little later in our office he seemed to want to talk less than usual – though he had greeted us all politely – content to sit in his chair in the centre of the room, raising his head to gaze round at the gaudy chains and strips of tinsel. They were less giggly with him this time, but still quite patronising, asking things like what Father Christmas was going to bring him.

His face was waxen, with little blue lines showing on it, and his lips bloodless. From where I sat I could see the veins standing out purple on the backs of his hands. Speaking for more than a few seconds made him breathless, but during a lull in the chatter he turned to me and asked, 'Miss . . . Thorne. What are you painting now?'

The others had gone silent. 'A girl. A girl at the theatre.'

'That's brave. The human figure isn't easy. My sister was . . . something of a painter; was taught, as a girl, to paint on glass. But only things that were . . . "improving" – flowers and sea-shells and so on.'

Jen asked, 'Was that Lady Alice, Mr Filey?'

He nodded. 'She longed to paint the human figure, but . . . in those days . . . girls didn't.' His words were getting quite slurred. 'My father was a self-made man . . . untaught . . . and he and our mother wanted their children to have greater . . . ease . . . in their lives. They hoped Alice would do no work, or, if she must, something . . . sheltered. But Alice was robust' – he smiled at the memory of it – 'she went into the glassworks, painting things. A dreadfully . . . hard life, but it kept her free from their . . . ambitions.'

Cheryl was shaking her head. 'He's got it all confused,' she whispered to Jen. 'I'm *sure* she never . . .'

'Now,' the old man said, 'I have talked too much and over-tired myself. It's only too easy.' He started to rise and the others ran to help him.

'Shall we get Mr John, Mr Filey?'

'Just a helping hand . . . down to my car,' he said. 'Perhaps you would be good enough to ring through to my son . . . and let him know I'm on my way home.' As Jen went to the phone he turned and said to me, 'May I ask you to . . . go down with me, if you can spare . . .'

Lynne and Cheryl drew away, and he looked gaunt and awkward standing alone under the bright paper-chains which hung close to his head. We went out slowly, and as the door swung to behind us I heard Lynne burst out, 'She *never* did – he's got it all muddled. She married Lord Something-or-other.'

I got him to the lift and he stood silent, breathing heavily, then on the ground floor we started slowly towards Reception. 'She did – she did indeed,' he muttered, smiling, 'and never once regretted it.' He paused for a moment, leaning against the wall close to the doorway of Accounts, and asked, 'And you? I keep wondering what Filey's will have to offer a creative girl.' We started off again and his hand felt cold against my wrist as he clung to my arm for support. Slowly he began, 'You know, I have never been able to decide . . .' and was suddenly falling, stumbling sideways against me. 'I am so very, very sorry . . .'

He had let go of my arm and was trying to get his hand to his collar but it floundered around its target. I tried to take his weight, to get him to the wall again, but suddenly he crumpled, and I saw his lower jaw shaking as his head fell towards my shoulder.

'Help me, someone!' I heard my shout, and the porter hurried out of his cubby-hole and Maurice and another boy ran out of Accounts, and suddenly it seemed that hands were stretching out towards us from all directions, supporting him, lowering him gently, freeing me.

His eyes were closed as he lay on the floor, and for a few seconds the usual clatter and murmur of voices came through the open office door. Then everything went silent in an abrupt, unnatural way, and I grew aware of faces, eyes staring, packed into the doorway. I could see people moving and speaking, but everything soundless, like a silent film, then noise came back with a rush into my head and I heard the lift whirring, saw Mr John and another man run out, and two others clattering down the stairs. The first-aid team brought a stretcher and carried the old man to a room across the corridor. I thought he was dead.

'You all right?' Maurice said, and I nodded, wondering if I ought to go back to the others upstairs. He stood awkwardly for a moment, then reached into his office and lifted out a chair for me. Mr Westbrook, the Chief Accountant, came out of the room where Mr Filey had been taken and asked me what had happened, nodding gravely as he listened.

'Is he dead?' I asked, and he shook his head.

'Another heart attack, they think. An ambulance is on the way. Now, you should go home. I'll call Mrs Weekes. Stay here, both of you.'

When a doctor with a black bag was hurried into the room opposite, Maurice said, 'That's Weston, Harley Street. And if you or me show worryin' symptoms we get sent to him for a check-up. All in the family – well – relatives of relatives; everyone gets done proud.' We could hear a siren, and an ambulance drew to the front door, flashing. As they carried the old man out, Mrs Weekes from Personnel ran down the stairs.

'Transport's arranged,' she said, 'and someone's bringing your bag and outdoor clothes. Is there anything else? You're going with her, are you, Maurice? I'd be glad if you would.' He went to get his coat and she whispered, 'I'd send one of your chums from your office, but I think you'll agree it's nice to have a man's support at such a time.'

Outside, the chauffeur held open the door of old Mr Filey's big Bentley, and we got into the back. Maurice seemed as awed as I was, and neither of us spoke till we were nearly home, then he gasped, 'Well, there's a turn-up for the books!' After that he leaned over and kissed me, and it was quite comforting, but when he put his hand up my skirt it seemed a dreadful thing to do in Mr Filey's car, and I was glad we were already slowing down.

'You're early,' Mother said, up to her elbows in flour. 'Whatever's wrong?' So I told her, then had to repeat it first to Ginny then to Dad as they came in. My teeth kept chattering, and Mother said that as I didn't want supper I should have a warm drink and sit by the fire. As she got up to get it she said, 'They must think quite highly of you, sending you home in a great car like that, mustn't they, Dad?'

'Well, you've got yourself noticed,' Dad said. 'It won't be forgotten.'

'I don't really want to go back there.'

'Now you're just talking silly!' Mother called from the kitchen door, and Dad began, 'But what else could . . .'

'I was thinking I could get a job in a factory or something.'

Mother hurried back in, and stood with folded arms. 'After all your father did, getting that job for you! Oh no, no daughter of *mine*'s going in for factory work, so you can put the idea right out of your head.'

'Surely I can decide for myself. I'm old enough.'

'Not while you're under my roof. Not in a factory. Let's hear no more about it.' She went for the milk and I sat feeling stunned by the threat in her words. Unlike Ginny I'd never seriously considered the idea of our family actually breaking up, and any of us living under a different roof.

Dad must have been shocked, too. After I'd gone up early to bed he tried to make Ginny beat the dog for making a mess, and when she refused he thrashed poor Bone himself. I lay with my fingers in my ears, sick with guilt because I'd triggered it, and when Ginny came up her face was still red with tears.

She took the yellow dress down from the picture-rail and hung it away for me, then sat cross-legged on the end of my bed, brushing her hair which had been cut short for her fifteenth birthday. 'Even if he does get better,' she said, 'he won't be well enough for dancing, that's for sure.' Then added quickly, 'I nearly cried when you said about his lips being all blue. It made me think of Grandfather Gordon.'

'I thought of him too. He and Mr Filey were quite alike – they both listened so politely.'

'We used to tell him every mortal thing, didn't we, when we went round there, Friday evenings. I do miss him.'

'Me too. Even when I started the curse he was the first one we told; went straight round and asked what we should do.'

Before she went she offered me a pink capsule, one of three a girl had given her for exam nerves. I was glad of it, and lay waiting for it to work and exorcise the pictures from my mind. When I woke in the night, certain that Mr Filey was dead, I kept wishing I'd said or done something to make his last minutes easier. He must have been scared, with everything going to pieces around him and the sight of me struggling to support him.

It occurred to me that I would have been in his last mental picture before he lost consciousness – perhaps before he died, even. It was a frightening thought, as if, by dying with a picture of me in his head, he might have brought me, suddenly, to God's attention.

Next morning at Filey's no one did any work. A notice in Reception asked all members of staff to meet in the canteen at a quarter to ten, and Mrs Boyd came out of her separate little office to wait with us. Quietly she asked me, 'Feel all right this morning? I hoped you wouldn't come in unless you felt up to it; see how it goes today.'

Jen, Lynne and Cheryl told over and over how they had 'just known' yesterday. 'I think you can *see* death on a person,' Cheryl said, and Lynne nodded hard.

'Oh, you can. Didn't I say, yesterday, seeing him get out of that car, how strange he looked? Different. And when he went out of that door I somehow knew as clear as anything that he wouldn't be back.' It made me wonder why she had been so worried about whether Lady Alice went into the glassworks.

In the canteen there was subdued chatter till Mr Westbrook went on to the little raised platform at the end and announced that the head of our firm, our much loved and respected Chairman, Mr Henry Filey, had passed peacefully away yesterday evening, 'shortly after leaving the office, which is how he would have wished it'. He told us some funeral details, and that it would be private, and said that the family were grateful that they could rely on our loyalty and support to help them through this time of grief. Then he said that under the sad circumstances the Board felt we should not proceed with the annual party, and it had therefore been cancelled as a mark of respect to the family.

When he had gone everyone stayed silent till one of the Area Managers got up and asked for volunteers to help take down the decorations. Quite a lot of hands went up but at the same time there was murmuring in several parts of the room, and as we all streamed back to our offices people began arguing quite heatedly.

In the corridor I saw Jen, red-faced, laying down the law to Maurice, and heard his retort: 'Well, the way I see it, with all due respect to Mr Filey, is that those decorations are up there to celebrate the birth of a Messiah, whether anyone believes in it or not, and nothing whatever to do with *this* establishment. There should have been a vote.' If there had been, I would have voted to keep them up, though not because of any principle that I could think of.

Back in the office Jen exploded into anger. 'Isn't he just . . . bloody awful!' Then she turned to me and looked abashed. 'I'm sorry. I didn't think. You're friends, aren't you?' I shook my head.

'I thought you . . . went out together.'

'No. They asked him to see me home yesterday, but we've never been out.'

'Ah. Well, I must say I *was* a bit surprised to think that anyone so . . . coarse . . . should think he stood a chance with one of us.'

When I told them at home about the party Mother said it seemed a waste of a dress, but Dad said he thought he'd get another flash-bulb and take a picture of me wearing it.

Chapter Sixteen

Work finished at midday on Wednesday, Christmas Eve, and during that morning Mrs Boyd called me into her office. She offered me a chocolate. There were sweets and soap and talcum on all the desks, as it was the custom to give presents to the others in your department, and the shiny wrappings were welcome now that the decorations were down.

Lynne had said, 'Pregnancy suits her,' and Jen had replied, 'It suits us all.' Certainly her eyes were lovely – clear, velvety and smiling – and when she took a chocolate herself I noticed how her plump fingers closed round it to lift it from the box and began to think of my picture with the big important arm and the still undefined girl.

I could give her a great swollen abdomen and a green-and-red checked skirt stretched tight across it, though it would create a new problem about how the arm should fall. On the left hand, holding the box, I would put a thin wedding-ring, and another ring above it with a stone like a ruby.

She said, 'Mr John won't be back now till after the holiday, and as you know, I shan't be returning, so I want to make sure everything's in order for my replacement when they get one. You seem to have settled in, and we like your work. Any problems, are there?'

Though it was sticking my neck out, I told her my doubts about Filey's being the right place for me, and she showed no surprise at all, and asked what I had in mind. When I suggested the factory idea she still wasn't surprised, but said at once, 'What do your parents think?'

'My mother's fiercely against it. My father – well, he's got ambitions for me . . .'

She was doodling on her blotting-pad, not looking at me. 'Lots of fathers,' she said, 'seem more involved with their daughters' happiness than the mothers are.' She put the pencil down and looked up. 'I do understand about you wanting to make your own way – it's only reasonable. Still, if you don't mind me advising you, I shouldn't rush anything. You can't get independent without upsetting your family in *some* way, but I always think you've got to pick your time. It could be that later on, say, they could take it better – your mother might not be quite so fierce. I know something about friction in families.' She pushed the chocolate-box towards me. 'Think it out over the holiday. If you do stay, promotion would be on the cards, of course. They wouldn't expect to keep you where you are for long.'

I thought she had finished, but she put her elbow on the desk, cupped her chin in her hand, and seemed to look through me, lost in thought. 'You have to give a fortnight's notice here, but we'd give you a reference, of course. I started a home of my own at your age, never regretted it.' She seemed to be advising me in two different directions, and to have my interests, and my family's, more at heart than the firm's, and I think she saw my bewilderment. Quickly she asked, 'Made any friends, have you?'

'Well . . .' I felt awkward.

'Some do it easier than others, don't they? Me – I've never found my friends where I've worked. I suppose it depends on sharing interests, and I can't at the moment think of anyone at Filey's who does drawing or painting. You'd most likely find kindred spirits at the Art School.'

Dad had often suggested I should go there, not so much for friends as for perspective and anatomy and what he called 'a few tricks of the trade', but coming from Mrs Boyd the idea was immediately attractive to me, and I told her so. She jumped up and stretched out her hand and shook mine, then held it between both of hers for a moment, saying, 'Anyway, we'll run up against each other again, I hope.'

I said, 'I hope you have a very nice baby,' and she pressed her lips together suddenly as if she were trying not to cry, and turned aside.

For the rest of the morning I was acutely conscious of her presence behind the glass partition. She had had her leaving presentation the day before, but just before twelve Jen brought out a bottle of sherry saying it didn't seem right not to make a bit of a fuss, and the five of us had a drink together. We all called her Heather, and I treasured every smile, each word she spoke to me, like a schoolgirl crush.

I hated losing her so soon after finding her. It was the same with old Mr Filey, and even perhaps Arthur, while my relationship with Lydia, though it had not come to an abrupt end, had never become real friendship. It felt like incredibly bad luck, but at the back of my mind lay the suspicion that it all pointed to some awful failing of mine.

The canteen wasn't opening that day, as we were finishing early, but I hadn't told Mother, who would have insisted on a proper midday meal at home. Already the thought of Thursday to Monday over Christmas with just the four of us was beginning to oppress, so I planned to get a sandwich at the Friendly Cow, calling at Lydia's with her present on the way.

For a time I stood outside the pawnshop looking at a tiny compass set in brass that Arthur had admired before he left school. I wanted to get it for him, and fought a battle within myself. What would it seem to mean? Would it be what Mother called 'making yourself cheap', and would that matter? Ginny would have said give it, Dad would have called it a waste of money, Mrs Boyd might have said . . . I wasn't sure who I was listening to any more, and walked away.

Perhaps I would get sweets for the little boys, which would embarrass nobody. But when I pictured myself choosing them in Ted Forrest's shop it seemed ludicrously like taking coals to Newcastle, so I hurried on towards Lydia's to deliver a present which I didn't even want to give, feeling resentful because I found it so hard to be a doer, or listen to myself.

Lydia's mother was handsome, with a good figure and a well-preserved face, heavily made-up. 'She's not back yet, dear,' she said, opening the pretentious Georgian door. 'Come in a minute, there's only me.' Her voice was la-di-dah and strident. I followed her to the dining-room where she poured two drinks almost automatically. 'We'll have a snifter together, just to say Happy Christmas. Don't laugh – she's got a job. Vacation job, she'll tell you all about it.'

Lydia had changed, she said, and was giving them a difficult time. 'I daresay it's just her adolescent rebellion, and will pass. They all have to have it, don't they – well, you know yourself. How's it working out, by the way? O.K.?'

I nodded and she went on at once. 'We shouldn't grumble really, she's working hard for university now, and that pleases us, but I don't think she meets the right people, not since you left.' She leaned forward and began to use her hands to help her speech along. 'A lot of these – fanatics, *you* know. Peace, she's into, and Youth for this, that, and the other – that sort of thing. You have to let them have their head, though, and perhaps it's better now than later on. We were ever so sorry you left; she was always so settled when she had you.'

After the drink I left the Christmas present with her and went to the milk-bar, but it was so crowded and noisy, as most working people had finished early, that I turned to go, then saw Lydia at a corner table, waving to me, twice as lively as she'd ever been.

She looked lovelier than I'd remembered. She never wore make-up or paid much attention to dress, because with a face like hers it would have been painting the lily, but perhaps because she had found someone strong to imitate, she looked more all-of-a-piece. 'We were just going,' she called as I fought my way over. 'Come with us? Neville's got a bottle. We're going through the park.' With her were two girls dressed alike in tight grey skirts and huge white heavy-knit sweaters with the sleeves pushed back to their elbows. Their hair hung over their faces and when they spoke they kept brushing it back out of their eyes. There was also an exceptionally good-looking boy with a girl's complexion and very fair curly hair. I remembered him from the boys at the County when I'd walked home with the rowdy ones, but now he wore dark, dirty overalls, as if he'd been working in a garage.

Lydia's friends seemed to hold her in special regard. They didn't mind me joining them, and they went on ahead, while she told me they were all working at Forman's Jellied Almonds. Neville was working full-time in the Transport Department till May, when he'd start a course something like Arthur's, and she and the girls had holiday jobs. 'Only part-time – I do it for the independence. I'm working for university, Elle, it's the only way I'll ever get separate from them. They've had me all worked out for years: nice little job, but not for long – not actually *with* Dad, but he's got fingers in everything, and strings attached – and after that, well, they'd even got the fellah sorted out. Dad's been giving him "opportunities". I was grateful to you for leaving – it pulled me up short.'

The park seemed full of people: workers bouncy after office parties, excited children, tired women taking the short cut home with shopping-bags laden with food for the long holiday. It was the park I used to come to with Arthur, but without the others would never have dreamed of coming in December. The sun was just managing to shine, and the noise of the ducks at the lakeside, the squealing of children and barking of dogs – even a bonfire of leaves crackling beyond the path – all made it feel like the centre of somewhere. I was glad not to be drinking a lonely coffee in the Friendly Cow.

We found a seat near the water and drank some wine out of paper-cups from Forman's vending-machine. At work I had drunk two sherries, with Lydia's mother my first-ever gin-and-tonic, and I had forgotten to have a sandwich. Now I began to feel that in this friendly place it didn't matter whether or not you spoke or what you said. Lydia sparkled, no longer a drag.

Not far from us, beyond a carefully-clipped golden-privet bush, a girl of about my age sat on a concrete boulder beside a small fold-up pram, rocking it gently. She looked fragile and waif-like, with a thin pointed face and very straight fair stringy hair, and was continually jerking her head around, smiling at each new sight or sound, like a child. By her shoe a little Jack Russell terrier stretched on the grass, and she kept putting out a hand, without looking, to pat its head and set its tail wagging. Sometimes it wandered off to look at other dogs, then trotted back to sprawl beside her. And every few moments she would bend her head into the pram to talk to the baby, who began to kick excitedly under the waterproof cover, and wave its arms about. She took off the cover and spread it under her on the concrete, then loosened the blanket, and I could see the blue woolly-covered arms and legs waving and kicking in rhythmic ecstasy, and could hardly bear to take my eyes from them.

I felt deeply contented yet strangely troubled, and inside the soft protective bubble of too much to drink, was able to hold the two feelings together in some kind of balance. This, something told me, is how it has to be – this is what people drink *for*. Nothing needed deciding or changing, the sun was still shining, and I wanted to run home to get Mother and Dad and Ginny and sit them on the seat to inhabit the same world for a minute or two.

Neville threw the empty bottle into the litter-basket and went off with his arms round both the girls. Lydia said, 'They're great – everyone at Forman's is – totally different from school. We all got to be the same, didn't we, day in, day out. I reckon that's what finished you.'

I didn't tell her about my plan to get something temporary while I sorted myself out – no doubt a bit of envy was beginning to creep in, even through the alcoholic insulation. After all, she was already doing what I wanted to, but supported by her rich, adoring parents, and the outcome hardly mattered because she was on her way to university and the things I'd been working towards for years. And she was beautiful.

As she went on and on about her fight for independence – the wine hadn't affected her, she'd been brought up to drink – I began to feel a bit irritated.

'They know by now that I'm not interested in their wealth, and I've told them what they can do with their despicable possessions. Mum said she bet I'd be saving up for the same sort of things myself in a year or two, but she's right off-beam there. Dad gets terribly upset, he's pathetic; keeps bleating on about too much money being O.K. so long as you've worked for it. Oh yes, and it's all above-board, everything is, if you've "served your country". You'd think he'd volunteered. He tried every trick in the pack with the Exemptions Board! Anyway, he just doesn't understand that if I were a man *nothing* would induce me to take up arms, not against my brothers in foreign countries. It's a different matter altogether fighting at the barricades *with* them, against the common enemy, but he can't see that.'

I think I would have gone along with quite a bit of what she was trying to say, and if she'd been someone else might have admired her courageous defiance. But not Lydia. She wasn't *in* it. She made it sound unreal, and you could pinpoint from her words just who she'd been keeping friends with at school.

So I went on watching the baby. The sun had gone in and the newness seemed to be going out of the scene, and I was glad when Lydia said she had to go. She said, 'Thanks for the present you left. Look, why not come round some time over Christmas and pick up yours? Try Boxing afternoon. You could bring Ginny if you like.'

The girl lifted the baby out of the pram, and I watched her hands as she held him for a moment first above her head, then with his face close to hers, while they held a conversation of smiles and sounds. Then she laid him back in the pram, fastened the small harness over his shoulders, and tucked the blanket in all round.

You could paint hands, I thought, for a whole lifetime – lifting things, holding them. It would *take* a lifetime, discovering how to make them convey the weight, even the value, of what they lifted. You could cover a whole canvas with them, single ones and pairs, all lifting different beautiful things – plucking or fondling or holding or grasping, even struggling to support. She'll go now, I thought, watching her stand and straighten her coat and look all round and up at the darkening sky.

The little dog was away on one of his trips, and now, from beyond the garden beds towards the gates, came sudden commotion – squealing and shouting and snarling and yelping. Dogs were fighting, and walkers stood still and turned their heads, while children ran, yelling, to investigate. The girl hurried across the path, pulling a dog-lead out of her pocket, then turned and ran back towards me, waving. She pointed at the pram. 'Keep an eye for a tick, would you?' she called, and in that moment I saw that she was Freda from the end. So I nodded and she raced off, calling over her shoulder, 'Don't like these clouds. Won't be a sec.'

When she had gone I looked round at the shadowed trees over to the right and began to dread the dusk. December dusk seems to me the saddest, most death-like time of all the year. It's easy to see why we hang on to the awful gaudiness of Christmas, tinselling it up more and more shiny so that we shan't be tempted to look outside.

It's difficult to say in detail what happened next because the day's dreams and plans and imaginings seem just as clear and sharp-edged as its memories. The clouds grew really black and I remember either walking towards the pram or imagining I was. I think you walk, when you've drunk more than you're used to, in a soft, cocooned way, never quite certain whether it's actually happening or not. And then I was smiling down at the baby – that was really happening – and its legs were kicking away beneath the covers, and I was gently unfastening the harness – I can see the chrome rings with blue loops and red tags – and lifting the baby out, thinking that the way your hands need positioning can only be determined once you've discovered the weight they must lift. I shifted them round to hold the baby flat against me, then I was running, hard, towards the trees, with other people running after me shouting and squealing, gaining on me. And suddenly I realised that cold rain was splashing in great drops into my eyes and on the baby's head, and I was scared of slipping over.

Into the trees I ran and just inside the first row of them felt a hand fall heavily on my shoulder from behind, and when I turned to ward it off, saw it was Freda, the waif-like girl, leaning against me, helpless with laughter, one hand on me, the other round the baby.

'Thanks ever so much. *God*, what a sprint! You should've *seen* yourself! Goin' like Ole Harry, clutchin' on to 'im like a bag o' washing. You could see you're not used to it – God, I thought, don't let 'er trip!' She took the baby from me.

All round us people were shaking out their hair and wringing out their clothes, chattering excitedly about the surprise of it all. 'I'm ever so grateful,' she went on, still bubbling uncontrollably every few seconds. 'I knew you'd never get that hood up in time – it's ever so stiff, and generally I just hold it with one hand and run like hell. It'll have half an inch of water in it by now.' She was laughing again.

Shopping and other possessions, snatched at the last second, were being handed over to their owners, and a man ran in among the trees wheeling the pram with one hand and holding the waterproof cover in the other.

'Cop 'old a minute.' Freda passed the baby back to me, stripped the pram, spreading the one dry blanket at the bottom, then laid him in.

'I'll get 'im home quick. He'll be O.K. Tough as old nails. Look at *you*, you're sopped!' She was smiling, pointing at my shoes and hair. 'You look as if you've seen a ghost! I'm ever so sorry. Come back with us for a coffee – we only live in George Street. You in a hurry?'

I shook my head, then I was following her along the path towards the park gates, with all the others. The rain had stopped, but without the sun there was nothing for anyone to be out-of-doors for. The little dog trotted beside her. Suddenly she said, 'My name's Freda.'

'Yes, I think I know you. Didn't you used to live near us in Selwood Road?'

'I was born in Selwood Road – lived there for ages, only I can't say I remember you. D'you feel O.K.? You look a bit ribby.'

'It was a shock, that storm. And I'm a bit whizzy; a few drinks and no lunch.'

I felt as if I'd been somewhere else for a long time, and was immensely tired. Perhaps the coffee she had offered would be black and put me right for going home. I seemed to have been caught up in some great muddle or mistake, with a feeling that there had been something dreadful at the heart of it, something I couldn't quite latch on to, though it kept swimming in and out of my mind. Till bed-time there would be no opportunity to go back over it all and work out whether, when I had unfastened the baby's harness and was lifting him out of the pram, there had been any sign of rain. It seemed terribly important, and though I remembered particularly how my hands had looked, the fingers nearly meeting round the woolly bundle, I could visualise them either dry, or splashed with rain, with equal vividness.

For a moment I wondered if it would be best to hurry off now, before the girl or baby became more real to me; it would make it harder to flesh out the memory, and perhaps it would fade. But in my muzzy state I hadn't much resolve, and we turned into George Street with its little terraced houses, and almost at once through the gate of number three. I said quickly, 'Will your husband be home? Will he mind?' and as she put her key into the door she said, 'I'm on me own.'

She pushed the pram through the tiny dark hall to the kitchen at the back, then through into a lean-to scullery beyond it, where I could see a bath with a wooden cover. She took up the baby and brought him back into the kitchen, which was warm. 'Dry your hair on that,' she said, pointing to a grubby towel on a hook. 'I'll just get his damp things off, then I'll put the kettle on.'

'I could do it, if you tell me where things are.' The kitchen was decorated with red and green paper-chains stretched between diagonally opposite corners, and a red fold-up paper bell which hung below the light. All over the door to the living-room she'd stuck the 'scraps' you find on Christmas crackers – Santa-Claus faces, pairs of bells, flower posies – and she called to me from beyond it as she dried the baby, telling me where to find mugs and milk and sugar and coffee. There was order everywhere – it seemed to me to reflect tremendous courage, and I wondered why Mother's kind of order irritated you while here it stood to reason. The dog slept peacefully in a basket in the corner, taking no notice of me.

When I carried the mugs of coffee through she was tidying away wet clothes and the baby lay on a rug on the floor with cushions and bundles all round him. It was the strangest room I'd ever seen. Stacked against one wall were boxes and boxes of Christmas crackers, dozens of them, and ranged along the sofa in open cartons were the separate materials for making them. Under the window stood a pile of boxes folded flat, and several of these, assembled ready to fill, were arranged in a pyramid shape on top of a chest-of-drawers. A formica kitchen table with a wooden rod attached to its side stood in the centre of the room directly beneath the light, with small heaps of the things from the cartons spaced evenly along it. The rest of the room – the space round the gas-fire – was arranged as a kind of miniature home, with a rug, low table, two chairs, a shelf of books, a radio and a British Rail wall-poster of a country scene in autumn.

She said, 'I'm doing a bit of outwork.'

'Are there *crackers* in all those boxes?'

'Yeah, bonbons. They're not pickin' these up till after the holiday.'

'Don't they want them for Christmas?'

'These'll be for next time – they can never get too many. Takes so long, see, 'cos there's no machine they can do it on.' She sat down on her haunches and sipped her coffee, then added, 'I've done hundreds and hundreds.'

'Is it well-paid?'

'You must be jokin'!'

'Are they hard to do?'

'Anyone could do 'em.' She jumped up and went to the work-table. 'That's the outsides,' she said, pointing to a heap of cut-out crêpe paper in bright primary colours. 'Then you've got the white liners, cardboard stiffeners, the bit you pull to make the bang, mottoes, paper 'ats, presents, scraps for the outside. You 'ave to take a coloured paper and a liner and a stiffener and a banger and a motto and fold 'em in order, and shape 'em round that stick, and crimp one end up with that string stuff – 'tisn't string, it's something special. Then you stick in your 'at and present, crimp the other end, stick the scrap on the outside – Bob's your uncle. Here, let's pull one . . .' She ran to a half-filled box on the floor and said, 'Choose a colour.'

'Green.'

She selected a cracker. 'O.K. Come on, over by the door – Philip's not all that keen on the bangs.'

We pulled the cracker and she laughed like a child as she ran about picking up the pieces. 'Here, you get the present and I get the 'at, O.K.? D'you want the motto? I'd like the scrap for the kitchen door. Let's just make a note of that one; it'll muck up me numbers if I forget, and we're going to my mum tomorrow morning, till Sunday night.' She made a mark in a small note-book, then suddenly clapped her hand over her mouth. 'God, my mum's present! That's what I went out for, then all that carry-on in the park, everyone enjoyin' themselves, then the dog, and the rain . . .'

'They'll all be closed tomorrow. What did you want to get?'

'Oh, just something from the chemist's – soap or bath salts or something. My mum's not particular.' She was looking at her watch, rubbing her hands together in agitation.

I offered her the bath soap Jennifer had given me, or the talc from Cheryl, and she chose the talc, almost speechless with delight and gratitude. I would have liked to give her Lynne's box of chocolate mints but it seemed patronising – there was at least a reason for the talc. Then we sat down to finish our coffee, and she told me she was just eighteen and had left home before Philip was born because her mother wanted her to have him adopted. The baby's father, who was married, had helped her find the house and paid regular maintenance.

I asked if she could get a job. 'Wouldn't your mother look after him?'

'I like doin' it meself,' she replied simply. 'Anyway, I don't believe in that. Not much different to getting 'im adopted, is it? We're O.K. I just work twice as long for less than half as much; but I've got nothin' else to do, have I?'

Hurrying home I felt glad, at first, to have got to know her a little, but when I began to speculate how it might have been for her if the rain hadn't come to my help, the ability to visualise her face so clearly was too painful and I started to run, though the lamplit streets were still crowded, longing to slot back into something familiar.

As I closed the front door behind me I could hear raised voices, and found Mother, Dad and Ginny facing each other in the kitchen. Ginny's face was streaked with tears.

'She's given that lovely dog away!' Mother spat out the words. 'Just like that – handed it over to a girl at school!'

'That's not the point.' Dad was trying to keep his voice softer than hers. 'She's told us a lie, that's what worries me – came home and said she'd lost it over by the bomb-site. Had your mother and me hunting and shouting and questioning people – God knows what – then she turns round and says she's given it away . . .' Ginny said nothing, and though I generally found the appeal in her eyes unbearable, this time it all seemed ridiculously unimportant – a charade.

I couldn't remember us ever having this kind of confrontation – usually it was just Dad taunting Ginny at the table. But there we stood, facing each other, Dad and Mother furious. They had no right to so much rage, not for a lie told, surely, in self-defence – not after what *I* had, probably, almost done. I put my carrier-bag down on a chair. 'Oh, for God's *sake*!' I shouted, cutting across them both.

No one fell dead, and in the silence I began to justify my outburst. 'There's worse things than lying, for Heaven's sake, or giving a dog away. It's not as if . . .'

'Now look here,' Mother was wagging her finger. 'It's a long time since you've been any sort of example to Ginny, and . . .'

'It's not as if what?' Dad asked me, turning away from her.

'It's not as if she's a liar, not Ginny, and none of us wanted the dog – it was just a disaster . . .'

'Of course she's a liar,' Dad said. 'She told a deliberate lie.'

'A liar's a person who *habitually* lies . . .'

'*And* we don't need the dictionary definitions!' Mother said, folding her arms and straightening her mouth alarmingly. 'By the sound of you, young lady, you've been drinking, so I suggest you keep your mouth shut till you're yourself again, instead of doing your best to undermine our authority . . .' And she went on and on, though I heard only snatches of it – 'without a thought for anybody but yourself' – 'not a scrap of responsibility' – 'not an ounce of gratitude'. I'd stopped listening since 'keep your mouth shut', which seemed an awful thing to hear our mother say – ugly and coarse, violent almost. She must have been beside herself, using Ginny as a scapegoat, but surely worried by something much deeper than any dog escapade, and suddenly I felt my eyes pricking with tears of frustration and helplessness, and anxiety I suppose, for all of us.

'Why can't we be happy!' I sobbed. 'Everyone else is happy – why do we seem to be on at each other all the time, even at Christmas!' Dad put his arm round my shoulder, he could never bear me to cry. 'Come on now,' he said, 'there's no need for you to upset yourself – *you*'ve done nothing wrong.'

'Haven't I? I could've done something . . . criminal, for all you know, or thought of it, and that's nearly as bad . . .' It was all getting out of hand; I was frightening myself. I ran out of the kitchen and up to my bedroom and shut the door.

For a while I lay trying to remember the afternoon's events in their proper order, but too much of it had the quality of dream rather than certainty. I could have *drawn* the little harness, in detail, showing just how it was made, but how and why and exactly when I came to be undoing it, and what was happening beyond my hands . . . There were too many versions, all looking like memories.

I tried to reason. Who in their right mind . . .? You did read about such things in the paper, and generally there was something behind it like the hopeless longing of a childless wife, or the depression of a middle-aged one. I'd made my choice at the time of Earl's Court – but didn't want to start thinking about that. All the same, something told me I could never, ever, really rid myself of my own suspicion.

I could hear Ginny in the next room, crackling paper – she would be wrapping her presents. I began to wonder whether the relief from the tension of protecting the little dog from Dad would be enough to ease her grief at losing him. Was she cross with me for letting a telling-off become a full-blown row? It broke the thread of my thoughts, and I must have given up trying to work it out and slipped into daydream.

In the dream, a girl in a sunny park snatched a baby in blue woolly clothes from a stranger's pram while everyone was watching a dog-fight, and raced off through the trees and out of the gates, across a recreation ground, through a housing development, past the corrugated-iron sheds of an industrial estate, then stopped, wondering perhaps what she had done, and where on earth to go.

She had neither seen nor been seen by a soul, and now she climbed a bank up to a broad highway, empty of traffic and bordered by grass verges. She crossed the grass and entered a little wood where the sun shone down through the trees on to the thickest, richest grass ever, and she laid the baby there at the foot of a tree, close to the path, where someone would find him, and arranged the undergrowth – no brambles, just pliant stems and soft velvety leaves – around him for protection. Then she ran back, and now there was traffic in the dream, and the noise and laughter of people. Curtains were open and lights shone in all the houses.

When you're tired, daydreams slip easily out of control. A fly hovered over the baby, then settled. A few ants ran about on the blue woolly clothes and swarmed up to his face. An earwig fell out of a leaf. And suddenly I was trying to free myself from a dreadful trap of too much of everything – millions and millions of mindless small creatures running into and over beautiful and delicate things – soft eyes and mouths and tiny nostrils, and ears like pink, miniature shells – and too much pity and revulsion to be borne. There was a shout, which I thought I had made, and I was sitting upright on the bed, scratching my head with both hands, shivering, and shaking hair out of my eyes.

'Golly, that startled you!' Ginny said from the doorway. 'I called three times. You must have dozed off.'

Shuddering with disgust I jumped off the bed and began to brush my hair over and over and couldn't bear to stop.

'You're shivering,' Ginny said. 'You must've been sopped through. Don't get a chill at Christmas, for goodness sake!'

'Is there any hot water for a bath?'

'I'll run it for you.' As she went out she pointed to a little pile of envelopes and a flat parcel on the dressing-table. 'You haven't even looked at your post.'

First I opened the cards, then the parcel, a little book of Samuel Palmer drawings from Arthur. It warmed me and I sat wondering if he'd stood in front of a shop window for ages, as I had. It was shameful to have fallen down on my resolution to be a doer, and even more shameful to have been so influenced by Mother's heartless warnings.

Ginny was waiting for me in the bathroom. 'Listen,' she said. 'I'm sorry about pushing you into a row; I did try to avoid it. Mary Sanders has always said she'd love to have Bone, but I couldn't face the trouble it would cause, so I tried to lose him – *that* wasn't a lie. I went over to the bomb-site and kept putting him down and walking away, but he kept following, then I ran so's he couldn't keep up.

'But on the way home I was thinking about what would happen – I'm sure there's rats and things out there, or he might've run into the road and got hurt – and once you start daydreaming it gets worse and worse, so I went back and found him, snuffling about under some brambles, and took him to Mary's, then came home and said I'd lost him. It got to be a nightmare. Better leave you to your bath.' She was crying again.

While we had tea I told the story of my afternoon – how I'd met Lydia and sat by the lake in the park and heard a dog-fight, and how a girl named Freda, with a dog, had asked me to keep an eye on her baby. How I'd seen the storm coming and run for the pram but couldn't raise the hood, so I'd grabbed the baby and rushed through the rain to some trees. The more I told it, the more real it would become, and easier to visualise.

'I'll bet she was grateful,' Ginny said.

'You should've run with the *pram*,' Dad began, but Mother interrupted, 'Oh no, not with the rain beating into his little face. Poor wee soul.'

So I went on telling – how I'd gone home with them to dry, and how poor the girl was, and all about the crackers. I said she was marvellously cheerful and hard-working and courageous, even though her husband had deserted her, and added foolishly, 'You'd never believe the awful odds she's up against.'

Mother reached over to cut a slice of bread. 'It puts me in mind,' she said quietly, 'of the first Christmas after Ginny was born and your father was away at the Front. Two of you I'd got, and precious little money – not that there was anything much in the shops. We lived in the Allinson Road flat then, one room and a bedroom, and a kitchen with a bath in.

'I'd got your granny's old machine and I tried to make a few shillings altering people's clothes – no one had enough coupons for new ones – and I had these things all round the room, dangling on hangers from the picture-rail, out of your reach. I made a couple of crackers, one for each of you, just a bit of fancy paper round some little present, and the ends pinched up so you could pull them. Nothing to bang – there was quite enough of that already.'

I was grateful she hadn't challenged me. We all seemed nicer and friendlier since the row, and Ginny helped things along by saying, 'Gosh, you were up against all that! I know it's daft, but when you've spoken about the other places you lived in I've always imagined them as just the same as here – nice house and garden and . . . all your things. I suppose all kids are the same.'

It reminded me of Lydia, so I asked if it would be all right for Ginny and me to go to her house on Boxing afternoon.

'You can't do that!' Mother was horrified. 'None of us has ever left the house . . .'

'No, you can't,' Dad said. 'At least, *you* can if you like, but Ginny'll have to stay with your mother – I've arranged to be out that afternoon.' His face was red, and he stirred his tea round and round and round, staring into the cup. It felt like the end of an era.

In bed I lay wondering at how interested and warm they had all seemed when I'd talked about the baby. A few months earlier, at the time of Earl's Court, whatever had anguished and embittered us couldn't have been the idea of a baby. I'd never even pictured one.

Chapter Seventeen

New years, till that one, had always felt hopeful, but back to the office the minute Christmas was over held none of the excitement of a new term at school. It was an anticlimax and I wondered more than ever what I was doing there. The canteen was the liveliest part, but without a friend it wasn't always easy to hide away in the crowd, chattering like the rest. In lifts and corridors and up and down the stairs, men sometimes tried to chat me up, leaving me agonising about what I could have said if I'd known they were going to. One or two had said quick, shameful things when no one else was there, and I guessed that if I had a friend I'd know whether they did the same to everyone or just enjoyed seeing the dreadful colour spreading up from my neck. Ginny said she couldn't *wait* for her turn, but doubted if they'd ever notice her.

I longed to leave and make a fresh start, but the factory idea which had once seemed a solution began to feel less so now that the ones who had supported it – Mrs Boyd and Arthur's mother – were out of reach. I lacked the courage to make any move at all, and wondered more and more at the strength of whatever it was that had led me to interfere so impulsively in the normal, safe plan that Mother and Dad had worked out for me.

Ginny, more often at home now than me, told of long silences between the two of them even apart from meal-times. Fearful, she watched my mood – it would have taken very little to 'start something'.

So I took to calling in at Freda's, where it was restful, and sometimes walked about in the High Street with Lydia who used to wait outside the office for me. She was trying to get me to go to meetings, but never succeeded, then as soon as I told her of Freda she wanted to meet her, desperate to know someone really exploited, and with Freda's permission I took her to George Street on a Saturday afternoon.

'Your labour's the most valuable thing you've got,' she soon started in, cuddling Philip on her lap while Freda turned out crackers at incredible speed. 'If you undervalue it yourself you can't wonder at the bosses taking you for a ride.'

Freda pointed at the baby without looking up. '*He*'s my most valuable possession,' she smiled. 'O.K. I know what you mean, only it suits me, see?'

'Doesn't suit most of them, and it'll take *all* of you to get things like this changed.'

'I'll make a cup o' tea, shall I?' Freda half rose, still twisting paper, but Lydia jumped up and handed me the baby. 'I'll do it,' she said, and hurried into the kitchen.

I'd grown used to holding him, that January, with his fingers gripping one of mine, and his tiny weight making a melting feeling in my belly like the beginning of the marvellous moment I'd first felt at Arthur's flat. It made me lethargic.

I was discovering that once you bring together two of your friends you start a world of your own, instead of just being attached by a lot of separate strings to other people's. Lydia was bossier here than I'd ever known her, but Freda seemed older and stronger than both of us. You could imagine her holding her own almost anywhere, giving as good as she got.

Over the tea I mentioned my factory idea to them for the first time, but said nothing about Mother's threatening objection, as Lydia would have jumped at it, certain that I was as keen as she was to be free of home and family. She wanted to pin me down, choose a factory; she'd make enquiries for me about conditions of work and pay and so on – you didn't want a treadmill. She suggested Bailey's, because among other things they made artists' materials.

'You must be jokin'.' Freda was folding banger strips between layers of paper. 'Packing them tubes into little boxes all day – Rose Madder, Burnt Umber, Chrome Yellow – it doesn't have to be *that* boring.'

'Boring or not's irrelevant,' Lydia told her. 'She's going to be a top painter one day – you seen her stuff? You don't get *there* without striking out a bit. I reckon if she'd done the course at Goldsmith's then gone straight into teaching she'd have said goodbye to all that. Making a break like she's done must mean there's something really strong in her, single-minded, no mucking about.'

'I did that,' Freda said. 'Could've gone to Tech. but got a job

146

instead. Sometimes you wish you hadn't. Still, I wouldn't have had *him* then, would I? No, I reckon nobody ever does anything they don't really want to, whether they plan it or not.' She wondered though, folding in mottoes, what was wrong with Filey's . . .

'Just that she'll stifle in any office. On the factory floor she'll meet real people.'

'I never met 'em. Specially piece-work. Everyone hell-bent on their targets and the minute they'd done they were into their coats and off home. So would anybody be.'

'She wants an opportunity to think – a bit of peace.'

Freda laughed, but didn't look up from her work. 'I've never been anywhere where there wasn't a hell of a noise – if it wasn't machines you got the radio. I've never thought of anything much at work – except roll on packin'-up time.'

I enjoyed leaving it all to them. Other people's voices chewing over the things that worried me seemed a lot more leisurely than the great sorting-out sessions all alone at bed-time. When Lydia left I went to the door with her. 'You could still go back,' she said, standing on the step. 'Just for exams; it's legal. You could still make Goldsmith's by October. I only mention it . . .' Her words agitated me, and Philip started to cry.

'Smashin' looker, isn't she?' Freda said, leaving her work at last to take the baby from me as I came back into the room. 'Know a lot of fellers, does she?'

'She's never mentioned any.' I hadn't thought it strange before.

'Let's have a sweet.' She stretched up behind her, reached down an expensive-looking box and fumbled with the cellophane. 'Sixty per cent off, from Ted Forrest's shop, corner of Crew Street. Been in stock so long I expect the choc'late ones have gone all grey.'

'Is he having a sale?'

'Clearing up a bit, ready to marry that dark-haired woman who serves there sometimes. She'll smarten him up, but I reckon he's brave, taking on three boys. One's grown-up, and there's two little tiddlers. I've never seen 'em but I bet those little 'uns are devils. My mum says you have to watch it when they're brought up without a father – that's why she sent me to the Catholic School.'

She arranged the baby's nest of cushions on the floor and

started to feed him tiny bits of chocolate, and I cleared the tea-things ready to go.

'I didn't know you did painting,' she called through the kitchen door. 'I knew a boy once who got to be a commercial artist. Did it all from evening classes at the Art School. D'you go there?'

'No, but I'm going to; you're the third person who's suggested it. Trouble with me is I nearly always need someone else to tell me what to do. I imagine you make your own decisions.'

'Just 'cos you imagine it, doesn't mean it's true,' she laughed. 'I only left school 'cos of this girl I liked – lovely red hair, she had – she left, so I did. Still, when you think of it, there was dozens of others I liked, all doing different things, and I didn't copy them. It's like I said: doesn't matter who suggests it, you only do it if you want to.'

At the front door I asked, 'Could I bring Ginny some time? She loves babies – it would be a treat.'

'Sure. And don't go givin' up your job for some old factory. Not yet.'

'I can't anyway – my mother wouldn't have me in the house.'

'Blimey, I didn't know you were that much up against it.'

Her smile was warm, and her concern moved me, particularly as she was used to accepting pot-luck for herself.

The late-afternoon streets were crowded with shoppers hurrying home, and people of my age who wouldn't be going home for hours. There was a Rock session at the Palais, queues outside the cinema and a group of young men and women handing out 'Ban the Bomb' leaflets on both sides of the road. Though there never could have *been* a time when the world wasn't changing, you could tell it was doing it faster than ever just now – everyone said so. Finding somewhere to fit into it, I supposed, was just a knack that came to people at different ages. One of these days, with Ginny out at work too, we could both be walking down this street of an evening, greeting our friends, deciding where to go, as easily as the rest. I began to put together a dream in which there were more people in the lives of all four of us, and Dad and Mother didn't mind so much about everything we did.

'Gosh, am I glad you've come!' Ginny said, hiding away upstairs. 'I was sitting downstairs reading the same paragraph over and over, praying for you to hurry – he hardly says a word till you're there.'

Home was beginning to feel like a trap, and I was glad to have started something outside. It was only then that I told Ginny who Freda was, and how I'd spent the afternoon. She clapped her hand to her mouth.

'*Never* tell them. They'd stop you going there.'

'They can't really, not now I'm at work.'

'All the same, don't let on. This family, at the moment, couldn't survive a row.' She took up a length of yarn, made a knot at the end and began to twine it round her fingers, in an elaborate cat's-cradle. 'Sometimes I even wish they'd brought us up religious, instead of just – well – timid. At least you get someone to turn to, even if you are only kidding yourself.'

'Freda says you could go there with me one Saturday. D'you want to?'

'I'd *love* it! Except that she'd find me pretty boring; but I could always listen.'

'Well – whenever you like . . .'

'If there's not a netball match the Saturday after next, could we go then?'

On Friday Mrs Boyd's 'replacement' – a Miss Lucas – kept me working with her through the lunch-hour, preparing figures for the afternoon's meeting, and sent me down to the deserted canteen well after two o'clock, while she went off to eat in the Senior Staff Dining-room.

In the kitchens beyond the serving counter the canteen staff were having their meal, and Iris the supervisor brought me my food on a tray. 'There's no hurry,' she said, 'they've still got the tables to do – you take your time.'

I was tired, and wished I'd brought a book. A small leaflet advertising an amateur dramatic production was on the table and I turned it over and began to jot down in pencil a few things we needed from Boots. In between I doodled, and my attention wandered to the far end where one of the women had started to clean the tables.

She was short, broad-hipped and quite plump, and supported herself with her left hand on the edge of the table while she leaned across it, a red dish-cloth in her other hand, washing the surface with big, slow movements. There was not an angle in her, and she rubbed anticlockwise, so that the circles she made were contained within the width of her body. I began to draw her, still doodling really, building her up from the middle outwards with tiny shallow curves that described her contours, and no outside edge. It was restful, after a morning of columns of figures, and sharp red ticks, and the clack of typewriters.

Iris brought coffee and collected my plates. She leaned over my shoulder. 'That's nice . . . *very* nice – come and look at this, Win, she's got you to a tee.' Win hurried over, wiping her hands on her apron. 'It's lovely,' she said with a Welsh accent. 'My youngster's good at drawing. He's fifteen, just started his first job, and can't wait to get to the Art School, evenings, only they don't take 'em till they're sixteen. Wonder how long that'll last! D'you go there, Miss?' I shook my head and she went on, 'Probably good enough already. I don't think we know your name, Miss.'

'Ella Thorne.'

'Ah. Just that little bit different. My grandmother was an Ella, but I'd never met another.' She smiled and hurried back to her table, and Iris carried off the plates. I decided to join the School of Art that day, if possible, and felt a kind of shame that the idea had needed to be spelt out to me so often. I could get the bus out there that evening to make enquiries and perhaps enrol before going home to tea. It would leave no time for imagining, and the chance of frightening myself out of it.

When I got back to the office Lynne and Cheryl were away getting tea. Jen told me, 'Heather's got a little boy. We're sending her a card – I don't know whether you'd like to add your name, would you? We think it's lovely.'

'Oh yes, please.' I signed the card, which was a picture of a stork carrying a Moses basket, and Jen went on chattering.

'She's calling him Thomas. I do think it's lovely – Thomas Boyd I suppose it'll have to be, for the time being. Sounds really masculine.'

A thin young man, the only one on duty in the Enquiries Office at the School of Art, said there were vacancies, though not in all subjects. Young first-time students were expected to start in General Drawing, but lots of them moved on, once they were in.

'Could you tell me what General Drawing actually is?'

'Well, copying really. Basics – drawing from plaster casts, a lot of busts and drapery. Doesn't sound all that fascinating, but they all do it different. Thursday nights is Mr Zimmermann, and he's good. There's vacancies that night.'

So I enrolled to start the next Thursday, and he told me where to buy materials, where to go for coffee in the break, and where to hunt out drawing-boards, which were in short supply.

And I stopped feeling apprehensive and went home and told Mother and Ginny what I had done. 'It's funny you never mentioned it before,' Mother said.

'I only thought of it this afternoon.'

'Your father might have given you some advice. As it is, I'm wondering how you'll manage. You can't expect him to come all the way out there for you. He's always seen you girls home, after dark, but not that time of night . . .'

'I don't expect it, not now I'm at work.'

Dad wasn't in for tea and she said he hadn't actually told her he'd be at Aldershot, but you couldn't tie a man down to exact times for coming and going, not when he was getting on in his career and taking on fresh responsibilities. We sat stiff and silent for a bit and I wondered if Ginny felt the same despair for her as I did, though it was difficult to tell from her frightened little face. She's even worse off than Mother, I thought; she's caught between the tension of his presence and dread in his absence. Mother at least wanted him at home.

So I said, 'My friend Freda has suggested I take Ginny along some time, just to see the baby, if it's O.K. by you.'

'Of course, if Ginny wants to go.'

Ginny flushed. '*Could* I? It would be marvellous. What should I wear?'

'No one's going to notice what you're wearing,' Mother said. 'People have got too much to be going on with.'

I wondered whether she had relaxed her views on dress because a very humble friend of mine was not someone to be reckoned with, or whether she now had too much to be 'going on with' herself.

Ginny clapped her hand to her mouth as if she had just remembered something. 'What about you though? You won't be on your own, will you?'

'Now you're just talking silly,' Mother said, and, jumping up, began to clear the table.

Ginny went up early to have a bath, then read in bed, and after a time I noticed how unusually tired Mother was looking, and said I wasn't thinking of going to bed for ages and would get whatever Dad needed if she didn't want to wait up. She seemed reluctant to go at first, and I hunted about for something she might have liked me to say to her, but between the bitterness and the bravado it was difficult to know how she was feeling – apart from tired.

So I shouted up the stairs for Ginny, who came at once in a pink nightie, looking worried, and we started larking on, running about playing bossy hospital nurses as we'd done years and years ago: 'Nurse Thompson, Mrs Thorne has been up quite long enough. Help me get her to bed please, and supervise the preparation of her cocoa.' It was something you couldn't do by yourself, and Ginny joined in happily: 'Now, Mrs Thorne, let's see if we can get you to your feet. That's right, lean against Sister on the other side.' And Mother went almost quietly, laughing despite herself and calling us 'silly little cats'. I went back to the kitchen to watch the milk, then followed up behind them with the mug of cocoa, calling, 'Are you having trouble, Nurse?' 'None whatever, Matron,' Ginny replied, dropping a curtsey, and Mother said, '*Matron?* You've gone up in the world. And don't imagine you're getting the better of me – I'm only coming so that Ginny can get back to bed. She'll catch her death of cold, after a bath, with nothing on her feet.'

As we shut the bedroom door behind her I whispered to Ginny, 'It wasn't *patronising*, was it?' and she shook her head, but I was never certain.

Dad wasn't very late. I told him we'd bullied Mother to bed, and he sat on a chair in the kitchen while I made tea for both of us. Though he'd been drinking he wasn't drunk, but seemed preoccupied, and sat with his legs stretched out in front of him, his hand across his eyes.

I put the tea on the table and sat down on the other side of it, and he lifted his head and blinked himself awake. 'What about you?' he said slowly. 'Have you . . . thought any more about your job? I don't like to mention it when your mother's around.'

'I'm staying at Filey's for the time being. Today I enrolled at the Art School, for evenings, and I'm starting next week. I don't think you should change more than one bit of your life at a time, do you?'

'Ah.' He stirred his tea slowly. 'Perhaps you're right, though there's times you feel you could give the lot up, almost, for a

152

fresh start.' He sat quiet, looking troubled, then seemed to become newly aware of me. 'Erm . . . No, you're right, one thing at a time, when you're having to do things on your own. You go ahead at the Art School. I can't be a lot of help to you, not just at the moment. Got too much on my plate.'

'You have to start with General Drawing, but there's Life and Portrait and Pictorial Composition . . . things like that.' But he wasn't listening.

'Just so long as you're here . . .' he was saying softly, stirring and stirring and staring into space. 'Just so long as you're here.'

Chapter Eighteen

You could be quite anonymous in the General Drawing class – it suited me. People came there and took what they wanted like shoppers in a supermarket, and everyone was doing something different. There were classical busts and plaster models and several groups of arranged objects with fabric draped behind them. When Mr Zimmermann saw me standing about at a loose end he drew up a donkey for me in front of a head of David and suggested I should draw it. People went in and out in the silence, and no one took any notice. It was different from school, where we sized each other up for ages, or the office, where a few of you were stuck together all day and could never have stayed separate.

Mr Zimmermann came across once and looked over my shoulder. He pulled up a chair, took my board and pencil and said, 'Don't worry with a lot of detail till you've made sure it won't fall over,' then made two swift, untidy lines on my neat drawing, which seemed to shore it up, and went away.

At break-time I took my first look round at the others, and waiting for me by the door was a girl named Daphne who had left my school about a year earlier. She was carrying all her materials, and on the way downstairs said she always moved into the Life Room after coffee and I should do the same, or die of boredom.

'Would anybody mind?'

'Who's to know, or care? Nip back and get your things, there's always room.' And she went on down because someone was getting her some coffee.

I collected my possessions and joined the queue for drinks. It would be the worst part, I thought, as I watched the others chatting in groups. Many of the students seemed to know someone standing just behind me, with a name I couldn't catch, and spoke some greeting as they passed, but I heard no reply. Just as I reached the counter a strong, bored voice with a marked cockney accent said to my back, 'Ten minutes for queuein', ten seconds for drinkin',' and I turned round and saw a woman who could have been forty, with a gaunt, sculptured-looking face and tousled black hair. She was oddly dressed in an old-fashioned, heavy, three-quarter-length fur coat, belted right round her, with her hands thrust deep in the pockets. No skirt showed below the coat, just bare legs in very high-heeled shoes, and neither was there any neck-line of dress or sweater showing at the collar. She took the cigarette from her mouth and said, 'You ever managed it in less?'

'It's my first time.'

We bought our coffee and she followed me to a space where there was room to stand, and we leaned against the wall and drank in silence, and glancing sideways I guessed from her faint smile and the narrowing of her eyes that she was imagining. People went on greeting her and when they did so she jerked the smile wider, focusing for a second, but never answered.

'Everyone knows you. D'you know them all?'

'Faces, I know, not names or anything. Faces, that's all I notice.' She came out of her trance.

'What is it they call you?' I asked.

'Clem. Short for Clementine – only it makes you think of old Attlee, doesn't it. You in Portrait?'

'General Drawing – Mr Zimmermann. But I'm going up to Life after this.'

'He's a lovely man. It was him got me these sessions – I'd never done any modellin' before, but it soon built up. Dulwich, I've got now, and the Central . . . And a little job, mornin's. What about you?'

'I work at Filey's.'

'You hardly look old enough. Zimmermann's got a couple of schoolgirls in there, so I wondered . . .'

'I'm seventeen.'

'Ah. I had my boy about your age. He's fifteen now, at the Grammar at Hammersmith. Doin' fine.'

'I expect you're proud of him.'

'Well, you are, when you've brought 'em up on your own.'

'I've got a friend who's bringing up a boy alone. She works at home all day, making Christmas crackers. She's got hundreds, all over the place.'

'Poor little sod.' She laughed. 'I was on the glasses, dozens and dozens of 'em, all laid out upside-down on the floor and over the furniture. You did two daisies and one leaf on each glass – I must've done thousands, *thousands* of 'em, all told. The stink of that paint!' She was smiling, and her eyes were huge, soft brown and lively. A bell rang somewhere and she put down her cup. 'See you up there then,' she said, and hurried out, and I saw her run up the stone staircase as if she weighed no more than a child.

Daphne was waiting by the door. 'I see Clem picked you up.'

'She's strange, isn't she, but nice.'

'She's a shocking old lesbian,' Daphne said lightly as I followed her upstairs.

The Life Room was already quiet, crowded with busy students. In the centre, on a small hessian-covered dais, Clem sat on a high stool wearing nothing at all. Her right leg was stretched out, the foot flat against the floor, the left knee bent with its foot resting on the crossbar of the stool. Her arms were folded against her belly, and she hunched over them, staring at the floor.

It seemed awful to intrude, and I would have hurried away if the tutor hadn't beckoned me over to the only vacant donkey. Clem looked so softly still that as I tried to settle myself quietly I felt, by contrast, a bundle of jerky, uncontrollable muscles and sharp bones.

I tried drawing her the way I'd done Win in the canteen, but it made her look too rounded. The tutor said I was trying to paint with a pencil and would do better to commit myself to a line. He took a pencil from his top pocket and at the bottom of the paper quickly drew a few thick lines which, though they didn't begin to look like a body, told more about the pose than all my tentative sketching and scratching and rubbing. He seemed to know, as if he saw beneath her skin, where the muscles were and what they would be doing.

Afterwards, with the two drawings rolled together, I waited about for Daphne, but she told me she was getting a lift home so I started to walk back on my own. Ahead of me, Clem and a middle-aged man with glasses slipped into the saloon bar of the pub on the corner. By now she was wearing slacks under the coat, a big polo-necked jersey, and a headscarf. With her, I thought, you get the feeling that thousands and thousands of us, all different, belong in the same world, and whatever you are, it's O.K.

I didn't want to go home – it seemed important to keep the evening going, and there was little of it I could share with Dad and Mother – so I turned out of the main road into George Street, and rang Freda's doorbell. 'Could I come in just for a minute or two?' I asked.

She was wearing a dressing-gown and holding a bundle of banger strips. 'Sure. You O.K.?' You could see from the state of the room that she'd been working all day. Philip lay asleep on the floor among his cushions.

'Don't you put him upstairs at bed-time?'

'No point in it – him lonely up there and me on my own down here. Let me just switch off the radio.'

'Doesn't it keep him awake?'

'He'd sleep through anything.'

She went on working and I told her about the school, and Clem, and she smiled as she rolled the coloured strips. 'I met a lot like her when I used to go up the West End. They were ever so kind to me. I really missed them when I was in the country – just to talk to.'

'Did you *live* in the country?'

'My mum sent me there when I was about thirteen, and gettin' a bit of a handful. She sent me to my old grandad. God, didn't I hate it! I used to go out and stand looking round and think there was nothing in the world but a lot of green. Nothing. Nobody. I used to long for the shops and the pictures, and the boys. And Mum, of course.'

'Did you go to school there?'

'Had to. They said I was up to harder work than the country kids my age, so they put me in a higher class, where you never got any sort of fun – not even Friday afternoons. At home me and Mum used to have the radio on while we had our tea, and she used to tell me stories – about her life, and that. But my old grandad never said a word; just sat and smoked his pipe. One day I said to him, "Tell us a story, would you?" And he looked like I'd asked for a fiver or something. He said, "You'm thirteen! Too big for stories!" So I said, "Not a fairy story – tell us a true one," and I kept on at 'im and at last he said:

"A cow and a calf . . . that's arf,
The cow jumped over the wall . . . that's all."

'Then he roared out laughin'. I could've killed 'im. Anyway, after that I gave 'im merry hell, and got sent back, only by then I was fourteen. That's when I used to go up the West End, with a girl from school. You're lucky, having a sister.'

'D'you ever feel like going there now?'

'No. Don't feel the same about boys – nowhere near it.' She was quiet for a moment, then said shyly, 'You're different to all the other girls I've ever known.'

'How d'you mean?'

'Well, they're always boasting about boys, and havin' a good time . . . You don't think all that much of yourself, do you? Perhaps you don't like boys – you're not going to tell me you don't know any. Not a smasher like you.'

'Oh, I do like them.' It seemed churlish to try to hide things, when I thought how freely both she and Clem had talked to me. 'And I think some of . . . sex . . . is lovely. I've tried to paint about it. Then it gets – well, I think it does – awful.'

She went on with her rolling, but I could tell she was suddenly concentrating hard. 'Always the same, is it? Always disappointin'?'

'I've only actually done it once, but I expect . . .'

She lifted a laughing, shining face to mine. 'God, you kill me, you really do! You been reading novels or something? No one gets it like that, lovely from the word go and happy-ever-after. You've gotta give it time.' She went on smiling as she worked, but I didn't feel for a moment that she was laughing at me, and in the silence, decided to tell her my secret.

'I think I lost interest. It went wrong, you see, and I had to have an abortion.'

For a second she closed her eyes, then looked up into my face, the work forgotten. 'Whose idea was that then?'

I shrugged. 'I told my mother, and I suppose she told my father, and they arranged it. I was glad they did – I wanted to be at school, and college, and so on.'

She was thoughtful, looking towards the window. 'You never got asked, really, did you?' she said. 'And you never got what you wanted either.'

'I only left because I couldn't concentrate.'

'Is that why you thought about a factory job?'

'I've given that up. It's no good trying to change too many things at once.'

'I'll make a quick cuppa.' She stood up and Philip began to stir in his sleep. 'You can pick him up if you like,' she called from the kitchen, 'it's time I moved him.'

As she brought in the tea I began to say that I'd never before mentioned to anyone what I'd told her, and she nodded quickly and said, 'If you should want to move out, in a hurry or anything, you could always come here till you found yourself something.'

We played with Philip for the rest of the time, then I left, and ran most of the way home, partly because it was late and partly because I felt free and – in a strange way – protected, with a foot in a world where Dad and Mother weren't in charge. Nothing had necessarily got to stay the way it was; there was room around me, room for movement.

Indoors I put my head round the living-room door and was surprised to find Mother waiting up with Dad, as she was getting into the habit of going early to bed, often with a headache. I ran upstairs and took off my coat and scarf and unrolled the drawings, dropping the sketch of Clem on the floor in a corner and rolling the head of David back into the rubber-band, then went down again.

Mother was making cocoa and I handed the drawing to Dad. 'Is that a whole evening's work?' he said at once.

'Oh no – lots of little rough sketches,' I lied. 'You don't keep them all. The thick lines are where the master helped me.'

Looking over his shoulder, Mother said, 'Well, to me, your bit looks a lot neater than his. How did you manage about getting home?'

'A lot of us walked back together. Everyone's very friendly.'

When she had gone up, Dad looked at the drawing again. 'Well, you've made a start, and I daresay you'll fall on your feet,' he said. It seemed to me that he said it with some relief, as if it lightened a small part of his own responsibilities. He had been home all evening, so not drinking, and it could surely do no harm now to try talking about our family muddle. I said, 'Mother looks better, no headache tonight.'

He started rolling up the drawing slowly, then pulled the elastic band round it and put it on the table. 'Your mother's letting herself become a victim to women's ills. You and Ginny must know more about it than I do.'

'What d'you mean, "women's ills"?'

'It's her age, I suppose. They get weepy and start fancying they've got all the ills there are.'

'What does Mother think she's got?'

He looked uncomfortable. 'Oh, one thing and another. Feels she's hard done by, not appreciated, taken for granted . . .'

'Who by?'

He looked at the floor. 'Me, mostly.' For a moment I thought he might speak of his feelings, as he had in the brown pub, but it came to nothing and I said, 'If only she wasn't so unhappy! She and Ginny are stuck with each other so much of the time – it's miserable for Ginny.'

Dad was staring at me, his mouth tense with anger. 'What you're trying not to say is that I should be at home, isn't it? Isn't that what you mean, that I should go off to work in the morning then straight back at night to share the misery? Just the three of us – with you otherwise engaged?' I wanted to stop him but didn't know how, and he went on, 'There's something you've conveniently forgotten, I think, when you're talking about happiness – something a few months back that didn't do a lot to make *any* of us happy, least of all your mother . . .'

'It wasn't that! Everything was changing before that – you know it was. And anyway you told me not to keep going on about it for ever . . . And I'm *not* "otherwise engaged" – I'm just doing something once or twice a week away from home. Everyone should, at my age . . . I only want to build a life . . .'

'Me too!' Dad shouted. 'And what about *my* age!' He had half risen, in his rage, but fell back again and we sat listening to the dreadful echoes, till he said softly, 'I, it seems, go on carrying the can for my mistakes for just about ever, but you and everybody else must have the opportunity to "build a life" – is that what you're saying?'

'No – I mean, Granny Thorne allowed you at least to grow up and be independent and finally leave home. She didn't expect you to be always around . . .' I didn't know how to put it. Girls at school had often told of rows like this. They'd said things like 'You've had your turn, your chance to put it right' and so on, but I knew it wasn't true, not with ordinary people who simply have to stay among the muddles they have made. The strange thing was that Dad expected me to challenge his right to make a life of his own, while a few months ago, on the night I went

160

to Arthur's flat, I'd felt such despair because neither he nor Mother ever *wanted* to.

The stairs creaked, and I guessed Ginny had crept a little way down to listen. Dad took our two mugs to the sink and washed them under the tap, and I think it was the first time I'd ever seen him do anything in the kitchen. I found a tea-cloth to wipe them, standing beside him, and as he dried his hands he said, 'Don't worry about it,' and a few seconds later, 'I had a dream for you, which isn't going to be much like I planned it. God knows what you'd dreamed up for me, but . . . you'll be no luckier, I'm afraid.' He put his hand on my shoulder and kissed me good-night as usual – though I felt his thoughts were elsewhere – then went to call the cat in and bolt the front door.

The light was on in my room and Ginny, showing no distress, was looking at the drawing of Clem. 'Did you go red when you saw her?' she asked.

'No, but I was surprised. We had coffee together and she told me about her life.'

'God, you do meet interesting people.'

'She's over thirty, and she's a lesbian.'

'I'd run a mile,' she drawled. 'There were two girls at school who were; everyone said so. They were quite nice, though they did look at each other a bit soppy sometimes. D'you have to be another lesbian to attract them, or does anybody do?'

'I don't know.'

'I mean, everyone assumes they're heterosexual, but suppose you'd never had a boyfriend and along comes this lesbian and you hit it off together. You might never know what you really were.' Her eyes looked puzzled, and she added softly, 'I know it's awful not knowing, but what do they actually *do* . . .?'

'Oh, don't go on! What does it matter?' I didn't know either, and she was saying things I didn't want to think about.

She turned aside quickly. 'You see! The minute you're out to work you join the secrecy brigade! Anything connected with any kind of sex – how's anybody going to find out *anything* at a reasonable age? Sometimes I wonder if there's even anyone in the world who really *knows* . . .'

'You said they talk of nothing else at school.'

'Yes, but not real – more like the stuff I used to say at bed-time. *I* reckon you learn about it from men, in the long run, and I think that's dreadful!'

'Why?'

In a slow, restrained voice she said, 'I don't know one really nice man. Not one. D'you realise that? Not one I'd want to tell me. All the kind ones, or interesting or romantic ones, they've been out of books or films. Yet I know women, and girls, who are far nicer than any out of books.'

I knew what she meant, but began lamely, 'Uncle Peter's nice, and Uncle Arthur, and . . .'

'They're idiots, Elle. One's a timid idiot and one's a blustering one, and you know perfectly well that if they weren't related to you, you wouldn't want to know them for a minute, but I know women who . . .'

'Dad's not an idiot.'

'It isn't fair to mention Dad.' She hung her head and I quickly changed the subject and tried cheering her up by telling things about the evening, but she soon began biting round the edges of her nails.

'You don't think, do you, that we might both be a bit – not so much odd, but a bit backward? I mean, I've never had a boyfriend and I've got this thing about women, and . . .' her face was reddening, 'you're the only person I've ever heard say that sex is awful.'

Again I fell back on my out-at-work superiority. 'It's the sort of thing I've been discussing tonight. You'll understand a lot easier in a year or two.' Though in that case, I wondered, why didn't I?

For a time I lay awake thinking of all the things that had been said that evening, with Ginny's fears about sex uppermost as I'd been trying for so long not to think about it. Freda had said, 'You've got to give it time' so confidently, but suppose I did and only confirmed my fears. What happened to people who *never* grew to like it? Did they avoid it, or pretend? Was it what 'frigid' meant? Should I forget it for a bit, taking time to catch up with myself, then try again? And would I ever be brave enough to do so?

My arms and legs refused to let me lie still, and I sat up and thought of Freda – warm, happy and easy, with the baby on the floor by her feet, the dog at her side and the coloured, shining paper filling all the spaces – like a Madonna really, with gold leaf everywhere. She was my best hope, for help. The day after tomorrow I would take Ginny there. Anyone could see we were coming to pieces as a family – the thing she dreaded most – and for her it was happening before there was any chance of having something of her own.

I heard her lamp-switch, then the creaking of her bed, so I got up quietly and went in. She was sitting up reading *The Return of the Native*. 'O.K. to go to Freda's *this* Saturday?' I whispered.

She nodded. 'I'm longing to see the baby. God, I do miss Bone! Should we buy some cakes or something, to make it fair? Will Mother really not mind if I go?'

'Of course not. She doesn't want to spoil your fun. She's only keeping you a bit close because Dad's been out more . . .'

'No, it's *you* she's missing, same as *he* is, now that you've got more freedom and come home later. It stands to reason . . .' And she went on trying to convince herself that nothing was wrong with our family that couldn't easily be identified and put right, almost as if she hadn't crept down the stairs and listened to Dad and me.

Chapter Nineteen

'It's usual, of course, for the groom to give some little trinket to the bridesmaids,' Mother said. 'Is Hester getting something?'

It was Saturday lunch-time and she was keeping afloat a long conversation with Ginny, whose friend's older sister was getting married that day.

'She didn't say, but they're sure to do it right. They do everything right in that family.'

'Very important, the bridesmaids are; at the reception the best man has to make a speech of thanks to them, on behalf of the groom.'

Dad was beginning to fork his toad-in-the-hole round his plate, picking among the debris like a child hunting silver in the Christmas pudding.

'Do pageboys get something?' Ginny went on. 'They're having the bridegroom's newphew and Hester's little brother Thomas.'

'Oh, that reminds me' – I was glad of the opening – 'Mrs Boyd at work, the one who left at Christmas, she's had a son. She's calling it Thomas. We sent her a card, just our office.'

Ginny said, 'It's lovely to hear of a *happy* event, instead of all the awful things in the paper.'

'What awful things?' Dad asked without looking at her.

'Well, bigger and bigger atom bombs – destructive things like that.'

'One of these days you'll say something original,' he said, then narrowed his eyes and stared at her as if he had only just noticed her presence. 'So you're invited to the wedding, are you?'

She had back-combed her hair for the first time, so that it stood away from her face, giving it a rounder look. To her usual simple skirt and sweater she had added a loosely-knotted scarf, and a bangle through which she had tucked a spotted handkerchief.

Her nails were lightly glazed with colourless varnish and she had shaded her eyelids so subtly and carefully I was amazed that Dad had even noticed.

'Oh no – I'm going with Ella to tea at her friend's.' She turned to Mother and me, the colour rising in her cheeks. 'I'm trying to look a bit more sophisticated. I don't look gaudy, do I?'

'No, dear, very neat and nice,' Mother smiled, and Dad turned again to his food.

'What happened to this? It's not up to your usual standard.'

'Happened? Nothing at all. It was prepared and cooked in exactly the same way as usual.'

'Gas pressure must have been lower than you thought, and . . .'

'It was the same as usual . . .'

'You *thought* it was . . .'

'It *was*! There's no reason why it should have been otherwise.' Mother was beginning to mind.

'It *has* been known, recently, for you to mistake the number . . .'

'Once! Once only, at a time when I had a headache, and the only reason it . . .'

'But why on earth are you getting so agitated? All right, all right, so it was done as usual, if it means so much to you . . .' To my horror I noticed that Mother, who had allowed her irritation to show more than I'd ever known, had tears welling up in her eyes.

'That's right,' Dad said gently, 'you have a good cry. You'll feel a lot better after that.' He looked across at me. 'There's probably a quite simple and logical explanation, and no earthly need for tears. I'm afraid it's the way you women tend to deal with things. Isn't yours a bit soggy?'

Oh no, I should have said, I'm not playing this game. I was already pushing back my chair yet couldn't move away from Mother who had hung her head and was crying freely. Standing behind her with my hands on her shoulders, I wondered which of us was trembling.

Dad turned a look of mock bewilderment on Ginny, who had gone so white that the tiny bit of make-up gave her a hollowed look. 'D'*you* know what all this is about?' he asked, and she bit her lip, but her desperate eyes finished me.

'W-w-what are you trying to *do* to us!' I stammered, then

yelled, 'You're despicable!' at Dad, conscious as I did so that there was a better way to do it.

'"Despicable,"' he echoed. 'In nearly eighteen years you've never mentioned that before.' He was half smiling, and I guessed it was the spectacle of me not really knowing how to be angry that amused him, and I turned quickly and ran, knowing it wasn't right, and already wishing I could have stayed put in my chair and just taken him on. At the top of the stairs I stopped racing, and walked slowly to the bedroom door, feeling strangely that I could leave the anger behind.

For a few minutes I sat on the bed and stared at the books on the shelf, trying to think of somewhere far away and keep out the echoes of the words we had all used, then hearing the front door being closed I ran across to the bathroom which overlooked the street. Dad was pulling on his raincoat as he walked; he didn't look angry and hadn't slammed the door. He wasn't even hurrying, and stopped to pull a dead twig from the privet hedge, then looked at his watch and walked off.

Downstairs Ginny was still at the table, her head resting on her arms. When she looked up I saw that her eye make-up had streaked itself away. 'We'll stay here,' I said to Mother, who was collecting plates with no sign of tears about her.

'You'll do no such thing. Your father's had to go out and you two'll need to smarten yourselves up a bit before *you* go. Look at young Ginny!'

'But I don't want to leave you on your own.'

'Why not? You often do.'

'But not after this sort of . . . nonsense.'

'Nonsense is quite right. Now just forget it – there's none of you had your pudding yet.'

'It's treacle tart,' Ginny said. 'Shall I get it?'

So we sat together eating treacle tart and I wasn't sure who was playing whose game. Afterwards Ginny washed her face but didn't bother to renew her make-up. She seemed to have lost heart, and hardly said a thing on the way to Freda's till I asked what had happened after I went upstairs.

'Nothing really. I just felt I had to eat every last scrap of my toad-in-the-hole, and it took ages to get it down, because it was quite right what Dad said, wasn't it – it was pretty soggy. I noticed he kept looking at his watch, and suddenly it dawned on me that they were waiting for me to finish. Then he got up and said he'd have to go. I didn't feel so sorry for Mother then, because it seemed as if she'd been making him wait for his pudding. I only hope he didn't think I was eating slowly on purpose.'

I said, 'You'll love it at Freda's.' And you could see she did. They greeted each other like old friends, though in childhood they had never played together.

'We used to envy you being allowed to play in the street,' she told Freda.

'There were a lot of kids down that street,' Freda said. 'I can't even remember ever seeing you.'

Then Ginny sat on a stool with Philip on her lap and hardly spoke for nearly an hour. She relaxed so much, freed from the feeling of responsibility for keeping the peace, that once or twice she almost nodded off and I saw her start out of a doze as Philip stirred.

'Lydia might come,' Freda said, folding papers and mottoes. 'Yesterday I saw her getting on a bus and she called "I might look in tomorrow" as it went off.'

It was half past four when Lydia came, and I was making tea. She brought Neville, the beautiful boy she had met in her vacation job, no longer wearing his overalls but a big pale-blue sweater and dark-blue trousers. From the kitchen doorway I saw Ginny's eyes grow big with incredulity, and watched her smooth her skirt down, shake back her fringe, and come alive.

'Hello!' Neville said, staring down at her, and she beamed up at him with such spontaneous joy that I felt my insides melt in a kind of second-hand delight.

So we sat drinking tea and eating the lop-sided little currant cakes Ginny had made, and she grew up about three years in ten minutes, and talked without self-consciousness or pretence. I saw how wrong I'd been to fear that her future might be only an endless battle to keep the family together, ending in despair. It lifted my spirits, and when Neville said, 'Look, let me take him from you for a minute, while you drink your tea,' and she stood up and they passed the baby very slowly and carefully between them, both biting their lips with concentration on the delicate task, it reminded me of the moment when Arthur and I stood looking at his childhood painting, the night I went to help them eat the goose.

Now and then, as we chatted and laughed, I wondered about

Mother at home, trying to imagine what she would have done when the front door closed behind us – weep, or work, switch on the radio, read a book, or simply sit and think? Ginny had managed, momentarily, to forget, and had made a hit with the other three. Watching them enjoying each other's company I felt proud that no one, surely, would ever guess what she had to endure from Dad.

'You're quiet, Ella,' Freda said.

'So are you.'

'But I'm working.'

So I told them, because it would interest Lydia, about meeting Daphne at the evening class, and how much she'd changed since leaving school. 'Made me feel I'd got stuck somewhere. Who wants a second cup?' I jumped up and took the cups to the kitchen and, standing waiting for the kettle to boil, heard Neville add his own experience to mine.

'You do get the feeling that your friends move faster than you do yourself. The other day I was thinking – I don't even start my proper job for another three or four months, but out of the boys that not six months ago I was walking home from school with, apart from the ones who went to university there's one who went to Canada and was married at Christmas, one in Africa at a mission station, one living next-door to me who's engaged to the girl at the record shop, one in the Midlands somewhere who was about to marry the girl who'd got his baby, only she pushed off with someone twice his age . . .'

'Good for her,' Lydia interrupted.

'I dunno, could be he's well rid of 'er,' Freda joined in, and Ginny piped up, 'He might have *wanted* the baby though. It's a bit sad someone else getting it.'

'Anyhow,' Neville helped the conversation away, 'they've all done something more than just leave school.'

I handed the tea round, feeling as if the organs inside me were changing places. I didn't doubt it was Arthur they were discussing, and couldn't think why it had never occurred to me that the boys from the County might still be part of each others' lives. Neville might never have noticed, or had simply forgotten, that Arthur and I were so often together.

'We mustn't be late,' I said to Ginny, and Freda told us, 'You'll *all* have to go by half past five or so. My mum's bringing her friend from Australia, and I'll need to do a rush job on the place.'

'I'll do it.' Neville jumped up, and we all offered to help him.

'Thanks,' Freda laughed. 'In that case you needn't go till six.'

As we ran about with brooms and dusters I kept wondering what she got out of our company. She was so still and self-contained, and made so little attempt to get to know any of us that I could hardly believe the way we'd talked on Thursday evening. It could not have been just the freedom of her room that brought us here, crouched on the floor or balanced on rickety stools while the boxes of crackers occupied the few bits of comfortable furniture – more likely something to do with her certainty, or the baby.

Neville dried the tea-things as I washed them. 'Your sister,' he said softly, 'is a lovely surprise. No one told me. How old is she?'

'Just fifteen. She's at the Secondary Girls.'

'What would happen if I came hammering at your door?'

'Just at the moment, please don't. I had to be terribly tactful just getting this afternoon arranged.'

After a moment he murmured, 'Wish you'd arrange it again some time for me. Why not come out to our place and bring her along – if she'd come.' He took a wallet from his back pocket and drew from it a little card. 'Have one of these – they're my dad's – everything's on it.' He took up a saucer, smiling at his recollections. 'Holding that baby,' he said, 'she looked like a flippin' angel – what other girl, round here, at fifteen . . .!'

As we walked home Ginny chattered. 'Lydia's changed a lot – still beautiful, and not half so dumb. Freda was a lot different from what I'd expected – I thought she'd be kind of saucy, but she's quiet, and calm. Even Philip is. He looks quite wise for a baby. You can't imagine him babbling, or waving a rattle or anything.'

'What about Neville, did you like him?'

'If you want me to be completely honest,' she said slowly, 'I'm going to *dream* about him. I'm absolutely green at Lydia, but I suppose if you're *that* beautiful . . .'

'Lydia couldn't care less about boys – he's not hers.'

She frowned up at me. 'Then surely she's his, or something?'

'He was quite taken with you, actually. He told me.'

She flushed quickly. 'He didn't! Oh Elle . . .' She walked in silence for a time, with a tiny smirk of pleasure as her imagination got to work. 'Would you say, then, that I've got a boyfriend?'

'I don't see why you shouldn't dream about it. It'll be O.K., only don't say a thing to Mother and Dad.'

She sighed. 'I'd forgotten all that. Isn't it strange how you manage to, when something lovely happens.' As we neared home she pointed to the chimney. 'Looks as if Mother's lit the sitting-room fire. Quarrelling does make you feel cold, afterwards.'

Mother was sitting very upright on the sofa. 'Your father's gone,' she said.

'Gone? How d'you mean?' It was the way she'd put it when Grandfather Gordon died: 'Your grandfather's gone; it was very peaceful.'

'Left. Gone somewhere else to live.'

Ginny and I looked at each other. It was a moment or two before we understood, then the colour left her face and she sat down. 'What happened?' I asked.

'You know what happened. Nothing – not after you'd spoken to him the way you did. He went out, didn't he, and about an hour ago he came back and said he'd got a room, and took some of his things.'

It struck me as an extraordinary way to go – just pulling on your mac the same as any day, stopping to pick off a bit of dead privet. 'You don't mean he went because I said – that – to him!'

'Your father wants a divorce.'

'Divorce! You mean he's *never* coming back, and wants . . .'

'To marry again, yes. He's not with her though, he says, not at the moment.' She had spoken so far with a kind of bravado, but now she bent her head and fished for a hankie in the sleeve of her cardigan. I put my arm round her shoulder and glowered at Ginny who was staring, cross-eyed, into space, and she got up and put her arm round Mother from the other side.

'It's not a bit of good crying, I realise that,' Mother sobbed. 'But it's a shock, you know, even when you're expecting it.'

'You mean you've known for ages?'

'You just keep going – there's nothing else you *can* do, with you girls to think about – but I think his affairs had come to some sort of crisis.'

'Do we know where he's gone, or who . . .?'

'Not yet. He'll come back for the rest of his things, and I suppose he'll give us all the particulars then.'

'I'll make a cup of tea,' Ginny said suddenly, running from

the room, and when we were alone I whispered, 'I'm terribly sorry, Mother. You must feel absolutely dreadful.'

'No,' she said thoughtfully, 'not altogether dreadful – these past weeks and months have been an awful strain. It's Ginny who worries me. She'll take it badly. She's got a real soft spot for him, in spite of . . . everything.'

'She can do without the strain too. I'm just sorry we weren't even *here*.'

'I think he'd got the idea you'd be pushing off just as soon as you could. He always said if you went he'd go too.' In Ginny's absence she was talking to me like an equal and I couldn't bear to think of the humiliation for her when he said such things. 'All the same,' she went on, 'he doesn't want you girls upset, that's why he came when you were out. He's put most of his stuff all together in the box-room. What I'd like you two to do is help me get it down into the hall so's he doesn't need to traipse up and down my stairs.'

'We'll do it later.' I went to look for Ginny and found her in the living-room, hunched back-to-front in Dad's big armchair with the cat on her lap. She had put the kettle on and then forgotten it.

That evening we did almost everything in silence, taking no notice of each other, dreaming our own dreams, and even in that there was a kind of relief. I think the two of them kept sliding between anger and sadness, and Mother said once or twice that life must go on, which made it sound like a death in the family. But I didn't really feel angry, and it was a long time since Ginny had felt safe enough to sit cross-eyed at the table, imagining, dabbing her eyes now and then with one of her picture hankies. Looking at them, it struck me that quite a few things might depend on me now, they looked so defenceless.

When we had finished supper I said, 'You two stay in the warm and I'll carry the stuff up and down from the box-room. It's cold in there, and we'd only get in each other's way.'

Dad had cleared the front of the tiny room and stacked bags and small boxes in a pile, then covered it with a sheet of polythene. You've beaten me to it, I said to the idea of him which filled the room; he'd always used it for private possessions that Mother thought made the place look untidy.

As I carried armfuls of them downstairs and stacked them neatly alongside the hall-stand so that they wouldn't be too obvious from the front door, I found I couldn't easily visualise Dad in new surroundings. He'd given up the dream he'd had for me and chosen to follow one for himself, but I was too uncertain of his feelings to be sure of the look on his face. If he was thinking of us he might look sad, or lonely, or relieved, or even guilty, surely not just bland and ordinary as I'd seen him from the bathroom window. But perhaps he wasn't even thinking of us.

It wasn't easy either to put a face to someone who would want to marry Dad, and though I first tried picturing a comfortable smiling widow of Mother's generation, it occurred to me that middle-aged men often choose quite young girls when they marry the second time round, and that was unbearable.

I didn't feel inquisitive about the bags and boxes I was lumping around, but I did notice that the red leather-bound box where he kept the snapshot albums wasn't there, and guessed he had it with him. Then a sudden suspicion appalled me, that he might simply have left it behind in their bedroom among the things he didn't need.

The bedroom door was ajar, and I crept in and gently prised open the wall-cupboard behind their bed, where the albums and his most private things were always kept. Nothing at all of Dad's was there; Mother had already filled the shelves with piles of clean towels and tea-cloths, folded cardigans and school blouses. I'd often thought there was something quite sick about the albums, but was relieved that at least he still wanted them. Mother had always loved arranging her possessions in neat order – perhaps it had been the only way she could manage the time, that afternoon, waiting for us to come back from Freda's.

Ginny slept with me that night, though I'd hoped she wouldn't. I wanted to go over what Neville had said about Arthur, and the others' responses, and to wonder about the way it was disturbing me. As she got into bed she said it had been one of the most light-and-dark days she could remember, then she went quiet.

'You don't blame *me* for it, do you, Ginny?' I said into the darkness.

'No. It's secret between them really. Today wasn't the first time he'd made her cry lately. Always evenings, before you got home. I didn't want to tell you.' Then neither of us spoke for ages, and I guessed that like me she was taken up with the struggle of trying to dream, through the sadness and shame, about the promise of something new and good that the day had brought both of us. 'If I blamed you,' she said suddenly, 'I wouldn't come into your bed. I was just thinking how awful it must be for married people, sometimes, with only the one bed. Like when he'd been on at her all evening about her cooking or something.'

'Mm. Awful.' I thought about it, then added, 'Only, of course, they do have a wider bed than this.'

Ginny began to shake. At first I thought she was crying, but soon she spluttered softly, helpless with giggles. 'It's . . . what you said about . . . a wider bed! I was thinking of people . . . quite old, married people, sort of . . . clinging on to the edge . . . like we do. One at each side.' For a few seconds she shook silently and I felt her scrabble under the pillow for a hankie. 'I'm sorry . . . it always makes me . . . giggle.' She blew her nose and settled down, but every minute or two she was shaken by another awful spasm, and though she kept apologising, couldn't get control. After a time she got up and crept away to her own bed, and I rolled into the middle of mine to think.

When Neville had mentioned the group walking home together, I realised I'd been caught off guard and had pictured the Arthur of that time – the one with thin arms who was always pointing things out, instead of the one who'd taken me to the country on a Green Line bus. So I lay half the night thinking of first the one and then the other, and though it was easy enough to imagine the Green-Line-one boasting to his friends that he'd been let off the hook by a girl he was about to marry out of duty, the other one, I agreed with Ginny, would find it awful to lose a baby to another man.

Chapter Twenty

Waking into a Sunday which Dad hadn't already organised for us was something new, and affected each of us differently. Ginny went back to sleep and couldn't be roused. I lay wondering if there were opportunities, to be taken quickly, for starting new things, and how to get Mother to see the necessity for them. She had risen as usual and started the day for us all, so that when I went down to breakfast the Sunday joint stood in its tin ready to roast and she had already prepared vegetables and made an apple pie.

'It's not like Ginny to sleep late,' she said as we sat down together. 'We'll leave her just this once. We mustn't let our standards slip.'

'Couldn't we have some new ones; not lower, but different? I mean, it isn't right that you should have to spend so much of Sunday getting dinner. We could have easier things sometimes – or Ginny and I could do it . . .'

Spreading marmalade thinly on her toast she said slowly, 'Changes there will certainly have to be – your father's commitments mean no one will have much money to play with. Still, that's my affair. But I don't think you've ever heard me complain about cooking a roast dinner of a Sunday. You may as well understand from the start that I'm still in charge, and I don't need dictating to in my own kitchen . . .'

'I wasn't, Mother, honestly.'

'We must all behave as if nothing at all has happened. If this gets to the neighbours none of us will be able to hold up our heads. You won't have to put up with it for long, once we know where we stand.'

'How d'you mean?'

'Well, obviously I can't stay here for ever, quite apart from the expense. The truth will out at *some* time. We'll have to sell the house and pay off the mortgage, then I'll probably move in with your Auntie Rose.'

'But that's Hereford! What about us?'

'Ginny of course goes where I go. Your auntie's agreeable to it; she's got the space since Uncle Edmund died. We've had an understanding for some time that if things got too bad with your father I'd take the two of you there.'

'I can't go to Hereford!'

'Not now you can't, not with your job, though I daresay you'd find one as good, if not better. Judging by what you've been saying to your father, you're all set to make your own arrangements just as soon as it's legally possible.'

So it had all been planned for ages, and the things I'd had the abortion for – school, and career, and everything going on as usual at home – could have come to a sudden end at any time; it had all been worked out with Auntie Rose! 'Does Dad know?' I asked.

'Not about Rose, but he knows I couldn't stay here. It was only a matter of timing, with him, and I daresay it was in his best financial interests, till now, to keep his feet well under my table.' Then hearing Ginny on the stairs she added, 'All I've said is between you and me, mind.' She was so different from the mother who used to move awful moments on for us, quietly protecting us from Dad, that I sat wondering whether she was putting on an act now, with the tense, softly-spoken little woman still trembling inside her.

Ginny looked heavy-eyed and tousled, her clothes pulled on anyhow, and you could see that the good memory of yesterday hadn't been strong enough to help much in her distress about Dad. Though Mother opened her mouth, surely to say Ginny wouldn't have come down looking like a rag-bag if her father had been there, she thought better of it, and for a time we sat at the table in silence.

In no time at all, I thought, we could settle into a tension just as bad as before Dad went. All of us needed something new, but for Ginny in particular time was running out. Alone, she would never be able to salvage the promise of yesterday. 'I'm going out for a breather when we've cleared this away,' I announced, and she roused herself. 'You must be mad,' she said, 'in this wind.'

Just before eleven, from the call-box in the alley alongside Ted Forrest's sweetshop, I dialled the number on Neville's little card, and his father got him out of bed to speak to me. We arranged that he should visit us unexpectedly that afternoon, bringing a book he might have offered to lend me at Freda's, if we had discussed one. He laughed with delight and puzzlement, and agreed not to mention Dad, and to suggest a walk.

'I'm terribly grateful . . .' he began, but I told him he would be helping *me* out, and though I would tell Ginny before he came, I couldn't vouch for her reactions.

I only told her when we were washing-up after the Sunday roast, and she was appalled, especially when I confessed that I'd suggested the walk because I had a visit of my own to make, and would leave them somewhere like the Friendly Cow and pick them up later.

'You can't!' she said, colouring up. 'If you want to go somewhere why don't you just go! No one stops you, now you're at work. Why bring *me* in! He'll think we've tricked him into taking me out – it's awful!'

'He did ask me to arrange something.' I showed her the little card, and repeated as best I could his words in Freda's kitchen, and she was unable to hide her pleasure.

'You should have told me that bit yesterday,' she said. 'When I woke up this morning it was the same feeling that you get when someone's died. You open your eyes and think it's the usual world for a minute or so, then you remember, and all you want is to go straight back to sleep.'

'We can't change Dad's mind,' I said. 'He's gone, and we've got to get used to it and think about our own lives.'

'I know,' she said, 'but it's awful what the early morning does to you. At least we three can stay together – that's a blessing.' Hereford, I prayed, might never come to anything.

Mother was quite taken with Neville's manner. He stood warming his hands, with exaggerated pleasure, at her sitting-room fire – we always had one on a Sunday – and pretended interest in the wretched little water-colour by Uncle Edmund, so high on the wall it was almost out of sight. When he suggested a walk she offered tea, as if she really wanted him to stay, but he wondered if it wasn't a little early, and explained that he'd thought of taking us for a coffee and a Danish pastry at the Friendly Cow, and would she like to join us?

Mother said she found the noise there unbearable, but it was what the young people liked nowadays, and we should go off and enjoy ourselves. She was just as nice and easy-going as Dad used to be when we first brought girlfriends home. As I put on my coat in the hall she crept out and whispered that if we'd rather not take Ginny she would think up some treat for her at home.

'No, let her come. She needs an outing. If you're O.K. for an hour or so.'

'Perhaps it's better anyway. You say he's Lydia's friend? I wouldn't like her to think . . .'

'It's not like that. Everyone's friends with Neville, and Lydia's seen a lot of him because they worked together in the holidays. That's all.'

Mother said she wasn't so sure, and that I'd got a lot to learn.

Ginny wore a red woolly hat with her shiny black hair sticking out all round it, giving her face a plumper look. As I left them at the milk-bar I decided I would do a picture of their two heads against a flat grey street landscape – Neville pale gold and ivory, and Ginny glowing warm with pink cheeks and red wool and the brown of her eyes. Then I went straight to Merton Street and rang the bell at the Knights' flat, trying not even to visualise what it would be like, or question where it might lead, because that was the way I was going to try to do things from now on.

Ted Forrest opened the door, with Ralphie on his shoulders, and on the way up the stairs told me, 'She'll be tickled pink to see you. She's always wonderin'. You've heard, I suppose, that we're getting spliced?'

Mrs Knight was sitting by the fire making a rug, with a rectangle of canvas netting and a heap of short lengths of yellow wool. When she saw me she dropped the work and drew Steve, watching at her knee, closer to her. 'Look who's come, Steve – look who's come to see us!' Ted drew up a comfortable chair and she filled it with cushions for me, then ran into the kitchen to make tea, with the little boys at her heels.

I asked Ted about the sale at the shop, but after a few moments he leaned towards me and said softly, 'While she's not about – I don't know if you've heard the latest about poor old Arthur?'

'I was last here just before Christmas.'

'Ah. She won't tell you, not with the lads about, but she'd want you to know.' He looked over his shoulder. 'Little cat's pushed off with someone else. Married man, lot older.'

'How awful.'

'Perhaps it's just as well – you're well shot of some people.

All the same, it's a rotten thing for the boy, whatever the rights and wrongs of it. He'll be home next weekend, then we'll hear more – taking a week of his holiday to help me decorate this room and the hall and kitchen. They say work's a good thing when you're down, don't they? Thought I'd just tell you.'

He filled his pipe and Mrs Knight brought in the tea. I kept wondering whether it was they or Dad and Mother who were unusual as parents, and would have liked to stretch out and stay for the rest of the evening. It was easier, here, to try and synchronise the two Arthurs of my imagination into one who might be lolling, if you turned to look, on any of these chairs.

So I talked about the Art School, and Mrs Knight told me the wedding plans, adding, 'At our age it's a lot easier than it was the first time round. All that fuss and heart-searching. You thought there was only one, then, in the whole world – one happy-ever-after – and you were desperate you might not have got it right.'

When I left she went down to the front door with me, and standing in the hall said, 'Look dear, say no if you'd hate it, but when they start the next term at the Art School, could I go with you?'

'Of course. I'll get you one of their time-tables.'

'I wouldn't tag on, don't be afraid of that – just the first night or so . . . show me the ropes. We'll be married by then and he's already bagged a free night a week for snooker. You've got to set things up for yourself – no one else is going to, are they? I won't be a drag.'

Ginny and Neville didn't ask where I'd been, and we walked back together to the end of our road. Neville said, 'Lydia tells me you'll be at her birthday party next Saturday. She said I could take a couple of friends and I'd like to take Ginny – would that be allowed?'

I'd forgotten the party, and my head was already filling with tentative plans for the next weekend, but they were both watching my face anxiously, so I said, 'I'll sort it out with Mother. Give me a day or two.'

When we left him we started to run, already worried about leaving Mother alone, and Ginny said, 'I hope it's O.K. but I've told him about Dad.'

'You shouldn't have. Mother didn't want anyone to know.'

'Well, he said I was quiet, and a penny for my thoughts. But

I just couldn't think any *other* thoughts. So I told him and he's promised not to tell a soul, and after that there was so much to say that he said I was like someone who's been sellotaped up for about six weeks. I'm a bit sick of secrecy. Where did *you* go?'

'Just to see Arthur's mum.'

'Not him?'

'Oh no. He's away, you know that.'

'There's something I want to mention, but we're almost home so I'll leave it till bed-time.'

Mother was sitting by a much bigger fire than she generally allowed, listening to the radio. 'I did just wonder if you might bring him back. What a very nice way he has.' As we sat listening to the Sunday-evening serial Ginny kept helping herself to Liquorice Allsorts without even bothering to ask, lolling in her chair looking perfectly contented, and just before the News, stood up and said with a smile that she was off to bed to read.

'She's taking it well,' Mother said when she'd gone. 'The trouble is, you never know what she's really thinking.'

I said I thought the outing had helped her, and mentioned the party at once. 'Is that going to be O.K.? It means leaving you alone again.'

She thought for a moment. 'If anyone should have to stop with me for any reason,' she said, 'Ginny never minds. She could always bring in a little friend from school, just to make a treat.'

'Just this time,' I said quickly, 'let *her* go, even if I have to stay. She never gets a party.'

'Now you're talking silly. You know I couldn't let her go without you – not a child of her age! Sometimes I think you just jump into things without ever looking at the rights and wrongs . . .' And though she was telling me off, a lot of the bitterness had gone from her voice, and for the first time for weeks she didn't mention headaches.

Ginny, sitting up in bed and looking serious, was grateful when I told her she could more or less count on the party. 'Look,' she said, 'would you think it a cheek if I asked if you're in touch with Arthur? Since that Christmas parcel or anything?'

'No, I'm not – not yet.'

'Well, I hope this won't upset you, but from something Neville said, I've got a suspicion that the friend he spoke about at Freda's – the one who was going to marry a girl and . . .'

'Yes, it's him.' I was sorry she knew, but now she did I told her how we went out on the Green Line bus on her birthday, and seemed to be saying goodbye, then about the bombshell Mrs Knight had dropped.

She closed her eyes, shaking her head with disbelief. 'All that stuff with Bone,' she said, 'me sitting on the wall crying, and you trying to make me stand up to Dad, and all the time your heart was breaking!'

'It wasn't really.'

'*Must* have been. And when she told you – the other – that must *surely* have been the bottom dropping out of your world.'

I said, 'You read too much. What people in books say – it never quite fits your own feelings.'

She took a drink from her bedside glass of water.

'I'll never manage the things *you* have. I'd go barmy, or run away or something. At really ghastly times I lose control, and . . . just giggle. Like last night, and the night you came back from Earl's Court – I was really ashamed of that. I'll never be perceptive.'

'You do all right,' I told her, remembering how she had at least perceived that there was awfulness in it, not just disgrace as Dad and Mother thought, or some kind of solution, as I'd believed till I began to wonder what had hit me. 'You helped me get up in the mornings, when I couldn't.'

She laughed. 'Well, it was so uncharacteristic. Anyone could tell you weren't yourself.'

And because she made everything seem to stand to reason, I would have liked to tell her more about that time, and see what she would make, for example, about the incident with Philip in the park. Sometimes another person can say a very simple thing that might free you from the dreary spiral of your own thoughts and fears. But there was already too much worry in her face – for a fifteen-year-old – and I said nothing.

'When shall we have to tell Mother that I've got a boyfriend?'

'Let's have the party first. I'm making some plans for myself for the weekend – it might bring an opportunity to tell her.'

'If you do get to see him again, will you tell him what happened?'

I nodded, still full of uncertainty, but she pressed on: 'And will you tell Mother that you've told him?'

'I haven't done the thinking yet. It could all come to nothing.'

'I'll do anything – anything at all, to help with it, and so would Neville. It could make all the difference, them knowing each other . . .'

'No, please! I'm O.K. Don't even think about it.' You had to be so careful when Ginny was in a crusading mood.

'If both of them came right,' she said, pushing back her fringe, 'it'd be absolutely dreamy . . .' Her eyes were crossed, and I felt like a traitor, and wished I'd never even heard of Auntie Rose.

Chapter Twenty-one

On Monday morning Cheryl called me to the office phone. 'For you,' she said, 'personal call.' I was embarrassed as they weren't allowed, but she whispered, with her hand over the mouthpiece, 'You should worry. Sounds like a super sugar-dad. You'll be laughin', won't you – nice little flat overlookin' Hyde Park.'

'You can be quite coarse sometimes, Cheryl,' Jennifer said.

The liveliness of Dad's voice surprised me. It had been tempting, at times over the weekend, to picture him moping in some bleak bedsitter, missing us, but he sounded organised and precise, dapper almost.

'Ella? Don't hang up on me. Are you prepared to come and see me? Have a talk?'

'You mean – just you?'

'Of course.' It was like the night he took me to a pub – a different voice from the one he used at home.

'All right,' I said. 'When . . .?'

'Well now, to save you embarrassment that end – I know calls are frowned on – I'll suggest, and you can agree or not. Would you come here? I'm at Chiswick – wouldn't take you much more than twenty minutes on the Tube. I'd rather not come . . . home, and it's awkward meeting in restaurants.'

'All right.'

'Fine. Let's make it daylight. What about Saturday afternoon?'

'I have to be back for a party in the evening, with Ginny. Mother's agreed.'

'About two then?' He gave me the address and careful directions.

'Does . . . she know the address?'

'Your mother? I'll tell her this afternoon. I'm picking up some of my things.'

And when I got home his boxes had gone from the hall. 'Was it all right?' I asked Mother.

'He came in a taxi – sure way of attracting everyone's attention.

I was never more ashamed in my life; him and the driver, backwards and forwards over the pavement with piles of stuff; anyone could see it wasn't the sort of things you'd take on holiday. It'll be everyone's business by now.'

'Don't worry about them. What did he say? Is anything decided?'

'What was there to decide? It's a long time since your father and me went in for chatting, if that's what you mean. Not with a taxi waiting.'

'Didn't he want to come in?'

'I daresay he . . . expected to, yes, but I'll see he doesn't. It's not the same as you young people, you know – leave each other at the drop of a hat and "still friends". There's a lot of hypocrisy about. He said he'd spoken to you at work – I told him he'd better not do that too often . . .'

'What else could he do? We've no phone.'

'That's his fault. If there are problems he must solve them himself, I'm no longer at his beck and call.'

Upstairs, Ginny was trying on the new dress she'd had at Christmas. 'Will it do for Saturday?' she asked. 'What I *want* to wear is my floppy old brown – I love it and don't feel all dressed up; but she'll never let me.'

'Why? What did she say?'

'I haven't asked – it wouldn't be fair. We've got to be specially kind to her . . .'

'It's all starting again,' I told her. 'Mother's got free of Dad and she's still going on at him, and you're starting a whole new set of crazy prohibitions *for* her, so she won't even *need* to change. You're fifteen – you should at least try for things the way you want them.'

'You didn't, not at fifteen.'

Dad only had to reappear, it seemed, to set us off at each other. At supper-time there was quite an edge to Ginny's voice as she asked Mother, 'D'you think Dad will ever ask to see *me*?'

For a moment I thought Mother's lips trembled, as if she sensed the hurt, but they were soon under control. 'We'll have to wait and see, but your father had better not imagine he just has to beckon and we all come running.'

It was strange how awkward it could still feel, round the table, now that we were past the first shock of Dad. I longed to dream, but didn't want to drift away leaving Mother to decide how we should all behave. At the same time I shrank from being too alert to her – there was danger in getting to know her too well, seeing through to the hold she must have had over bits of our lives where we'd always thought Dad made the decisions.

For Ginny's sake I raised the subject of the dress. 'What are you wearing to the party, Ginn?'

'The child's only got one decent dress – the red one from Christmas.'

'That's not really suitable, is it, for that sort of party?' I asked.

'What sort of party?'

'Well, informal – not dressed up or splendid.'

'"A well-dressed woman,"', Mother recited, '"gives as much time to her personal appearance for the smallest of functions, as for the greatest occasions." It gives you confidence.'

'You don't feel confident if you're all spruced up and everyone else is in casual things.'

'Just because the rest of them are slapdash doesn't mean Ginny's got to copy them. She must learn to have a mind of her own.'

'What would *you* like to wear then, Ginn?' I crossed my fingers under the table and Ginny fought a quick little battle.

'I feel well-dressed and comfortable in my loose-fitting brown dress, strangely enough,' she said, and seeing Mother's appalled expression added, 'It's less . . . gaudy than the red one. It's in better taste to wear subdued things, and you can add nice touches with the right accessories.' She could have been quoting from any one of the magazines stacked on the sideboard. And so began our gentle bullying of Mother.

'After all,' I said to Ginny as we stood side by side looking out of my bedroom window, hating ourselves a bit and thinking up words to justify the bullying, 'she's not really old, is she, and might well want to marry again one day, but no one's going to want to marry a scold.'

'She's not really a scold,' Ginny said generously, 'or Dad would never have married her.' But it must have occurred to her where that thought could lead, and she quickly changed the subject. 'Neville came to the school gates today at dinner-time,' she told me. 'I don't know when I've felt so proud. Maureen and Joyce kept cave because of the mistress on duty, and every-one was terribly impressed.'

'Did you know he was coming?'

'Yes, we arranged it on Saturday. He's the most important thing in my life now, but the awful thing is, when I was thinking about it, how to tell you, it all came out just like the stuff I used to make up about boys with names like Lucifer. D'you remember? It was all very well making fun, but now I find it's not so daft. You never told me.'

During that week I couldn't tell whether the feeling that I was different from the week before was due to Dad, or Ginny's happiness, or the urgency about the dream I felt I must make, in a hurry, for all of us. It could start next Saturday, when after settling Ginny at the party I would go straight to Merton Street without thinking about it, and warm myself among the Knights. Arthur would be glad to see me and gradually each of us would tell about the past few months and it would become clear that at our last meeting both of us had worn false personalities – he because he was in a trap, and I because I was not myself after Earl's Court, as Ginny had reminded me.

We would slip easily back into the times when we seemed to share eyes. I would paint pictures, and we would give sex a chance and I would grow to like it the same as everybody else. We would surround ourselves with friends, at Freda's or the Knights' flat, and sometimes go to the West End with Neville and Ginny. In May I would be eighteen and could move to a place of my own. Mother would allow Ginny to stay with me, and I pictured us cooking, on a gas-ring, meals for people on their own, like Clem from the Art School, and Mrs Boyd, whose baby would be a toddler by then.

It wasn't, I told myself, an unrealistic dream, like winning the pools or marrying a film star, and I tried not to notice the childish over-simplification in its assumption that just about everyone I knew could find a solution, and happiness in someone else, the minute I did. Dad had made his own happiness already, and so had Freda, and now there would be Ginny and Neville and Arthur and me. Lydia would find someone to love at her meetings, Mrs Boyd must have someone already in mind as she'd just had a baby, and Clem, whom I'd only met once, would find support and happiness with one of the older men who drew her and took her for a drink after the class.

None of it was very different from the vows we'd made as toddlers, that when we grew up I would marry Dad, and Ginny would favour Uncle Edmund. And just as I found myself laughing inside at its silliness it occurred to me that Mother stood alone outside it, the only one I wasn't considering.

At the Art School on Thursday evening I greeted Clem in the coffee-break and she gave the nod and quick automatic smile she gave to all the others, as if she had forgotten me. Drawing her afterwards – in a new pose – I tried to see her as a set of padded cylinders rather than a person, and the tutor came and said, 'Good evening, I don't think we've met before. You seem to be on the right lines. I'll leave you to it.' But no one else spoke to me, and compared to my first evening there, this one was bleak.

When it was over, I left by myself and began to walk home along the High Street, and after a moment or two a large black car, hooting loudly, passed me and drew into the kerb a few yards ahead. Lydia jumped out and ran towards me. 'Want a lift!' she shouted above the traffic. 'Dad and I have just been to the club to get discount booze for Saturday.'

'Thanks, but I'd really like to walk,' I said.

'O.K., I'll walk with you.' She bent down to shout into the car, and her father, with a friendly wave, drove off.

We had hardly fallen into step together when Clem caught us up on my other side. She was wearing slacks under the fur coat and a big polo-necked jumper, and her head was tied into a scarf. 'Goodnight,' I said. 'Shall I see you next week?'

'No, dear. Dulwich next week. I'll be back about April. Funny, I thought I'd seen you somewhere before.'

'We had our coffee together last week.'

'Ah. You're the one who makes a lot of Christmas crackers, are you?'

'That was my friend.'

All the time she was speaking to me she kept looking at Lydia, then back to me to answer, and now, as we passed the corner pub she stood still and said, 'I generally have a drink before I go home. Want to join me?'

'We're under-age. Is that O.K.?'

She smiled, looking at Lydia, and held open the door. And after I had introduced the two of them I remembered she didn't even know my name, but it didn't seem to matter.

I can't remember all we talked about, but from even the first seconds it was clear that she was unusually alert to Lydia, watching her closely when she spoke, and nodding and smiling appreciatively. She drank gin-and-tonic, and we drank beer. She had bought the first round herself, and in a little while Lydia, sitting next to me, facing her, took out a pound and gave it to her saying, 'Same again? Only you'll have to get it – we mustn't stick our necks out.' Then she went off to the Ladies, and Clem, standing waiting at the bar, turned to watch her out of sight.

'Lovely friend you've got,' she said, bringing the drinks. 'You've got to be a lovely person with eyes like that, I reckon. Close friends, are you?'

'Oh no. We were just in the same form at school.'

A little later it was my turn to give Clem a pound, and she went to the bar again. 'She's a lively customer,' Lydia said at once. 'Trust you to pick the interesting ones!'

I said, 'She's a wicked old lesbian, Lyd,' quoting Daphne, but hardly knowing what the word meant. Ginny, bemoaning her ignorance the other day, had lessened mine a little, but it was not so long ago that Lydia and I had both been caught out at school when someone said the art mistress was bohemian and we thought it was a nationality.

Now she turned to me and said slowly, 'God, you sound about as prejudiced as my dad!'

'I didn't know I was.'

'Well, you don't have to saddle people with labels. She's someone who's suffered – you can see it in her face.'

Before the evening was over Clem had agreed to go to one of Lydia's meetings, and once or twice, laughing warmly at her jokes, had clasped the back of her hand as it lay on the table. She sought Lydia's eyes the whole time, looking straight at them when she addressed us both, and leaning forward whenever Lydia looked away from her, to keep sight of them. She was amazingly different from the night I met her in the coffee-break, when she'd acknowledged everyone's greetings with the little mechanical smile and nod, and never seemed to raise her eyes to a soul.

At ten o'clock, already in a cocooned, hazy state, I said I had to go, but neither of them showed any sign of coming with me, so I jumped up. 'Goodnight,' I said to Clem, 'see you in April. See you Saturday, Lyd. Cheerio.' And hurrying home, grateful for the cold air, I tried not to notice the little nagging worry about Lydia saying I was prejudiced.

What had happened in the pub made me feel that my dream

for the future had already begun, with two of the people in it probably finding their solution. It seemed oddly different, though, from any of the solutions I'd imagined, and not particularly pleasant, as I sensed I might have lost them both.

Ginny ran down the stairs as I went in. 'Mother's at Mr Brewster's,' she said. 'Phone call from Auntie Rose – he came down for her in his car.' Mr Brewster kept the corner-shop and quite a few neighbours without telephones gave his number, with his blessing, to relatives for emergencies. It kept him their custom. 'I suppose,' Ginny went on, 'she'd need support from someone like a sister at a time like this.'

Mother got back before I had my coat off. 'Your auntie wanted to come tomorrow,' she said, 'but I persuaded her to wait till Saturday. There'll be more of us about, and perhaps one of you could meet her at the station.'

'D'you want me to move in with Ella?' Ginny asked.

'Not this time. She won't mind sharing my bed, it'll give us a chance to talk privately.'

Inside my fuzzy head I heard alarm bells; the dream, for Ginny at least, could stop right here.

Chapter Twenty-two

While I dressed to go to Dad's, amazed to find myself taking so much care, Ginny prepared for the party, trying herself out with pendant earrings lent by a schoolfriend, armfuls of bangles, and a stiff petticoat to give the old brown dress the 'lampshade look'.

'It's not *meant* to stick out,' I told her. 'The cut's not right for it – it pulls.' She had grown a bit panicky when other girls offered this and that, all saying they wouldn't go to a party without them. When she put it all together, going overboard a bit, it looked really tawdry, and she gradually gave up some of the 'looks' she was aiming at. Half the school seemed to have been involved, and I guessed she had told just about everybody.

Before lunch I went to the Underground station for Auntie Rose. 'Don't keep her waiting,' Mother said, 'she'll have got up early for that train. We ought to have gone to Paddington, but you can't talk with that Underground noise – she might just as well be by herself.'

'Anyway,' Ginny said, 'it's not as if she's old . . .'

'She's eighteen months older than me, and not finding it easy.'

'What, hot flushes and things?' It was amazing the way Ginny had given up editing her thoughts before she spoke.

Auntie Rose behaved just as she had at Grandfather's funeral, shaking her head slowly without a word, then suddenly clasping Mother or one of us to her, patting us on the back as if to comfort a weeping child. 'A party!' she exclaimed when we told her about it. 'You poor loves; I'm sure you don't feel much like *that* sort of caper at such a time. Still, I suppose you can't let your little friends down.'

Nothing was said in her presence about Dad's departure, but from time to time she referred to him in such a detrimental manner that Ginny and I bristled but said nothing, feeling in a superior way that we understood better than anyone else because we were part of it. 'So you're off to see your father,' she said when I stood ready to go. 'I find that a *very* funny thing, asking you to go traipsing out there – *very* funny.' Then she suddenly fished for her handkerchief and dabbed at her eyes. 'You was the apple of that man's eye,' she said in an incredulous stage-whisper. 'How could he *do* this to you . . .' and I wondered if she'd ever known what he'd done to Ginny down the years. She blew her nose. 'Off you go to see your daddy then. I must say you're a brave girl – isn't it always the innocent ones who suffer!'

Taking the Underground to see someone in a new home is unsatisfactory, because you end up with little idea of where they are in relation to you. You go down in your own district and come up in theirs, and the bit in between is unexplained, making it difficult to place them later, when you're imagining. I seemed to be starting a cold, and my throat ached; I hoped Dad would have bothered with a fire.

He was watching from a first-floor window as I approached the tall yellow-brick house. Before I had reached the top of the outside steps he was at the front door, holding it wide, wearing a new jacket and shoes and, for the first time, a bow-tie. Looking cheerful and alert, it seemed as if he was expecting good things to happen.

In the shadows at the back of the entrance hall a middle-aged woman in a checked nylon overall stood smiling. 'My daughter, Mrs Murray,' he said as he led me up the stairs. 'My eldest daughter, Ella.' She nodded and beamed then began to shake her head slowly and solemnly, like Auntie Rose. I guessed it would always be like this – Mother's people shaking their heads in disbelief at what he'd done to us, while those around him shook theirs for what she'd done to him, with Ginny and me siding first with one and then the other, according to who was being maligned. It could go on for ever, and I was thankful we weren't going to have to decide, as some children do, which one to live with.

Dad's room was long and narrow and quite small, like a piece partitioned off a larger room. The window was in a short side, and the door in the middle of a long side, so that you walked straight into the middle of the room. Looking left there was a double bed in shadow, while to your right a table and chairs, and a sink and gas-ring in a sort of cupboard were arranged near the window. And though the furniture was someone else's, the walls were already hung with things of Dad's: sketches he'd done on holiday, an army photograph, and a diploma about

190

surveying with Leonard Humphrey Thorne, hand-written in a beautiful flowing script. I guessed it had been a first priority, for him, to get his diploma up on the wall.

Dad put his hands on my shoulders and kissed me. 'All right?' he asked, and I nodded, looking around. There were no photographs of any of us about, but the red leather-bound box where he kept the snapshot albums stood with other boxes against the wall under the window. He had arranged cups and saucers on a tray, with a plate of Garibaldi biscuits, my favourites.

'You look smart,' I said. 'So does your room – everything in order.'

He smiled. 'I've been well-trained. You look smart too – and not too miserable . . .'

'You don't look miserable either,' I said quickly.

Dad moved the cups around, then put the kettle on. 'We'll have some tea in a minute. Tell me about this party . . . you and Ginny. Is this a boyfriend?'

'No, Lydia's eighteenth birthday. I took Ginny to a friend's house and Lydia came, and some others, and she's asked them all. Everyone liked Ginny. Anyway, she's a bit sweet on one of the boys.' His new, alert appearance invited confidences.

Dad laughed. 'Does he like her?'

'Hard to say.'

'She's a nice-looking little kid,' he said, and I felt proud that he could chat with me so easily and pleasantly, and might have told him almost anything, without the usual editing. But suddenly it was as if he too had to tell, quickly.

'I daresay you've had some of all this explained to you, but I doubt if it's been pointed out that neither Joy nor I went into this with the intention of breaking anything up. Events overtake you – *you* know that. Men change as their children grow into adults, and women change when they see middle-age ahead . . . she's in her late thirties. Suddenly you have to make decisions from a different standpoint from where you were when you met. I couldn't see how waiting around would make things any easier for you . . .' By now a kind of impatience had crept into his voice, as if he had been told just what to tell and found it a burden.

'You'll like Joy, I know,' he went on, 'though she's bound to come as a bit of a surprise to you . . . but more about her later.' Suddenly he smiled and sat up straighter. 'So, you like the bow-tie? Now then, let's hear about *your* plans; you've already intimated that you have some.'

He began smiling in the sudden way Jennifer at work did and straightening his tie against his collar, so that for a few moments I wasn't sure where I stood. There seemed to be a kind of gloss over him now, a smugness that reminded me of the man in the advert in Mother's magazine, who says he can improve your memory, help you reach your full potential, and make everything right.

'I shan't leave Filey's yet,' I ventured.

'Good. What about friends, are you making any? A boyfriend perhaps . . .? You won't mind me asking.'

'Well, quite a few friends. I'm going to try to see more of a boy I've known for quite a time . . .'

'Good!' He kept saying it, decisively, as if it was one more thing to tick off an agenda and count as settled. 'You see, I want to be sure you're doing what *you* want. Most of us waste a lot of our time being submerged by others, never quite getting going in our own direction . . .'

'It's the boy from . . . last September; the Earl's Court time.' I'm pretty sure I was trying to stop Dad slipping away too smugly.

He stood up and turned off the gas under the kettle which had been boiling for ages. 'Ah. Yes. That was – well – I'd have liked things to have been a little different, of course, but – didn't get a lot of say . . .'

'I thought it was both of you; both ashamed of me.' I felt, after all this time, a ridiculous kind of indignation. 'You said I was in no position to tell other people how to run . . .'

'Look, last September my own affairs were in crisis, to say the least.' He had made the tea and was looking for something in the little cupboard. 'Damn!' he said suddenly, 'I forgot the flippin' milk! Look, hang on – I'll nip down.'

'To Mrs Murray? Shall I go?'

'No – I try to keep her at bay a bit – the shop's only about a hundred yards along; you get it in cartons.' He hurried to the door then raised a finger 'Sit tight, don't move. I'll be back before you know I've gone.'

The front door slammed. I thought, we'll both use this respite to get the things we want to say in order. Then I heard a car horn outside and went to the window and looked down. Dad was crossing the street to a young man standing by a black Morris-Minor, who was inviting him to help push it round the corner and out of the traffic. After they had talked for a moment Dad went to the back and the man pushed from the side, with his arm through the window to control the steering.

He'll be a time, I thought, and looking down at him, with his new jaunty manner and smiling confidence, wondered whether we had all failed him and it had taken the new woman to help him climb back into his proper personality. Or was he acting even now? Whichever it was, you could tell he was confident in the choice he'd made. I had noticed, though, that there seemed to be only three of us in his explanation or justification or whatever it was – Joy and himself and me. Perhaps he was coming to Mother and Ginny later.

The red leather-bound box was down by my knee, and I pictured myself taking a quick look through some of the albums which had always worried me so much. Surely he wouldn't mind – none of us had ever really given him credit for the idea, or praised his camera-work.

I lifted the box to the table and opened the clasp. The albums were upside-down and a bit jumbled, as if the box had been shaken about on its way here. The lilac-covered one was uppermost, and I turned it over to the front with its green-lettered label, 'At Play', and opened it, but there was nothing inside, just empty pages covered with little diagonal slits for photo-corners.

The next one down was the first of all the albums, the white one, 'Ella, born 1941', and when I turned it over something snatched inside me, catching at my breath. A new label had been pasted over the old one, and in the same gold, Gothic letters, it said, 'Thomas, born 1959'. With my heart pumping frighteningly fast I opened it, clumsily, and it fell to the floor and I sank down beside it. There was only one picture inside, on the first page – Mrs Boyd, sitting up in bed plump and smiling in a blue woolly bed-jacket, cradling a tiny, sleeping baby, with its head against her shoulder.

'Not Mrs *Boyd*!' I shouted, and heard it, alarmingly loud and harsh, then jumped up and scrabbled with useless cold fingers through all the pages of all the other albums. There wasn't a single picture in any of them, and the latest, the blue one with 'Sweet Seventeen' in white, was missing altogether. Down on my knees I hunted among the other boxes for the photos – there were dozens of them, they would make quite a parcel – but hopelessly. None of it could be true – no one as nice as Mrs Boyd could like Dad. It wasn't likely, hardly even *possible*. Angrily I turned to the picture again, then stood up, staring out of the window and seeing nothing, with a kind of hollow grief wrapping round me and holding me rigid and still. Mrs Heather Joyce Winifred Boyd, I kept thinking, over and over, remembering how Lynne had explained the initials at the bottom of all Heather's memos to us.

Gradually I became aware of the things out there that I was staring at, unfamiliar things, and I wanted to get away, down underground again, and come up in a place I was used to looking at. I snatched my coat and scarf and ran down Mrs Murray's stairs, with everything suddenly twice as hateful because I needed to go to the lavatory urgently, but not here. Outside I didn't turn back the way I had come because it was past the shops and Dad was in one of them. So I ran back to Hammersmith and had to stand, on the train, strap-hanging among the football fans, and trying not to start my thinking till we plunged underground.

It was snowing a bit when I came up from our local station, but though I could feel the cold in my head taking hold of me I walked straight to the park, because Auntie Rose was at home. The hateful pictures that had streamed through my mind in the train were threatening now to overwhelm me: Dad and Mrs Boyd, *months* ago, long before Aldershot, or Arthur, even before my birthday; Heather lending him money for Earl's Court, helping with a job for me. I was wondering now if Mother knew. When did he throw out my pictures? *Did* he throw them out, and did he want me to know? Did anyone else know?

I'd never stop minding. And I'd lost them both at once . . . and Thomas. Access to Thomas, someone like Philip in our own family, seemed like something I wanted more than I'd ever wanted anything before. I circled the lake, torturing myself with things I couldn't bear to think about, but couldn't change – *fait accompli* things. If I circled the lake enough times it would surely grow easier.

Anger dies down, but there's nothing you can do with jealousy. Thomas had been a 'happy event' the other day, but Dad with a son! Mrs Boyd and Dad with each other! Dad with another life, not moping and missing us – but turning his back on us and choosing something better. Dad taking me to Earl's Court because Mother had said so. Anger is something you feel entitled to, proud of even, but not jealousy. And there's no one you can go to with it.

There was hardly a soul in the park – it was too cold. My throat was sore, my head ached, and because I'd left my gloves at Dad's my fingers had lost their feeling. A man of about thirty with a little white dog caught up with me. 'You've been round this lake a good few times,' he chuckled. 'Keeping warm, are you?'

'Oh, just thinking,' I said. It hadn't occurred to me that it might attract attention, so I sat down on a bench, to be less noticeable, and the man sat beside me.

'Doesn't come to anything much, does it?' he said. 'Bit of a flurry and that's it, and still bitter cold. Do better with a good old blizzard; finish it, and get warm again.' I rubbed my hands together and after a moment he added, 'You all right?'

'Oh yes, thank you. I left my gloves in Chiswick, that's all, and wish I hadn't.' He had no gloves, I noticed, and his coat was threadbare. He spoke with an educated voice, and for a brief moment I wondered what had happened to him.

'Is that where you're from, Chiswick?'

'No, from here.' I said it brusquely because I wanted him to go away. The little dog jumped on to the seat between us and sat trembling with cold, or excitement. I put my hand on its head and it turned quickly, licking at my fingers, wagging its stumpy tail. Never let a dog lick you, Mother always said; you never know where they've been with their mouths, round the lamp-posts and places. I let him warm my hands with his pink tongue, and sat fondling his head for a few minutes.

'D'you have the correct time?' the man asked. It was ten to four so I jumped up and the little dog leaped down, eager to go.

'No, you can't go with her. We've got to get home anyway. She's got pups – a nice pair, one like herself and one brown. God knows where she's been. You don't happen to want one, do you? I noticed you were . . . good with her. There'd be nothing to pay, of course, only I can't keep them, not in the one room, and you don't like putting a living creature down.'

'I do like dogs, but my father won't allow it.'

195

'The men don't want the bother, do they? It's always the women do the looking after.'

I smiled and pulled up my coat collar then started to walk away. The dog trotted at my side, and the man jumped up and quickly caught up with me. 'You were nice with the dog,' he said, 'stroking her, and letting her lick your hand. It quite excited me. Made me imagine all sorts of things.'

He worried me now, and I didn't know what to say. He went on, 'You're very good-looking – must have known a few men. You can always tell a sensuous woman. I can anyway; tell from the way you touched the dog. All the same, I'm sure I could show you things you've never experienced.'

I wanted to run, but was afraid. There was something tense and keyed-up about him, and he seemed to pitch his voice lower, so that it faltered now and then. 'There's different ways of even just kissing – not just straightforward . . . I could show you. I'd certainly know how to excite *you* . . .'

'I must hurry,' I said quickly, walking faster. 'My father will be waiting.' Dad always said you should mention a man who'd be watching out for you.

'All right.' He was raising his voice, sending it after me. 'I simply thought – I've no wish to . . . molest you.' I guessed he was standing still. 'Bonnie!' he called, and the little dog ran back to him. I continued walking fast to the gates, then slowed down, amazed and a bit horrified at the intensity of my own excitement. It was as if the marvellous feeling I'd experienced at Arthur's flat had grown quite out of my control and become a great hollow ache, almost too much to bear, but strangely inevitable. I think I was only hurrying because in the park there had been fear and shame all muddled up with it.

When I got home my throat was hurting badly and my eyes felt hot. 'I hoped you wouldn't be much longer,' Ginny said. 'We've got to have our tea and then get ready.' She'd washed her hair and had a towel wrapped round it.

'You look frozen stiff,' Mother said. 'And where's your gloves?'

'I left them behind. It's all right, we can get them back.'

Auntie Rose was slowly shaking her head again. 'Marvellous, isn't it,' she said to Mother. 'Probably had her sat there all afternoon without a bit of heat or nothing – you know the way men live – then sent her off without her gloves.'

'It was warm,' I said. 'But I think I've got a cold. Can I miss tea and go to bed for an hour? I'll be O.K. if I catch it in time.'

They ran about with drinks and hot-water bottles, and when I was warm in bed Ginny came in with an anguished face. 'Don't let them know I've been in,' she said, 'they'll think I'm only worried for myself. Listen, Elle, you've *got* to come tonight, whatever happens, even if you've got a cold. *Please* come. Don't wreck it all!'

'Course I'll come. I promise you'll get there.'

'No, promise *you'll* get there . . . otherwise nothing's right. You haven't mentioned Dad. Was it an awful day?'

'They didn't ask, downstairs.' I was so full of things that needed thinking out, and felt so weak and impossible, it was too hard to try and keep it to myself. 'He's got a bow-tie on, and a new jacket. His "girl" is Mrs Boyd, from work, the one who was my superior . . .'

Ginny had clapped her hand over her mouth. 'You said she'd got . . .'

'A baby, yes. He's our half-brother.' She was silent for a moment and I remembered her with Philip and guessed her thoughts.

'It's awful really, isn't it?' she said, narrowing her eyes. 'All the same, d'you think I'll ever get to see him, or hold him or anything? They'll probably only ask you. Did Dad even mention my name?'

'Several times,' I lied, then told her about the empty photo-albums. 'Not a single picture – I think he's thrown them all away.'

Ginny had begun to redden and bite her lips. 'Hang on,' she said, and darted out of the room. I heard her open and shut her wardrobe door, then she was back with a large buff envelope.

'Promise not to say anything. Look, on Thursday when Mother went up to Mr Brewster's I went and had a look in the box-room. I was looking at the things Dad didn't want to take with him, wondering, really, if he'd left that little pirate's-head wall-plaque I made him at Christmas. It was the first piece of pottery I'd ever finished so I thought if he . . . Anyway, I didn't find it, but I did find these.' She opened the envelope and we looked through the photographs. They all seemed to be there, except the latest 'Sweet Seventeen' one.

'I was terrified you'd find them and feel awful, but now you

197

know, I suppose it's different.' We looked at them in silence for a little longer then she said, 'Can I hang on to them, please? After all, it is stealing, and I did it.'

Whoever had them, it could make little difference to the bereft feeling I had about Dad, so I agreed. Ginny left me to rest, but as I lay looking up at the ceiling which had become too glaringly white, it was easy to guess from the ache behind my eyes that I had a temperature. I was shivering, and felt light-headed, and when Auntie Rose looked in a little later I took her into my confidence. 'I can't stop shivering . . . I'll never make it tonight. Ginny must though, or I'll never forgive myself. D'you think you could settle it with Mother?'

She put her hand to my head. 'Good Lord, girl. You ought to have the doctor. You stay right there – I'll see your mother – Ginny'll have her party. Poor little mite, she's that excited . . . all dressed up in her plain little frock, like Little Orphan Annie. You'd think your mother would have got her something decent to wear, though I must say the broad sash at the waist gives her a lovely little figure.'

She went and settled it with Mother, and must have done so in her usual cack-handed manner, for I heard voices raised downstairs then Ginny burst in. 'I won't go without you. *Please* try and go – I can't bear you to muck it all up.'

'I won't muck it up. They'll let you go and . . .'

'But for *you*, I mean. It's got to be a special night for *you!*'

'Look,' I lowered my voice. 'I wasn't even going to stay there long. I'd made up my mind to see you in then go round to Arthur's.'

She looked down at the floor. 'He wouldn't be home,' she said softly. 'He'll be at the party. I got Neville to invite him – we only did it for you . . .'

'Oh Ginny!' The thoughts that bombarded me kept blurring and muddling together, and I wanted to get her away and save the day for one of us at least. 'Look, it doesn't matter – I can go there tomorrow, or if I'm not better, Monday. It's so long since I've seen him, a day or two more can't matter.'

So she went off, with instructions about not coming home alone, and what to say to Lydia. 'It's lovely,' Auntie Rose murmured, shaking her head slowly. 'It puts me in mind.' And somehow I managed to sleep.

It was after eleven when I woke to find Ginny staring at me

from across the room. She crept towards me. 'Ssh! They said I wasn't to disturb you. You all right?'

I nodded. 'Was it good?'

'Yes, it was dreamy, really – in a way.' She sounded flat. 'The best thing I've ever been to.'

'Neville enjoy it?' She nodded. 'And the others? Freda?'

'She sent her love, but says she won't come round because of Philip. It made my blood run cold when I thought of her turning up here.'

'And Lydia? Lots of presents?'

'She'd got a woman there, some model with a funny name. I can't remember. I did wonder if she was the one you had coffee with, but she looked too old, and not a bit like your drawing. Still, I suppose clothes make a difference. There were some even older people from Lydia's meeting. Honestly, I think this model one's nuts on her – I never felt so sick.'

'Meet Arthur, did you?'

'He said hello to me. He knew a lot of the boys, from school, I think. I've never *seen* so many boys. Philip was popular.'

'Philip there! I thought Freda's mum was having him.'

'She couldn't, so he came. Everyone liked him.'

'Who brought you home – Neville?'

She nodded, then sighed very deeply and began to shake her head slowly. 'Oh Elle, you should have *been* there!' she said, looking down at me.

It was easy to see that the evening had somehow disappointed her, and I tried to think of something positive to say. 'Listen,' I said, 'you remember you were worried the other day about whether we'd grow up backward, or . . . frigid or anything? Well, I'm pretty certain, now, that I'm not, so you won't be either. It's O.K. I haven't done anything awful.'

'That's all right then,' she said calmly. 'Actually, it wasn't frigid so much as quirky I was worrying about, but not any more. *I'm* O.K. too, and I haven't done anything awful either.'

She tiptoed out of the room and I lay feeling insulated, inside my fevered head, from the day's events, uncertain which of them had actually happened. Tomorrow or the next day would be time enough for me to start being a doer again. So I thought of all Ginny had said, and planned my next picture. It would be of a room decorated for a party, in which people moved about, eating and drinking, with some of the younger ones jiving and the older ones dancing sedately. And all of them, no matter what they were doing, would somehow be paying attention to a baby lying on a cushion in the centre of the floor. The more I pictured it, the more dramatic the gestures and the lighting became. The colours would all be jewel-deep, and I would buy a small quantity of student's-quality gold. Before I got to sleep it had become a sort of Nativity scene, but strange and rather bawdy.

Chapter Twenty-three

'It isn't considered good form,' Mother said, 'to push your plate away like that the minute you've finished eating.' She was addressing Ginny, who daydreamed freely now, no longer burdened with the need to monitor the conversation for danger signals.

'School dinners they get it from,' said Auntie Rose. 'Anthea was the same. And of course there's the reaction – that's bound to affect their ways for a time.'

It was bitterly cold. I was still in my dressing-gown, feeling weightless and distant, but had insisted on getting up for Sunday lunch. The visit to Arthur's would have to wait till Monday evening – provided I could make it to work in the morning.

Mother had brought me early-morning tea. 'Looks as if you've had a rough night,' she said, picking up the eiderdown from the floor. 'Get on all right with your father yesterday, did you?'

I nodded. 'Did you know his girlfriend is Mrs Boyd from work? And they've got a baby?'

'Something about it,' she'd mumbled, turning away and tidying things. 'Keep your mouth shut about it though, while your Auntie Rose is here.'

'Doesn't she know?'

'Even if she does, there's no need to keep going over it.'

'None of you asked how he is or anything, yesterday. Is it going to be one of those unmentionable things?'

'If it was just ourselves it would be different.'

In a few days' time I would give in my notice – half the night I'd thought about it, picturing Heather turning up at the office to show off the baby, or later on, taking our name. Sending me to Filey's, I could see now, had been about as arbitrary a way of choosing a career as picking one with a pin, and mine would just peter out, coming to nothing, like almost everything I'd ever started.

My shrunken world was beginning to centre round Freda's little house and the Knights' flat, places you could more or less guarantee staying the same, with people whose faces were benign in your imagination. I wanted to be well again only to sit holding Philip, watching the gaudy crackers shaping up; or run up the stairs at the Merton Street flat and lean back into the warmth and welcome and colour of it all, though I'd hardly thought about what to say to Arthur once we were alone. And in a way it didn't matter – there was a certainty about the need to be with him again, like the times I'd abandoned a half-finished picture in a muddle, and much later known suddenly, without even looking at it, what I'd meant all along.

Ginny took out the dirty plates and Mother brought in the pudding. It was steamed, shaped like an upside-down basin, with red jam covering the top and running down the sides. I'll never forget it, because of her words as she cut into it and removed a wedge-shaped slice on to a white, blue-rimmed plate for Auntie Rose.

She said, 'Now that we're all together your auntie and I want to tell you girls what we've been talking about. Custard in the jug, Rose; take care, the handle's hot. Well now, I shall have to think, sooner or later, about giving up this house . . .'

Ginny had come to. 'Oh, could we have one of those new little ones behind the hospital! They've all got different-coloured front doors, and they're not in a straight line like a street, they're . . .'

'Now don't talk silly! I've got to get right away from here, you know that well enough. Moving house isn't easy for a woman left alone, and your auntie's got that great house standing half-empty . . .'

'But it's in *Hereford*!' If it had been Hell, Ginny couldn't have spat it out with more shock and contempt.

'A lovely city,' Mother began, 'you know yourself how you enjoyed the shops.'

'But not to *live* in! Anyway, it's no good for me, is it, with school here. You can't change schools, just like that, so near the end of your time.' Staring hard at Mother and screwing up her eyes she went on desperately, 'And there's Ella's job. No one gives up a good *job*.'

No one spoke for a moment, then Mother said, 'Ella's coming up to eighteen. She'll be launching out in a place of her own . . .'

'Then we could get a flat together, couldn't we? I could have food ready for her when she comes in at night . . .'

'Now just listen.' Mother was trying not to get cross but her neck was already pink. She carried on cutting up the pudding, handing out plates and custard. 'I've made it quite clear to Ella that quite apart from what she does, you go with me, so there's no point in the two of you making plans.'

Ginny turned on me. 'You knew! You knew and kept it secret! Just because you're in the bloody grown-up league now . . .!' She must have heard the echo of her dreadful words, and in a second she had scraped back her chair and run from the room shouting, 'Well, I won't *go*!' and slammed the door.

'They're getting like it everywhere,' Auntie Rose said through a mouthful of pudding. 'It's not just yours, dear. The tales I hear! Kids layin' the law down – *I* reckon it's the schools.' Then she recited in a flat voice, '"Can a child presume to choose/ Where or how to live!" That's what it says in the old hymn we used to sing at school on the first day of term. They teach 'em different these days.'

I was fed up with her. 'It goes on, "Can a father's love refuse/ All the best to give!" It's not talking about Ginny's world.'

'That's no way to speak to your auntie. I'm surprised at the pair of you, after she's been so kind.'

'Ginny wasn't rude to her – it's the distance she's worried about. When's she to see Dad, or her friends? She's only started making any since he went.'

'Whatever it is there's no call for such language, and when we've finished you'd better go up to her.'

'It's a lovely pudding, Doris,' Auntie said, but Mother and I could only stare at our plates.

Ginny, upstairs, was red-faced but dry-eyed. I told her I'd only kept Mother's plan from her in the hope that nothing would come of it. 'People who've had a shock think up all kinds of plans they don't really mean.'

'I meant what *I* said. I'll *never* go. I'd die without Neville.' Then she said more calmly, 'He's at Southend till tonight, helping another boy build a boat, so I can't see him till tomorrow dinner-time. He'll know what to say.'

I told her not to worry, and said I'd mention it to Freda, and Arthur's family – though I didn't know what we could expect of them. I also said we'd find a chance for her to see Dad, then as

I put my hand to my thumping head she threw her arms round me – the first time for years. 'You ought to be in bed. I'm sorry I was sharp with you. After all, I've harmed you more than you've *ever* hurt me.'

The outburst puzzled me, but it was after all her first proper rage, first boyfriend, first chance really. 'Go on,' she added, 'lie on your bed or something, and I'll go down and say I'm sorry for the bloody.'

I got to work next day, and by lunch-time had the strange sensation of shrinking that you get after flu, when you dread climbing stairs for fear of hitting your chin against each step. Miss Lucas said I should go home, but I preferred to work through the lunch-hour – I didn't want to eat – then feel free to leave if it got too bad.

At three o'clock the phone rang. 'It's switchboard, for you,' Jen said. 'A Mrs Halliday – shall they put her through?' Halliday was Auntie Rose's name. We were expecting her to leave next morning, but I hoped this was to say she'd changed her mind and was off today.

'Ella? You better come home, dear. Young Ginny's gone.'

'How d'you mean?'

'Pushed off from school, dinner-time. They sent round. One of the girls had told on her – there was a boy, you see, only they wanted your mother to know so's she could decide about the police.'

I didn't feel particularly alarmed. It would be one of Ginny's small protests and come to nothing. She couldn't bear to give real trouble. 'You better come, dear,' Auntie Rose repeated. So I went home.

Mother was white-faced, Auntie Rose red-eyed and longing to tell. 'The school-teacher came. Middle-aged sort of person. There was this ring at the bell. It seems young Ginny never turned up at her class after they'd had their dinner, only they never noticed till the end of it. Then this young girl came forward – crying she was; worried, you see . . .' Auntie took out her hankie and was speechless for a moment. 'No one likes telling on a friend, do they, though of course she never knew any details, just that this boy had come along . . . She'll be in the West End; that's where they all go, these young girls. There's a terrible lot of it.'

204

I said that was the last place on earth Ginny would think of going, and that she was most likely just playing hookey from school for an afternoon with a boy, and that I'd once done the same myself. As Mother had done nothing about the police I told her to wait while I tried friends Ginny might have gone to. It seemed wise to keep it to ourselves until we'd looked about a bit, and Mother was in favour of anything that might keep it from the neighbours.

Perhaps because of my light-headedness I felt strangely detached. I thought I'd go straight to Forman's factory and try to speak to Neville. And if he wasn't there I would try Freda's, and once school was over, Lydia's. So I took another Aspro, and went upstairs for a woolly hat and scarf, desperate to get no worse before the evening, when, I was sure, Ginny would be sorted out and I could get around to Merton Street.

The bus stopped outside Forman's, where I had little idea of what to expect, picturing a large building with a porter in a cubby-hole by the door, who would use the internal phone to get Neville sent down to me. But the Transport Department was like an aeroplane hangar with an open side, where men and boys in overalls worked on lorries and fork-lift trucks, whistling and singing against the piped music, banging on metal, revving-up engines and shouting to each other. There was no place to enquire and no one seemed in charge, so I spoke to the nearest boy, who straightened up and looked at me.

'Where's Neville?' he shouted to his mate. I got the feeling they were quite used to girls turning up.

'Neville? Why, who wants him?' I could hear the name being called from one to another, and some laughing, and words I couldn't catch because of the noise. Then a boy came out of the workshop to peer at me. 'Got the wrong day, 'aven't you, sweetheart?' he called, and when I stammered that it was important and asked if I could see someone in charge he went back in and spoke to an older man at the far side. The man turned to look, and said something funny to the boy, then walked out to me. His voice was kind as he told me Neville spent Monday afternoons at the Technical College, and if it was *really* important I should go there and ask for the Vehicle Maintenance course.

The Tech. wasn't far enough to bother with a bus, and I went straight to the Enquiries Office where the clerk looked at me suspiciously, then said I should wait in the outer office while he

205

rang through. But I stayed near enough to the door, burning with indignation and fever, to hear his conversation, and it was clear that he wasn't having any luck. 'Not here,' he called to me, and when I went over to the desk, added, 'Never turned up,' and went on with his work. I felt less sanguine about Ginny now, and hurried to get the bus back and go to Freda's, though I had meant to stay away from Philip till I was free of germs.

It was the first time I had visited and not found her making crackers. She was sewing a dress, while the baby kicked in his nest on the floor. I longed to pick him up. 'Don't get too close,' she said. 'You poor soul, you don't look fit to be out! Let's make you some coffee.'

I told her what had happened and she didn't seem to think it was anything to worry about. 'Not *those* two. They're not the sort. They were lovely, Saturday night. They'll just be off some-where for the afternoon – I was always doing it.'

'Ginny never has.'

'How d'you know? She'd hardly say. Anyway, I reckon she'll be doin' quite a lot o' things now, things that she's never done before.'

'They sent a teacher round.'

'They always do if they notice in time. Look, you could catch your death wandering about in your state. They'll be back at tea-time, thinking no one's noticed. Sit down and stop worrying.'

I was grateful for the warmth, and peace, and Philip across the room. Freda would take all the silly drama out of the situation and say funny, sensible things and I could go home and reassure Mother.

She brought the coffee. 'Got something to tell you,' she said, and I was glad, because she rarely talked to me about herself.

'Something good?' I asked, stirring the lovely hot drink.

'Well, I'm keepin' everything crossed, if not actually countin' chickens. Listen, I think I've found somebody. Actually, there *was* someone a couple of months ago, but I'm glad I packed that in – wouldn't have done for him,' she said, pointing at Philip. 'Well, Mum couldn't have him Saturday so I took him to Lydia's party, and there was this chap – ordinary-looking, bit younger than me. Kept picking him up, and asking things about him – it was lovely. I could see why – remember that friend of Neville's, chap he spoke about who was going to marry this girl who'd got his baby, then she pushed off with someone else. Remember?'

I nodded. My teeth were chattering, and my head seemed to have filled with a kind of thick silence which, though she went on talking, most of her words didn't penetrate. I could see her lips moving fast, and the marvellous radiance of her face, and now and then a phrase burst through, banging into my ears like the metallic hammering at Forman's factory . . . 'bowled me over really, know what I mean? . . . lovely ordinary sort of talking . . . holding old Philip just like he was his mum . . . coming round tonight . . . praying, I am, absolutely praying.'

'Be lovely. I hope it works out,' my voice said, and she held up crossed fingers, smiling, so I crossed mine and held them up too, but could have cried with the ache in my arms. So I jumped up and said, 'Must go. See you soon. Good luck.'

'Go the back way,' she called, running to open the kitchen door, 'it saves a step or two. Don't worry about old Ginn. Whatever happens, she knows what she wants. Give her a break, Elle – let *them* look for her. You get to bed.'

And in a moment I was hurrying along the little back-garden path that led to the alleyway running behind the houses, forcing myself to think of Ginny – the only bearable thing, because even if they didn't come back tonight it was after all no more than you could have expected of someone as spirited as Ginny, faced with the prospect of Hereford, Mother and Auntie Rose. She had *done* something. Good luck to her.

It was already dusk. My arms ached like toothache, and I crossed them tight in front of me. Cabbages grew beside the path, and at the end of it a weedy bush twined over the gate, leafless, but with a few black, poisonous-looking berries still attached.

A group of little shabby children was in the alley, the oldest – a girl of perhaps seven – pushing a pram full of wood, while two smaller girls in dirty frocks walked in front of her, holding on to the sides of the pram. They were singing,

> 'If you bang 'im on the 'ead
> 'E will 'ave to go to bed
> And we won't vote for Morris any more.'

The littlest one – it must have been his pram – was several yards behind, trailing a bit of firewood tied to a long string, and stopping now and then to negotiate it over bumps. He stopped beside the bush, and I noticed that when I looked directly at him everything about him seemed clearer in detail than you would have expected in such poor light, while around and beyond, out of my focus, was quite deep shadow.

I saw him pull a berry, dropping his string and concentrating hard. He let it roll into his hand and looked at it, then as he bent his mouth over it, he lifted his eyes and saw me. I said, 'Ugh! Don't eat that, have this one,' fishing in my pocket for something to offer. There was a peanut and a few scraps of crisps, and I went down on one knee, holding out my hand with them lying in it.

The little boy leaned forward and put his mouth over my hand, sucking them up, and licking at the bits of salty crisps with his tongue, warming my hand as the little dog on the seat had done. Then he stood up, smiling and licking his lips, and looked round for his string.

I picked him up – he was quite heavy, but his weight was strangely soothing to my hurting arms – and started walking in the opposite direction from the other children, half afraid I might hear them running and calling out to me, coming to collect him. And though, once or twice before, I had done something very important without even imagining it first, this was the first time I'd ever known so certainly that I was doing what I wanted.

He turned, once or twice, looking back over my shoulder so that I felt his warm breath by my ear. At first I thought he might be wondering where the others had got to, but he was only looking at his wood, checking that it was trailing properly on the end of the string.